# Dragonsbane

Impervious Book 1

Brady Hunsaker

# Contents

# Chapter 1

## Visitor

Ven Yashke didn't want to run away, but what else could he do? He couldn't keep going swimming, playing tennis, or waiting for college to start, pretending like he didn't know his parents were murdered.

"Ven, do you want a ride home?" Gabriella asked, looking up at him with her sad, brown eyes as she exited the gym's door behind him.

Ven looked back and shook his head at her. "No thanks, Brielle," he said, flashing her a smile as he tucked his tennis racket under his arm.

Gabriella nodded back to him and waved goodbye, heading for her car as Ven crossed the parking lot and started down the road. At her encouragement, he'd started coming back to play tennis just to take his mind off of things since last week, but it didn't offer the healing he needed.

It had been three weeks since his parents' funeral, and it was driving him mad. The scribbled note his mother left him before leaving on their trip to Egypt only made matters worse. It said, "If we don't come back, destroy the dragonblood."

What did that mean? He wanted to pull his hair out. It sounded crazy. Too crazy to share with a cop or a lawyer. The note made no sense. If it hadn't been in his mom's pristine handwriting, he would have thought it was fake. His fingers rubbed the worn paper in his pocket. He didn't need to keep the note with him everywhere he went, but he did anyway. Mom would have had some psychological explanation for why he carried it, but Ven didn't care to analyze himself.

His parents hadn't driven more than three minutes out of town before his dad either fell asleep at the wheel or they hit some massive animal, went off the road and smashed into a tree while swamp water flooded the vehicle. The autopsy report stated that they were probably both dead before the water level mattered. Both their throats had been cut during the accident. That didn't make any sense, but they pinned it on the idea that crazy things happened during car accidents.

Not only that, but the accident hadn't happened on the way to the airport. No, his parents had been heading down a road that would have taken them in the opposite direction.

The other oddity was that they didn't have him come with them. Most of the time, he'd go along to whatever country they visited, but they'd told him to stay so he could focus on his college applications. Firsthand experience working with them would only go so far without the proper credentials, after all.

He clenched his fist, angry with the whole situation. If he had gone with them, would he have died as well?

A slow breath escaped his lips. He inhaled deeply through his nose, the scents of pollen assaulting his senses. His shoes scraped against the pavement with each step as he forced his eyes up. He imagined his mom telling him *it's okay to have questions and not know all the answers*. But boy, he wanted answers.

His parents hadn't gotten into some simple car accident. Somebody killed them. He just knew it. But the authorities wouldn't see it any other way.

He checked his phone. 3:32. Sunlight blared down and warm, humid air clung to the earth. It rained just a few hours ago. A typical day in Southwest Ranches, Florida. Most properties rested on large plots of land. Well-trimmed hedges blocked the view of his home from the street. He owned a car and got his driver's license a couple months ago, but he chose to walk whenever he could. The trauma of his parents' accident left him cringing at the idea of driving.

The gate in front of his long driveway was supposed to be closed. Instead, it was wide open.

Maybe the landscapers or Oliver, the housekeeper, forgot to close it.

Ven hurried up the driveway lined with palm trees and orchids. The modern-style home was blockish in blacks and whites. A large yard, bursting with greens, surrounded it. The three-car garage was closed. He followed the curve of the roundabout driveway and heaved open the ten foot door at the front.

Overhead, a gold and crystal chandelier cast white light through the wide hallway. At the end of the hall stood Oliver, who quickly set down a large, rubber ball. "Welcome home!" he said in a cheery voice.

"Are you bowling?" Ven asked, leaning his head to the side to see the bowling pins set up at the end of the hall.

Oliver shrugged. "I can't be cleaning all the time." He was twenty, four years older than Ven, and he'd been working for them for about three years. He was the closest thing Ven had to a brother. Or a friend. Well, Gabriella counted too.

This was probably just another self-imposed insecurity.

"Right," Ven said, "well the gate was open when I came home."

"Oh, yeah. My bad," Oliver said. "You had a visitor. I forgot to close the gate."

"Who?"

"I dunno, some lady. Said you'd be expecting her and that she brought something back from Mérida for you."

Ven raised an eyebrow. "Mérida?" He and his parents visited the Venezuelan city on a few medical missions.

"Yeah, she left her number." Oliver held a folded paper out to Ven. "Seems a little sketch."

Ven gave a weak smile as he took the paper and unfolded it, reading the words. *If you want answers* with a phone number written down in elegant handwriting.

"Thanks. When's dinner ready?" Ven asked.

"About 30 minutes."

"Okay, thanks." Ven hurried over through a french door just down the hall. The walls of the room were covered in bookshelves, paintings, and shelves with trinkets from various countries. There were three large sofas where Ven preferred to do most of his reading, but he took off his backpack and set it down on one of the two desks, right next to his acceptance letter to Harvard Medical School. He graduated high school last year and earned quite a few college credits, courtesy of homeschooling, while he traveled around the world with his parents so they could provide medical aid. Both of his parents had dual degrees as medical doctors and psychologists, though they'd done most of their work outside the United States, publishing endless papers and receiving broad international acclaim.

Venezuela was the last place they'd visited together before his parents died.

A single picture of his family from last year hung on the wall. They all wore scrubs, and both his parents wore white lab coats. Even then, at fifteen, Ven had been taller than his mother. He was over six feet tall now.

He pulled his phone out and opened his texts to create a new message, thumb hovering over the screen as he regarded the note in his other hand.

It was cryptic, that was sure, but what harm could it do? He put in her number.

*This is Ven. You came by earlier–could I help you with something?*

He shook his head and sat on his favorite couch. Dark green fabric, wooden inlays, depictions of dragons as armrests. They'd shipped it back after some time in Thailand.

His phone buzzed no sooner than he sank into the cushions.

*Ven. Pleasure. I'll be over in just a moment*

Wait. Ven didn't know how to respond. His text wasn't meant to be taken as some kind of immediate invitation. He still didn't know who this person was, but at the same time, if she had information, he wouldn't turn her down.

*OK*

He didn't know what else to say. He tucked the phone back in his pocket and rubbed a finger across his lips. A long breath leaked out. Maybe this was what he needed. Something out of the ordinary to distract him. Maybe he should sell the house and move to a different country. His parents would be sad to see him so down. He wasn't his normal, optimistic self, but two different quotes came to mind. His dad had often said, "Sometimes healing others heals yourself," and his mom had told him, "Just because we're doctors, it doesn't mean we're always healthy. We need help too."

And Ven needed help. He needed healing.

Ven jumped as the doorbell rang. Did she arrive already? He stood and took a few steps towards the door as Oliver's footsteps thudded through the hallway.

Ven clenched his jaw. It was time for business. He'd been in emergency situations so many times. When somebody was severely injured, he would often be the one comforting the patient as his father or mother performed unmedicated surgery, something that was all too common on many of their trips. He learned how to act like everything was alright even when it wasn't.

Their voices were muted as Oliver and the mysterious visitor spoke, then their footsteps approached the study. Ven would glean whatever information he could.

Oliver entered the room. "The visitor I mentioned," he said as an introduction, gesturing behind him as the woman strode in.

She wore a crisp, tan suit that made her look like she belonged on an African safari and black leather boots, a fine brimmed hat held lightly in one hand. Her face was youthful, but he guessed her age to be mid-thirties, her skin a light brown. Her most striking feature was her eyes. Surrounded by long, dark lashes, they almost had a hint of... violet.

"That was quick," Ven said, offering a smile that didn't reach his eyes.

She didn't respond, but looked back at Oliver. "I'd like to speak with him alone."

Ven nodded to Oliver, who quickly backed out of the room, raising an eyebrow at Ven as he left.

"I don't get many visitors," Ven said, eyeing her suspiciously. "Especially from Venezuela. What brought you here?"

"You are taller than I thought," she said, ignoring his question as she tapped her chin. Her voice was low and slightly accented, but it didn't quite seem South American. "I mainly wanted to make sure you could pass as a 19 year old." She looked him in the eyes. "You have questions, I'm sure, Ven. I want to help you find answers."

Ven remained standing, unsure of how to respond. He narrowed his eyes at her and took a step back, feeling increasingly uncomfortable under her scrutiny. "Indeed, I do have questions. What's your name?"

She tilted her head and raised an eyebrow in a way that suggested she was bored by his questions. "Dayelle. Now ask the deeper questions. The true unknowns." She cast her eyes at the picture of his family on the wall.

Ven folded his arms. "Did you know my parents? Is that why you're here?"

"That's exactly why I'm here." A smile curled at the edges of her lips. She came and stood beside him before turning to look at the picture of their family on the wall. "I know everything about them."

A chill went up Ven's spine. He needed to play this calm. He had no idea who this woman was or what her motive would be for coming here. "Like what?"

"Like the secret jobs they would go on when they didn't invite you along." Her eyes glinted at him with amusement. "Like why somebody would have wanted to have them taken out because of their research."

Ven bumped into his desk as he took a step away from her, startlingly aware of his blood pulsing through him, strong and warm. He eyed her more closely, both intrigued and suspicious. For all he knew, she could have been involved in whatever it was that happened to his parents. "What do you want?" Her motives would provide better insight into whatever it was she was trying to do.

"To offer you a job," she said, strolling over to Ven's favorite chair and taking a seat.

Baffled, Ven folded his hands in front of him, assuming a professional air to try and hide the excitement that writhed in his chest. "I fail to see how this correlates with my parents. Or is that not what you came here to discuss?"

"In due time, yes." She arched an eyebrow at him. "You want to know what happened to them, don't you? Why did they lie to you? Why were they murdered?"

Ven gulped, eyes widening despite his best efforts to maintain his unperturbed facade. She knew they were murdered. She'd addressed his unasked question. He set his jaw, hoping she would continue.

Instead, Dayelle smirked at him, showing her brilliant teeth. "I can tell you everything. I can answer all the questions."

Ven waved a hand at her. "Then, by all means."

"Unfortunately, there are conditions," Dayelle said, sparking a flare of annoyance. "Your parents were involved in very sensitive research. I'm not at liberty to disclose such information without knowing I can trust you."

Ven shook his head, failing not to sound too snappy as he said, "They were my parents. I deserve to know whatever you have to share. And don't try to convince me they worked for the CIA or something, I know that's not true."

Dayelle crossed her legs. "Nothing like that. It was a private endeavor, but the information remains classified."

Ven scoffed. "So you're going to offer me a job as a means of proving myself, holding alleged information about my parents as potential compensation?"

"Precisely. I would offer you money, but..." She looked around the room before resting her eyes back on him.

Ven was a seventeen-year-old millionaire.

"I think information will be much more persuasive," she finished.

Ven shook his head. "What exactly could you even tell me?"

"Who killed them and why." She arched an eyebrow at him.

"And I'm just supposed to believe that what you say is true?" He couldn't shake the feeling that this whole conversation seemed crazy. Who even was this woman? How dare she throw false hopes at him to take advantage of him when he was in such a state? His parents would have thrown her out of the home, albeit, politely. "I think you should leave."

Dayelle rose to her feet, her eyes never leaving his as she withdrew a hand from one of her pockets, holding the palm closed. "I thought you'd have a little more faith than this, Ven, but I have some proof for you. Something you might find interesting."

Ven folded his arms. He was done with the conversation, and he could tell she was toying with him. He *wanted* to see what was in her hand. He *wanted* to believe that she could tell him everything. His heart ached for truth. For resolution.

When she opened her palm, his jaw dropped. He clamped it shut, glaring hard into her eyes, waiting for her to explain.

"Have you seen one of these before?" Dayelle asked, holding her hand up closer to him.

The object she held looked like a marble, but it glimmered with metallic sheen in hues of amber and gold.

He knew exactly what it was. Every summer, their family took a week-long horsebacking trip through southwest Montana. At one part of the ride, his parents always told him to close his eyes. He'd done so the first couple years, but faked it after that. His parents rode on either side of him, and they'd hold one of his hands. His dad would pull out the marble and pop it into his mouth as they rode between two large, stone pillars. After that, they were a few minutes' ride from a small town that looked like it was straight from the 1300's. His parents said it was an isolationist society, but they always went to provide a little bit of medical assistance. They never stayed there for more than a couple days before they rode back out and continued elsewhere.

It was a strange tradition—to close his eyes and hold their hands. The marble was the strangest part, but he couldn't bring himself to ask his dad why he'd put it in his mouth. He figured they would tell him when he was ready. He'd never gotten that chance.

"It's a marble," Ven said, smiling as if it was a silly question, trying to hide the squirming feeling writhing in his stomach. He didn't tell her that it looked exactly like the marble that had been recovered from his dad's pocket. The marble that Ven kept in the drawer of the desk behind him.

Dayelle wasn't having it. She tilted her head at him, eyes intense. "You know it's more than that, Ven." She withdrew her hand and placed the marble back in her pocket. "So? You've had your evidence. Do I have your answer?"

Ven gulped hard as the room swirled. He believed her. Or maybe he just *wanted* to believe her. It would mean answers. Answers he couldn't get anywhere else. He shook his head and asked, "What's the job?"

Dayelle smirked. "There's a research facility that has been running experiments on people. It's inhumane. They will be looking for fresh, young doctors, specializing in psychological treatment. I want to plant you on the inside."

Ven pursed his lips, emotions raging inside, both nervous and eager. "Where is it?"

"Very far away," she said, holding the marble up with two fingers, "but I can get us there quickly. I know how to use the portals better than your parents did."

"Portals," Ven said, voice nearly cracking as his eyes flicked to the marble. He smiled, but Dayelle's expression lacked any sense of amusement. "And how long would this take?"

"Likely a few weeks. Possibly two or three months even."

Ven shook his head. He could very well miss the first several weeks of college. His acceptance at Harvard was a big deal. They didn't often take younger students, so missing his opportunity to start would potentially soil the entire arrangement.

"The job, Ven. What's your answer?"

Ven gulped. All logic screamed at him to say no. This was a complete stranger, but the marble... it was a secret nobody would have known about. His parents hadn't even told him about it—he'd only learned of it by sneaking a peek when they'd told him not to.

But somebody really had killed his parents. Mom and dad were his best friends. His only family. Somebody had taken that from him.

Justice demanded that he do *something* to find the truth. He grit his teeth and leveled his gaze at Dayelle. He took a deep breath, soothing the writhing in his stomach as resolve settled over him. "I'll do it."

"I'll come back Wednesday morning," Dayelle said, turning to go. "I'll explain more on the drive. It's best if you don't tell anybody about our meeting. Till then." She winked before leaving the room.

Portals. Magic marbles. Murder. Secret jobs.

The only thing Dayelle *hadn't* mentioned was the dragonblood.

Good grief. What did he just agree to?

# Chapter Two

## Chapter 2

## The Subjects

Mia emerged from the toilet room. The walls churned as she fixed her eyes on her doctor. The effects of the poison diminished enough for her to notice his ancient jowls jiggling slightly with a shake of his head.

"Did you vomit?" He said, voice escaping as a strong wheeze. He barely glanced up at her over his spectacles before continuing to write furiously on his notepad. Her pain was merely a basic procedure to him.

"No." The burning in her throat and gut faded rapidly as her imperviousness worked its magic, adapting to the trauma.

"Symptoms?"

Mia knew the routine. "Mild trembling after initial ingestion, burning sensation everywhere it touched, dizziness, pain in the stomach followed by revulsion and an urge to vomit before the adaptation started taking over."

The doctor grunted as he took notes, glancing at her only twice more as if to confirm what she'd said. After knowing him all seventeen years of her life, she didn't know his name. He never offered it, and she made a point not to ask. She had to wonder if he'd ever once been human. Thinking of it twisted her guts even more than the poison.

"I'm no longer experiencing any symptoms," she said. A warm sensation flooded her skin as her body completed the adaptation, like a reassurance that it had finished.

The doctor clicked a button on his stopwatch and wrote down the time. "We'll compare with the other subjects and post results later this evening."

He said the same thing every time she completed a test. Didn't he realize that she knew how it all worked by now?

She rolled her eyes. "Am I dismissed then?"

"Indeed." He didn't look up, too absorbed in his analytics.

Mia tramped away. She pushed open the aluminum door, leaving the sterile whiteness of her lab room behind. Every test she took made her *angry*, like she wanted to shove her doctor to the ground to see if it would break his hip. See if *he* recovered quickly. But fear of getting put in the box again prevented her.

She passed her bedroom to the left, a stairway to the right. The stairway was to be used by staff only. She didn't know what was up on the higher floors, but she suspected that's where her doctor slept, always within short walking distance of her. These details escaped in a blur as she all but ran to the end of the short hall, bursting out the door at the end.

The inner courtyard of the facility lay beyond. A concrete walkway lined the perimeter of this open-sky area, surrounded on all sides by the four story building. More concrete walkways crossed the middle of the open space, splitting the courtyard into four quadrants where grass and a few small plants grew.

Her urge to find respite from the synthetic world around her took hold, and she stepped off the concrete path and dropped to one knee beside a newly growing plant. It broke out of the blackened soil beneath it, two small, green leaves already sprouting from its tiny stem. A meager sem-blance of calm began to wash through her.

"Mia," a young male voice called from behind her. "I see you're out here before everyone else. You must've done well."

Mia stood quickly, cheeks burning ever so slightly, not only because Dami had come to talk to her, but because she felt nervous that others would know about her fondness for the plants.

"I'm sure I at least did better than you," Mia said steadily, holding back a smile as she ran her eyes across Dami's handsome features. His black hair was trimmed thin. Like all other subjects, imperviousness gave him a lean and healthy body, but he was taller than most. He carried himself with a posture that evoked confidence. His deep, black eyes glittered with hidden wisdom.

Dami breathed a laugh, his smile revealing perfectly white teeth. "Never speak before the scoreboard reveals the results. Not all of us run out here to watch the plants grow."

*So he noticed that.* She offered a nervous smile and glanced up at a facility worker watching them from the second floor rampart that ringed the courtyard area.

Dami looked over his shoulder at the worker and gave the man a small wave. The worker nodded back.

Mia frowned at him. The subjects usually ignored the workers, talking only to other subjects or their doctors. The workers were almost just an-other accessory of the facility itself. Always there. Always watching. They didn't even seem like humans to her.

Dami didn't care about any of that.

Other subjects entered the courtyard, crossing the space to the canteen on the opposite end to receive their rations. Dami waved or nodded to most of those who walked near them, but otherwise remained silent.

Did he know how much they all adored him?

"How was your experience with the poison?" Mia asked, hoping to capture more of his attention.

"Same as all the poisons," Dami said. "I immediately vomited all of it out, but there was a lingering burning and vertigo. Your body doesn't do that though, does it?"

Mia shook her head. "No, I never vomit."

"Interesting," Dami said, nodding with genuine interest.

The volume in the courtyard picked up as more subjects exited their lab rooms. They wore the same kind of clothes made of black synthetic, form-fitting fabric meant for athletic performance. At least, that's how Mia's doctor described it.

Dami stepped closer until he stood right beside her, looking down at the small plant she'd been watching. When he spoke, it was so quiet she could barely pick up the words. "We shouldn't be here—getting tested like we're some kind of experiment. It's wrong."

Mia nodded, drinking in the words. She knew every subject must think the same thing, but dared not speak it. Not since it had been burned out of them in their childhood. Nobody wanted to get thrown into the isolation rooms again. And now she heard it from Dami, the subject who'd been getting first place rank the most consistently for the last few years.

"I hear you," she said, finally forcing out the words, trembling that their very utterance would mean sitting in a dark room by herself for a week.

Dami's plump lips barely moved as he said, "I intend to break out of here somehow, and I'll take you with me."

Warmth flooded Mia's cheeks, but their conversation was cut short before she could respond.

"Hi, Mia. Dami." Mia's friend, Ambrose approached them. Ambrose's skin and hair shone like gold, not with actual light, but reflectively as though made of metal. She'd seen the same colorations among facility staff, but on Ambrose it was flawless. Her very skin spoke of warmth. Whatever it was that made the subjects different, it seemed to affect them in unique ways at times. If they weren't good friends, Mia would probably hate her for it.

And she hated her right now. At least a little bit. She wanted to throw Ambrose across the room for interrupting her conversation with Dami. Didn't she know better?

Ambrose's big smile bespoke enthusiasm.

"Hi, Ambrose," Dami said. "Should we head to the canteen, Mia?"

"Of course," Mia said, stepping back onto the concrete path.

More workers lined the second floor, glaring down at her with those emotionless eyes. What would it mean to be free? And how would Dami break them out? However it would happen, Mia could hardly wait.

# Chapter 3

## Investors

Footsteps clacked down the hallway behind him, signaling Taye Mansen's approach. She always wore heeled shoes that made her look taller. Zein Huan never understood his assistant's sense of fashion.

He stood before a set of aluminum doors that led into the conference room, waiting for Taye to join him.

"You have the results ready?" He said as Taye stopped beside him. He adjusted his doctor's suit, smoothing creases that didn't exist.

Taye held up a folder. "Of course I do. Are they all here, then?"

"I believe so," Zein said. "Let's just hope they give us more time." As the founder of this facility, he was responsible for its success, but he had investors to please. He walked forward, opened a door, and held it open for Taye to enter with him.

The conference room waited on the other side, a large office with two rows of wooden desks facing a raised platform. Several people sat behind the desks, many of them dressed in the finest clothing money could buy, gaudy suits that made Zein's look like rags. A few of the women wore sharp dresses. Technically, their research here was illegal, but that didn't stop many of the richest and most powerful people from investing.

Large windows on the far side of the room let in enough natural light from the midday sun. Chatter in the room drew to a halt as Zein stepped up onto the podium.

"Thank you all for making it here," Zein said. "I assume you all received our latest annual report sometime in the last two weeks. I'm happy to summarize that the subjects continue to adapt physically to every conceivable condition. We'll be—"

"But when do we start making profit, doctor?" It was the distinctive nasal voice of Feriz Cadwol, a disreputable merchant with little respect to formalities. He'd unfortunately dumped a large investment into the facility, making him one of the primary voices. He had pale, freckly skin with unique, orange-red hair.

Zein cleared his throat. Money. They always focused on money. "You'll have read that our medical research results are as optimal as possible. The subjects are completely immune to any disease, sickness, or radiation to which they have been exposed. Our effort to isolate those immunities into practical treatments is currently our primary focus."

"Why does it need to be isolated?" asked a man with a small investment. Zein didn't even remember the man's name.

"It's easier to develop a saleable product," Zein said. "We want it to be isolated for particular treatments. In its raw state, it grants *all* characteristics of the Impervious Project, some of which are not attributes we'd want distributed in an uncontrollable environment."

"That's all good and well, doctor," Feriz said, "but that doesn't make us any money. It's been seventeen years, and we haven't seen any return yet. You've asked us for enough of our time, now we've reached the point where we need to start applying it to profit."

Zein was about to respond when a woman's voice cut in, clear and commanding.

"I have a proposition." Lady Sitena Rosars stood from her seat. All eyes shifted to her. She was a handsome, ambitious, wealthy woman in her mid forties, and one of the few women present who wore a dress, magenta and laced with white and gold.

"I thoroughly read the reports on all the latest experiments." She raised her thin eyebrows. "I haven't failed to notice that, in addition to the subject's impervious nature to sickness or disease, their physical structure also displays considerable resistance. Needles cannot penetrate their skin, and they seem unable to harm each other while sparring. Can you confirm these reports?"

Zein held back a sigh with great effort. "They do show some resilience in that area, yes."

Sitena pressed on. "And if I were to say, attempt stabbing one of them with a dagger, what level of success might I have?"

"They have training with fighting," Zein said. "They block the attack."

"If they did not?"

"Then." Zein swallowed. "Then it would be very unlikely to pierce the skin."

Sitena paused and ran her eyes across the other investors. Many of them nodded with understanding. Feriz Cadwol in particular smiled and rubbed the red beard at his chin.

"I have a proposition," Sitena said. "A way for us to turn a quick profit."

"Surely you don't mean mercenary work," Zein said, already anticipating what she'd bring up.

"Of course I do," Sitena said, raising her eyebrows again. It was perhaps the only expression she ever made. "In fact, I already have a job in mind. I have connections, and I happen to know that this opportunity would pay well to pursue."

Zein shook his head slowly as more investors nodded. "I know you to be thorough in your analysis before you would propose it here to the group, Lady Rosars, so I assume you have also read through their psychological reports?"

"I have. I don't believe complete sanity is required to perform military work."

Zein wiped at his brow. When had he started sweating? "It is often quite vital. I also hesitate to give the subjects any opportunity to express violence against those who are not equally resilient. It will open up doors from which they can never return. I hate to imagine what they might feel once they see how effectively they could destroy another human. Psychologically... I predict devastation.

"We started this project with the objective to improve human life. To find cures, to help those who are in need, to save lives. This would go against the very purpose for which the Impervious Project was initiated." Zein's left leg trembled ever-so-slightly. Was it from rage, nervousness, or terror? His entire life's work crashed around him. If Sitena pressed any further, he doubted he could sway the investors. Most of them, after all, invested solely for wealth.

"All good and true, doctor," Sitena said. "I imagine this avenue to be something difficult for you to accept, but you may still continue your studies. We won't be stopping that at all. Even on a personal level, I'm sure each of us wouldn't mind having access to the amazing results you've been able to discover once you can develop them into specialized treatments. These... jobs would only require a select few subjects, and they would come intermittently as the right job presents itself. We can start with one and see how it evolves from there."

"Brilliant idea," Feriz said, jumping to his feet. "Let us vote on it. Who says aye?" He raised his own hand, muscular frame stretching the limits of his tight suit.

Almost every hand went up, save for two of the investors who happened to be doctors as well. Two of thirty-five. Only two saw how catastrophic this would be.

Zein turned his face away. Taye offered him a consoling frown, and he found no comfort there. He knew what this meant. They said he could continue his research, which he would, but he understood the implications. He'd trembled in fear the very first time the thought occurred to him, even twelve years ago now. The subjects would make terrible warriors, a force so destructive...

"Doctor Huan," said Sitena. The other investors bubbled, talking excitedly amongst themselves. "Prepare a few of the subjects. You'll want some psychological specialists on hand, so I expect a turnover of staff who can assist in that area. Your concern regarding their mental state is certainly valid. I'll speak with my contacts and provide further details."

"Very well," Zein said dismissively. "I assume this meeting has concluded then."

Without awaiting response, he turned to leave. Defeated.

# Chapter Four

---

# Chapter 4

## Portal

Ven was 13 years old the first time he stitched up a severe wound. Dad had just finished performing a surgery on a broken femur, and Ven helped restrain the patient, since they didn't have anything other than a local anesthetic.

Now the man stared blankly at the blue sky, a ruined building surrounding them. Dad moved onto the next patient while Ven finished the stitches. The building had collapsed after an earthquake, killing many of the occupants. Mom was off to Ven's right, holding a woman's hand who was probably about to die unless she got a blood transfusion quickly.

This would be Ven's first and only visit to Haiti.

"Kijan ou rele?" Ven asked the man for his name. It was one of the only things Ven knew how to say in Haitian Creole.

The man only blinked at the sky as Ven continued to do up the stitches. It surprised him how little blood there was. He almost expected a scene of terrible gore, but Dad said his main arteries had avoided damage.

Ven spared a glance at the man's face, asking for his name again before refocusing on the stitches. His hands moved with precision. He'd been in dire circumstances like this several times already, and he had full confidence in his ability. The man still didn't answer until the third time Ven asked.

"Samuel," he said, eyes blinking at Ven for the first time.

Ven finished the stitching and placed his whole attention on Samuel. "Samuel," Ven said with a nod. "You survived. Your leg will heal." He wasn't sure the man would understand him, but he hoped his words would at least convey a sense of hope. Ven demonstrated some deep breaths and placed a hand on the man's chest, indicating that he should do the same. Samuel caught on, and together they took deep breaths for a couple minutes.

After Samuel's nerves seemed to calm down and his shaking diminished, Ven smiled at him and pointed at his leg before giving an enthusiastic thumbs up.

Samuel nodded shakily, biting his lower lip, tears welling in his eyes, repeating, "Mési," their word for thanks.

"Ven," Mom called, beckoning him over.

Ven grasped Samuel's hand, locking eyes with the older man. His heart warmed. They nodded to each other before Ven got up and hurried over to Mom. She handed him one of their few remaining bandages and pointed at a teenage girl who held her hand over a serious head wound.

Mom held Ven's arm before he left. "You did well with him," she said, pointing her eyes at Samuel. "Healing the soul is often more important than healing the body. Our minds can do incredible things. Like you. You are just a boy, but you are not *just* a boy. You can do incredible things."

Ven nodded with a smile, then she released him, and he ran off, hoping there were ever more incredible things in his future.

***

Ven paced around the driveway in front of his home. He'd been walking around since 7:30 and now it was nearly 10:00.

"When's she supposed to show up?" Oliver asked. He plopped down on the front step.

"I don't know, she just said it would be in the morning."

"How long will you be gone?"

"I don't know."

"And you're not taking anything with you?"

"No. She said I won't need to bring anything except one of my parents' lab coats." Ven tugged at the white garment around his shoulders. His dad's lab coat fit perfectly. He wore a loose pair of slacks and a polo underneath. "I can't even bring my phone or my wallet."

Oliver narrowed his eyes. "This sounds like a kidnapping."

Ven shook his head. "I think it's too elaborate for that."

"If you say so. You might be a little too trusting in my opinion."

He was probably right. Ven stopped pacing as a dark blue SUV entered through the open gate.

Oliver came and stood beside Ven. "You have my number memorized, right?"

"Yeah, I'll call you if I need anything." Ven paused. "And if I can find a phone."

"I feel like I should be calling the police."

Ven laughed. "It'll be alright, Oliver. On the bright side, with me gone, you'll have more time for bowling in the hall."

Oliver shook his head.

The SUV came around the loop. Its tinted windows were impossible to see through, but it stopped directly beside Ven. The window of the passenger seat rolled down. "Hop in, Ven. Adventure awaits," Dayelle said from the driver's seat.

Ven gave Oliver one final smile, then opened the door and hopped in, ignoring the discomfort roiling in his stomach. He had to do this. He deserved to know the truth about his parents.

"You didn't bring your phone, right?" Dayelle said as she steered them off the property.

"Nothing but the clothes on my body, just as you'd requested," Ven said as he buckled himself in. He didn't tell her about the small marble in his left pocket. If it was something important, he would keep it with him. "Why does that matter?"

"It won't work where we're going."

"And where is that exactly? Can you tell me now?"

Dayelle's lips curved in a smile. "You've been there before. I can sense the lingering smell of it on you."

That seemed an odd thing to say. Did the woman possess unique senses? He could only imagine such a talent to be animalistic in nature.

"Did your parents ever make you leave your phone behind somewhere?" she asked.

Frequently. Especially when they were in other countries, and for the whole week long horsebacking trip they'd do in Montana. "Yes," he said, hesitant to mention Montana.

Dayelle gave a rich laugh. "Then this will not be foreign to you. There's a portal just a few minutes west of here in the swamps. It's why your parents moved here in the first place. They could easily go between worlds as part of a day trip."

"Between worlds. Right. That's normal," he said, voice laced with sarcasm. Maybe Oliver was right. This whole thing was crazy. He sank into his seat. The twisting feeling in his gut only got worse.

Dayelle gave him a long look as they came to a stop at a light, her eyes glinting with that violet hue. "Remember why you're here. You want to know what happened to your parents. I'm going to provide those answers. It'll be easier to process after we use the portal."

They headed west down I-75 and drove in silence for several minutes. Ven turned the AC away from his face and Dayelle turned it down.

"Did you know my parents?" Ven asked.

"No, but I knew of them." She turned right down a road that led to the Big Cypress Reservation. "We're getting close." This was the same road on which his parents had died.

He swallowed hard. For all he knew, this woman could have been involved in his parent's death. What if she knew all the answers because she was the one responsible? Even then, he didn't have any other option to discover the truth.

Ven stared out the window at the swamplands, wondering if he'd recognize the place where their car was found, grinding his teeth. It was thick with trees and bushes, and he couldn't pick it out. Despite living here off and on over the last eight years, he'd never been up this way. His family wasn't big on fishing or boating. They'd stuck with swimming, tennis, hiking, and horseback riding.

"What's this job you want me to do?" Ven asked, focusing instead on the task at hand.

"I'll tell you more about it once we're through."

Ven shook his head at the insanity of the situation. "And you're sure I'm qualified for it?"

"Oh, absolutely. You're motivated and you care about people."

"Do you really know so much about me?"

"I know just about everything about you, Ven. I also know that you carry your parents' key in your pocket, despite telling me you only had your clothes."

Ven's eyes widened and he opened his mouth, but no words came out. He patted the marble as if to make sure it was still there. Key? That was the first time he'd heard it referred to as a key. It drove his curiosity wild. If only Mom had explained more about this dragonblood concept before leaving him with only questions.

Dayelle chuckled. "Don't worry. It was wise to bring it. You may need it." She turned off down a gravel road and parked in a small turnout. "We're here," she said, turning off the engine and getting out.

Ven got out of the car and looked around. The area didn't seem significant at all. Certainly not the place he'd expect to hide a portal to another world. Though it would potentially make a great place to hide a body if she wanted to get rid of him. He set his jaw. If she tried anything crazy, he'd be ready. He was tall, but a little lanky as a result of his sudden growth spurt last year. He knew he wouldn't be much of a fighter, but he'd at least push her in the water and run away if he needed to.

"Follow close behind me," Dayelle said. "It's not a long walk, but you'll want to keep on the trail I lead or you could slip off into the water."

Ven did as told, relieved that she took the lead. Dayelle led him down a narrow trail directly into the swamp. The path they followed was completely covered in green leaves. The swamp hummed. High pitched croaks abounded. Various animals rumbled at each other in a discordant song. Cypress trees rose up from the water, providing a shaded canopy. A subtle smell of decay and rotten eggs filled every breath. The murky water rippled with movement, but Ven didn't dare to take his eyes off Dayelle's feet.

She stopped after a couple minutes of walking before a large cypress tree. "Here we are."

"It's a tree," Ven said, looking around to see if there was something he'd missed. At least with the supposed "portal" in Montana, there'd been stone pillars beside the path. There was nothing of the sort here.

"It has more to do with the aura." She placed her own marble—key as she'd called it—into her mouth and held her hand out to him.

Ven bit his lip and shook his head, eyes focusing on her hand. He knew what grabbing that hand meant. If this really was a portal, it would take him somewhere else completely. But this was his only way to get answers. If he didn't take her hand, he'd always wonder. The questions would never leave him. He let out a breath and grabbed her hand, stepping up beside her.

She rolled the key to her cheek and said, "I knew you'd have an idea of what we're doing." Her eyes looked more violet than ever. "Take a deep breath. Walk forward with me. You may want to close your eyes."

Ven pointedly kept his eyes open as they took two slow steps forward. On the third step, before his foot touched the ground, the world lurched and spun. It felt as though his skin was stretching, almost to the point of ripping. He screamed but the sound was lost. The noises of the swamp vanished as well, replaced by a high-pitched whine. Ten seconds passed. Then thirty. A whole minute. The greens of the swamp blurred into gray, black, and brown. Branches overhead disappeared, slowly replaced by a growing blue sky.

His foot touched the ground. He crumbled in a heap, gasping for breath. He wasn't sure how much time had gone by. "That was the longest step I've ever taken," he said, face close to the ground. His palms pressed down against gritty tan sand.

"Quite literally," Dayelle said. She bent down and helped Ven to his feet. His vision spun as he looked around, jaw hanging loosely. It was like they'd been transported to a place that was a mixture of southern Idaho and the African safari. Black, volcanic rock formations jutted out from rolling hills, covered in gray grass. Sparse trees with thin trunks were scattered at the bottom of every hill.

"Where are we?"

"The natives of this world call it Orund."

There was no denying it now. It was real. Ven had just traveled to another world. And this wasn't his first time doing it. "Okay." He turned and vomited on the ground.

# Chapter 5

## The Facility

Ven sat on a large, blackened rock. His vision hadn't stopped spinning.

"It should pass in a moment," Dayelle said. She held a canteen out to him. "I did tell you to close your eyes."

He grabbed it and drank deeply, slowly realizing that he hadn't seen her bring a canteen with her. As his vision cleared, other details came into focus. Dayelle held a cloth backpack. A dusty trail nearby led off through the hills. The sky was blue, but deeper and richer than what he was used to.

"What just happened?" Ven asked.

"We traveled through a portal," Dayelle said. "Your previous experience with this was a simplified version. Most people can only travel from one portal to its immediate connection in the other world. I am skilled in traveling from one portal to any other portal, allowing me to cross great distances in a single moment. Which, fortunately for you, brings us within a couple hours ride to the facility."

Ven blinked, trying to process. How many portals were there? Did other worlds exist, or just Orund and Earth?

The familiar sound of horses tromping drew Ven's attention to the trail.

"Our ride is here," Dayelle said.

"What the…" Ven started. Two horses tethered together pulled a carriage behind them. A man on a seat at the front of the carriage guided the horses along.

"Technology is different in this world," Dayelle explained. She climbed into the carriage when it came to a stop.

Ven took another swig of water and looked around. The dizziness was gone, but his mind spun. He took a deep breath of the dry air. It smelled of sand and ancient wood. With a glance behind, he confirmed that the swamplands of Florida were indeed gone. There was no turning back. With a deep breath, he resolved to see this through. He climbed into the carriage. Seats faced each other on the front and back ends. He sat opposite Dayelle.

"Not what you'd expected," Dayelle said knowingly. The carriage lurched forward.

"I'm not sure I expected anything."

"Nonsense. You've seen *Avatar* and *Star Wars*. You thought there'd be dinosaurs or spaceships."

Ven laughed. "Dragons maybe, not dinosaurs or spaceships." He snapped his mouth shut and looked away, hoping he hadn't just revealed anything about his knowledge of dragonblood.

Dayelle leaned forward in her seat, face suddenly serious. "The dragons are dead."

"Okay," Ven said, scooting back, worried that he'd said something he shouldn't.

Dayelle sat back and crossed her legs. "There are some things you should know about Orund. The biggest difference you'll notice is in the technology. Electricity and engines as you know them don't exist here. However, though illegal, many people use dragonblood technology. It functions as a very raw energy, but can be used to power lights and machines."

"Why is it illegal?" Dragonblood. There it was. It was illegal, but his mom had asked him to destroy it. Perhaps that's what this was all about.

"Public fanaticism if you ask me, but it's rooted in the popular opinion that anything to do with dragons is evil. Dragons used to lord over Orund before people overthrew and killed them all. During the overthrow is when dragonblood was found to contain considerably powerful qualities which is when the research and technology around it was born."

"Okay." He was so fascinated by the idea, but couldn't help thinking it sounded too fake. Then again, how could he deny anything she said? He'd just walked through a portal. He might believe anything she'd say after that.

She smirked at him. "You'll find the technology here to be comparable to Earth in both the 1000's and 1800's. Orund's medicine is fairly advanced, which is probably what interested your parents. Also, most everyone you're likely to meet will speak English."

"Prepping me for the quiz later?"

"The context will help keep you from sounding like an idiot at the facility."

Ven nodded, knowing he'd need to be serious. "Right. What about the job itself?"

"Firstly," she said, "there's the job that *our* employers have given you. The job for the facility is a ruse. Remember that. Your true purpose here is to help us bring the facility to ruin. They are involved in dragonblood research, but they've been running tests on human subjects. Their studies are abhorrent." Her lip curled up a bit as though she'd come across a horrid smell. "It must be stopped, and we can't let their research spread. Your task is subtle. Merely sabotage. We have agents there working with other delicate tasks. I understand you have a history of theft."

Ven's eyebrows rose. "You know about that?"

She smiled. "We know everything. I admit I find it interesting when a kind, wealthy young man with no great need simply enjoys putting things in his pockets that don't belong to him."

Ven's cheeks burned and his throat instantly dried.

Her smile widened. "It's okay, I'm not calling the police."

"It's not that," Ven said, shaking his head. "I'm just not proud of it." It was something Ven couldn't understand about himself. Why would he want to help others so much, why would he want to be such a force for good but still allow himself to do something so *wrong*?

She shrugged. "Well, it's not like you stole anything of value anyway."

"Except for another doctor's pen," Ven said. "I didn't know it was something rare—but I did sneak it back into his office when I found out." Still, a weight of guilt crushed his conscience as he thought of the box of stolen goods under his bed that *hadn't* been returned. In truth, he hadn't taken anything for a few months, but he'd been avoiding the impulses more effectively of late.

"Point aside, your role here will be important." Her expression returned to seriousness. She leaned forward. "We don't have anybody among the researchers or doctors yet. You'll have access to information that has of yet been inaccessible to us. The danger of what this facility is doing cannot be emphasized enough. From what we know, they've somehow successfully applied a dragonblood infusion on humans. Such a thing should not be possible. We need to know how they did it so we can prevent such a thing from happening in the future.

"Your task is simple: if you come across valuable documents or information, we need you to steal them and transfer them to another of our agents who will be able to extract the information from the facility. This information would be anything related to the dragonblood transfusion procedure. Once we have enough intel, we should be able to bring down the organization and arrest the researchers involved in developing the study. Also, anything that can be done, subtly, in the meantime, to delay the advance of their studies would be helpful as well. The fewer discoveries they make, the better. Ultimately, we want the facility to meet a brutal end. Even the poor subjects may need to be cured of whatever the doctors did to them."

She leaned back in her seat. "Any questions?"

"A million," Ven said, pinching the bridge of his nose. "But when do you tell me what happened to my parents?"

"I will once we take down the facility. I anticipate that it will take no longer than seven or eight weeks."

Ven nodded. He was finally closer to learning what happened to his parents. A tingle of excited energy ran across his skin. "What about the job the facility will have for me?"

"About that," she said. "You'll get one of two assignments, either as a researcher or as a subject's physician. You won't know which until after you arrive. This will put you closer to the kind of data we need and make it easier to sabotage the results. Either of the assignments shouldn't be a problem for you, but I suspect if they evaluate you first, they will assign you to a patient. I understand you have extensive studies in psychology. You will need it."

Ven wondered what she meant. He certainly had more experience treating illnesses and injuries than he did with psychological things, but he'd already passed basic college courses on the topic and had found it quite interesting. It wasn't something he'd really practiced in a professional environment other than in communication with patients.

Dayelle pushed aside the curtain covering a small window on the side of the carriage and looked outside, sunlight spilling in. "I should be getting out soon," she said. "Any last questions?"

That was all the prep she was going to give him. But somehow, deep down, he knew he could do it. He knew how to work with patients and other doctors. "How do I get back to Earth when I've done the job?"

"Confident," Dayelle said with a smile. "Good. We'll come back the same way we came."

Ven nodded. He would help take down this facility. He would get his answers. "Let's do this."

"Very well." She looked out the window again. "One last thing. Should you find information or feel it necessary to contact us, the first time you may do so is while you are collecting your meal from the employee canteen. Just say that you wish you had some grapes loudly enough that others may hear you. Spoiler," she said, holding a hand to the side of her mouth as if telling a secret, "they never serve grapes there. Horrible place."

"You'll also want this." She held up a paper folder. "It has your paper-work to get in. I should be off." Dayelle made as if to leave, then added, "remember not to lose focus on your real job." With that, she opened the carriage door and jumped out, door closing behind her.

Ven looked out the window beside his seat, but she was already gone.

The carriage lumbered on for another hour, its steady rhythm and bump providing Ven a bit of comfort through the loneliness of waiting. Would this all be worth it? He'd possibly ruined his future career as a doctor by taking this job and coming here. Given the timeline, he'd likely miss the first few days of college. Would they still let him proceed if that happened? His heart pounded.

Without warning, the carriage came to a halt. Ven's chest bubbled with anticipation. He checked the windows on both sides, the one to his right revealing a massive mansion that looked like it belonged on a university campus. Only it lacked the ornamentation. He leapt outside the carriage to get a better look, his brown leather shoes grinding gravel beneath his feet.

Red bricks formed the walls of the four story building. There were no windows on the lower floor, but the three upper floors were heavily lined with them. A large, wooden, double-doored gate hung open. It led into what looked like an inner courtyard, and it was big enough for the carriage to fit through, but they'd stopped outside. A few, small cottages were also scattered around the trail they'd ridden. They reminded him of homes he'd seen in South America.

Ven wasn't alone. Several other carriages stopped in front of the facility. Their clothing looked different, and Ven felt a little out of place. Most of them, including the women, wore leather boots and long, light colored lab coats of woven fabric. Ven wondered if he'd stick out too much, but Dayelle didn't even comment on it at all, so maybe it wouldn't matter.

"Doctors," said a man at the gate, "please present your contracts here and then you'll be ushered to a conference room for orientation."

A barking laugh caught Ven's attention and two other doctors approached him. "Who brought their child?" the man in the front asked. He had a sharp nose, thick eyebrows, and short cut hair.

"The name is Ven," Ven said, almost laughing at the idea that somebody had already noticed his youth. This was his role. Dayelle had complete confidence in him. Enough so that she brought him in, even at seventeen years old. Ven had traveled all over the world providing healthcare services with his parents. He could do this. "Doctor Ven Yashke. And yours?"

"You may call me Doctor Makarr," he said, a smile at the edge of his mouth. "And this is Doctor Henze." He gestured at the doctor beside him. Both of them were relatively young, perhaps in their early twenties. Certainly not as young as Ven.

"I just didn't know they let children become doctors," Makarr said. "Is this your first time leaving your parent's home?"

"Yes," Ven said. The haughty glint in Makarr's eye hinted he was making fun of Ven, but he decided to play along. "I've never even seen the sun till now."

Henze laughed, but Makarr merely narrowed his eyes.

"Well, try not to get lost out here, eh," Makarr said.

"Thanks for reminding me! I was just about to head back down the road. I suppose *inside* the building is the correct way." Ven hurried towards the gate without a glance back at the other doctors, handing his papers to the servant.

The servant looked over the contract for an agonizing few seconds. Ven picked at the hem of his coat and held his ground. *I'm a fraud. They know it.*

"Welcome Doctor Yashke," the servant said, handing the contract back. He pointed to a door beyond the courtyard. "Enter through that door and take a seat anywhere on that second row."

"Thank you." Ven let out a long breath and crossed the courtyard area, noting how empty the space seemed. The facility vaguely reminded him of Harvard University buildings, but here there was less life and more sterility.

He entered the door as instructed and another usher helped him find a seat in the second row. The place was shaped like an amphitheater, a rounded room with four rows of seats facing a stage. Some thirty indiscernible voices chatting away provided an undertone like that of bees and wasps buzzing in a blossoming tree. About half of those seated wore the doctor uniform while the others wore suits. Whatever he was becoming a part of here, it was certainly a large undertaking.

He took his seat beside a small, young man in a brown suit scribbling furiously into a notebook. "How are you, sir?" the man asked.

"Quite excellent," Ven said with a smile. "And yourself?"

"Oh, excited to say the least." Indeed, the man seemed to bounce as he spoke, and he had an accent that suggested he was from somewhere like India. "Name's Tem, by the way. Tem Porodukuz. You can call me Tem."

Ven smiled. "Pleasure to meet you, Tem. You can call me Ven."

"Doctor Ven Yashke?" Tem said.

So Tem knew Ven's name already? When Ven nodded, Tem seemed like he would say more, but a loud tapping from the stage silenced the crowd, all faces turning. On the stage stood an older man in a doctor's suit with a bald head and squinty eyes. He held his hands together behind his back, examining the audience with a steady gaze.

"Welcome," the man said, voice deep and rumbly with age. "I'm Doctor Zein Huan, founder and director of the Impervious Project. When I started this project, I had a simple vision—to cure anything and everything. Many of you will scoff at the idea, but be prepared to be surprised. Here in this facility we have indeed developed such a solution, and you are joining near the later stages of this research.

"There are two primary goals. Each of you, both doctors and assistants will receive assignment either to research or subject treatment. For those hired to research, you will be tasked with developing a practical treatment that can be administered for individual needs. For those hired for subject treatment, you will be tasked with ensuring the ongoing health of the test subjects.

"Neither assignment will be simple and must be treated with utmost diligence. We are on the cusp of changing the world. At our very fingertips is the power to reduce the suffering of the human race." He held out his hand, fingers raised for emphasis.

It was a bold vision. Ven could already feel a fire burning his chest. Was such a thing truly reality? There was so much about this world that was unknown to him. He had to remind himself of his true purpose here. To end the research so Dayelle would trust him enough to give him the information about his parents. Something about this place was darker than Zein tried to portray. At least, as long as Dayelle was to be trusted.

"Ms. Taye Mansen will hand out your assignments," Zein said. He dismissed himself without another word, vanishing behind the stage.

A tall woman wearing high heels and a narrow dress clacked her way through the rows of seats, shuffling through sheets of paper and handing them out one by one. When Taye handed Ven his sheet he scanned it quickly.

He'd been assigned as a subject doctor. Just as Dayelle predicted. He rubbed two fingers across his lips in thought. What would the job entail? Was he expected to be an expert on psychological treatment? Mom always talked to him about emotional management, metacommunication, and a slough of other things. They'd also had to treat many people suffering from depression, PTSD, OCD, and nearly any mental condition imaginable, but those often required more long term treatment than his family was able to provide. He knew most of the basic principles, but in practice, this would be new territory.

He chewed his tongue as he read through the rest of the document. He'd been assigned to work specifically with one of the top performing subjects. Surprisingly, she was the same age as him, only seventeen years old, though the facility was under the impression that Ven was 20. His role would primarily be focused on helping provide psychological well-being. He was to run analysis and treatment according to her specific needs.

*Shouldn't be too bad. I can do this.*

Beside him, Tem grunted in his seat and said, "Ven, I'm going to be working as your assistant."

"My assistant?" Ven said. "What do you mean? You're not a doctor as well?"

Tem laughed. "No, I'm not a doctor." He looked back through his paper. "Change bed sheets, fetch hot water, prepare notes for examinations.

Basically anything you need it seems. Well, it doesn't say anything about foot massages though, so I wouldn't get any ideas." He laughed at his own joke.

Ven smiled, glad that he'd at least be working with someone who was good-natured.

"I've already been working here for a couple years though," Tem said. "So if you have any questions about the facility, I can help you there too. All of us assistants already have plenty of experience here so help acclimate the new doctors. Say, how old are you anyway? You're quite a tall one, but look so young."

"I'm seventeen," Ven said, hoping it would come out as sarcastic. He'd said his real age partially because he just didn't feel inclined to lie to Tem.

Tem humored him with a good laugh. "Right you are, doctor. Take every year while you can."

"Well," Ven said, "my assignment says to make contact with the subject immediately, even before settling in. Perhaps you could show me the way to make introductions."

Indeed, several other doctors were already up and leaving the room.

"Very well, Ven. I'll take you to meet Mia."

# Chapter 6

## The Doctor

Mia folded her arms across her chest. She sat on a bench in the inner courtyard, her back resting against a table behind her. She'd been told to sit here and wait for someone to come meet her. The other subjects were similarly seated at their own tables.

The large space was silent, several staff glaring down at them from the second story railing. She couldn't remember the last time she'd seen so many staff all at once. Perhaps they were worried about something.

This was the first morning of her life where she hadn't been summoned from her room by her doctor. In fact, she hadn't seen that ancient man all day. She could only hope that he'd finally withered away and died.

Doors opening on the far side of the courtyard drew her attention. Several new faces emerged, many of them dressed in light gray doctor suits. They were relatively young, none of them bore canyons of wrinkles, and there was sparsely a gray hair to be seen. She sat up straighter. The doctors began pairing off with her fellow subjects.

She'd never seen behavior like this. Mia scooted to the edge of her bench, mouth hanging open. As soon as she noticed, she snapped it shut and slumped back in her seat.

A young doctor emerged from the crowd, heading straight for her. He was tall and slender, with light blonde hair and sun-tanned skin. His thin lab coat hung loosely on his shoulders. A small man in a brown suit accompanied him.

"Mia?" the doctor said. Even his voice sounded a little high. It reminded her of the other male subjects' voices from a couple years ago.

"No," Mia said. "Sorry, I think Mia left."

The doctor smiled. She'd *never* seen a doctor smile. "Pleased to meet you, Mia. I can appreciate a little sarcasm. My name is Doctor Ven Yashke." He held out a hand.

"Wow," Mia said, cocking her head. He'd just gone and blurted out his name already. She'd never known her doctor's name. "Did my doctor die? I know people do that when they get old."

"Uh." Doctor Yashke dropped his hand and glanced at his assistant who shrugged. "I don't actually know, but I'm your new doctor."

"How old are you?"

"20."

"Wow. That's raz."

"Raz?" Ven rubbed at his lower lip. He shrugged. "What's that mean?"

"Oh, yeah, I guess docs never say that. It means something is interesting, or good?"

"Oh, an expression."

Mia folded her arms, shaking her head. She'd already spoken more casually to this doctor than she ever had to her old one. What was different? His youth. His casual tone. His *smiling*. It was disarming. She frowned. Maybe it was part of the facility's ploy. Everything was a ploy.

"I know this is a different experience for you," Ven said. "Doctor Brogerman worked with you your whole life so far, but like my dad always said, 'change offers a way for us to grow that we might never have experienced otherwise.' I'd like to get to know you better before we dive in. Should we head back to your examination room to talk some more?"

Mia's head reared back. "Talk?" Her heart pounded in her ears. The way he spoke to her almost sounded *kind*. And he *asked* her to go to the examination room instead of *telling* her. Something was off.

Ven clasped his hands together. "I take it you and Doctor Brogerman didn't talk much. He probably wasn't a very personable individual..." He glanced at the other people in the courtyard. The frown on his face looked sad and confused. He shook the frown away a second later. "If you don't want to talk, that's fine. You could just listen, but I'd prefer to speak somewhere more private. Is your examination room acceptable?"

"I suppose," Mia said with a shrug. She was up to anything. This new tactic of theirs, whatever it was, wouldn't faze her, despite that pounding in her ears. Or the tightness in her chest. Would the other subjects notice how she was reacting? Perhaps somewhere private would be much better. She launched to her feet, leading the way back to the exam room, steps quickening the more she thought about that tight feeling in her chest.

The courtyard passed her vision in a painful blur. Once she dropped onto her seat in the exam room, she gasped for air.

Ven entered a second later. "Fetch us some cold water, please," he said to his assistant before closing the door behind him. Instead of taking a seat, he crouched down in front of Mia. The frown was back on his face. He scrutinized her for a second, then went to his chair, sitting a safer distance away.

"Sorry about that," he said. "I didn't know how you'd react. Do you experience those feelings very often?"

"What are you talking about?" A reactive sneer tugged at her lips.

"Right... you didn't talk much..." The sad frown didn't leave his face. "I assume your conversations were more analytical?" He nodded to himself, rubbing his lower lip again before speaking. "We can address that later. To begin with, I want to make sure we have a mutual understanding here, so I'll review some things. You grew up here in the facility. They ran regular tests on you as part of the Impervious Project to test how your resilience would develop. They've reasonably concluded that you're fairly resilient to everything physical. I still need to go through your papers in more detail, but I don't think I'll be running any tests on you. It's quite clear the results would be the same."

Mia blinked up at him, digesting the words. After a moment of silence, she finally said, "No tests? So what are you here for?"

Ven nodded. "That's the question." He sat forward in his seat. "Mia, your physical resilience is without question a miracle." He held up the folder in his hand. "You are a living marvel. From my quick glance through your papers, you've survived things that normal people wouldn't be able to. I've usually worked with people who have physical injuries, but I was asked to help you in a different way." He shook his head as he glanced at the floor. "You've been through some difficult things that may have been rather traumatic, and I've seen that break people down before, so I think they want me to help you develop resilience.

"Right now, this is a different concept for you. Your body's resilience is automatic, but your mind isn't set up that way. Emotional resilience has to be learned.We'll focus on creating a  deeper emotional awareness, so I might often ask you how you feel. This will start you down a process of identifying those feelings and actively responding to them."

"What about the ranking system?"

"I haven't heard anything about that yet." Ven shrugged, looking back at the papers. "I'm not sure how to put emotional resilience into a ranking system. I suppose we'll see what the facility recommends there."

Mia slumped in her seat. This was something new. It was both exciting and nerve-wracking. Her initial panic had faded, but there was still some strange horror lingering in the back of her mind.

Ven cleared his throat as if he'd say more, but the door opened. "Thank you, Tem," Ven said to his assistant as he placed a pitcher and two cups on the counter.

"I do have one more question for you," Ven said, turning his attention back to Mia. "I'd like to know what you want. What do you want for yourself?"

"Freedom," Mia said, the word bursting from her mouth.

Ven nodded. "What does freedom mean to you?"

Mia shook her head incredulously. "To be able to make my own choices. To dictate what happens in my day of my own accord. It means…" she paused and took a deep breath. "It means going to the mountains and seeing flowers grow."

"I see." Ven rubbed his lower lip again.

He was analyzing her. She could see it now. He was testing her mind, testing her words. They weren't going to be testing her body any more but how she responded to things emotionally. She was still just a test subject to them. She shouldn't have told him what she really wanted.

"Well," Ven said, "I think that's a great thing to want. It reminds me of a town I've been to. Beautiful place. I'd go there every year growing up." He looked at her, and for the first time she noticed a joy in his eyes. She realized now what it was about him that was so disarming. It wasn't simply his youth, but it was how *real* he was. There was *sincerity* behind his words. At least it seemed that way. It had to be a farce. He was a doctor. He was testing her, as they always were.

"For my part, I want you to get there, Mia." Ven rose to his feet. "I understand there's quite a routine here from day to day. Let's meet here again tomorrow morning and look through the schedule." He went and held the door open for her. "Thanks for your time, Mia."

Mia stood, her movements mechanical. The pain in her chest returned as she realized something else. She wanted to keep talking to him. He was the first person she'd ever opened up to. He'd gotten her to talk about flowers, of all things. She wished she could say everything she was feeling, to burst into tears and tell him all the pain of the constant comparison to other subjects and the mandatory tests. She wanted to share about her urge to run outside and see the beauty of nature, and even the burning desire to want to hug someone and feel the warmth and strength of somebody actually *loving* her.

But of course she couldn't say any of that. She clenched her fists and her jaw. She forced back all the thoughts, but the pain remained. Thankfully, her feet took her from the exam room and straight to her bedroom, the one place of privacy she had. She dropped to her knees beside her bed, buried her face into her pillow, and wept.

# Chapter 7

## Climb

Ven let out a deep breath as the door closed behind him. He filled his lungs to capacity before letting it out slowly. "All is well," he told himself. It helped him to resettle and refocus. The pain in her eyes was so striking. Her initial arrogance was a thin farce. It reminded him of helping his mom work with abused children at an orphanage in Mexico. He hadn't even made that connection until he'd sat down with Mia.

He forced himself not to watch Mia as she walked away down the hall into her room. To say she was beautiful would be an understatement. She had flawless skin and luxurious hair. In fact, all the other subjects he'd seen in the courtyard were equally beautiful, male and female. They wore the same, form-fitting attire that accentuated bodies of optimal physical condition. It had immediately made him feel self-conscious of his own gangly form.

He cleared his throat audibly and shook his head. This helped to clear his mind. He couldn't shake the pleading look in her eyes, that moment of pain that crossed her face. She needed help, that much was sure.

Tem excused himself to go make sure Ven's room was in order.

The chair creaked as Ven plopped onto it and withdrew the folder of paperwork. He flipped through the papers, astounded by the entire operation. She and the other 39 subjects were essentially prisoners. How they'd ended up here to be raised in the facility, he had no idea. Nothing of their origin was revealed. Most of the notes about Mia were statistical. She'd survived diseases and poisons. They'd even attempted surgery on her once, which had proven to be impossible.

Apparently in her younger years, tantrums were not uncommon. She'd scream, kick, or bite, which they only ever treated by putting her into an isolation room. In fact, that appeared to be the previous doctor's only and immediate resolution to any discontented behavior. Ven couldn't begin to imagine the kind of trauma that might have instilled in her.

He closed the folder, shaking his head with a sigh. *Help me*, her eyes had said. It might as well have been verbal.

Tem entered the room. "Your room is all in order, sir."

"Thank you."

"How did she seem?"

Ven sighed again. "Hurting. This won't be easy. She opened up more than I thought she would, but her emotional needs have been all but ignored or intentionally smothered. She rightfully may have very little trust in doctors."

Tem offered a laugh. "I'm sure you can work that out."

"Thanks again, Tem. You've been extremely helpful today." Ven stood. "Can you show me to my room?"

"Certainly." They proceeded down the hall and up a flight of stairs.

"And tomorrow morning, I'd like you to go over her previous schedule so I can see what her old routine looked like."

"Easy enough."

They reached the second floor which boasted a featureless hallway similar to the one below: white walls, white floors, white ceiling. A fluorescent light stretched the whole distance. It was similar to electricity, but instead of glass, it looked like a glowing bar of metal. It was the first sign he'd caught of anything related to that dragonblood technology Dayelle mentioned. Nothing in Mia's paperwork mentioned the origin of her condition at all. He could see why Dayelle had recommended he try to get on the research team. But then he wouldn't have met Mia and seen that pleading look on her face.

But why did that matter? That had nothing to do with his objective or learning about his parents.

"Here it is, sir," Tem said, pointing to a door with his hand. "I'll see you in the morning."

"Thank you, Tem."

Tem smiled before disappearing down the hall.

Silence greeted Ven as he entered his room. It was small, but it had a bed, a drawer, and a desk. There was never a shortage of desks in this place. He walked straight for the window on the far end of the room. His window faced west, towards the dropping sun. The uneven ground outside grew long shadows. Dark gray stones sneered back like blackened teeth at the edges of every hill. It was a marvel they'd found an area flat enough to place a building this large.

He took a deep breath, thoughts returning to his task at hand. How would he locate any information? What type of information did he need in order to earn Dayelle's trust? Now that he was in it, the task seemed more daunting than he'd originally anticipated.

But the image of Mia's pleading expression kept coming to mind. It was people like her that had inspired his family to travel all over the world and do what they'd done. *No, I need to help bring down this facility. That's the real task. They're clearly doing something to these subjects that is unacceptable.* But Dayelle had said the research was extremely dangerous. What was dangerous about making people immune to disease? Perhaps it was the idea that dragonblood research was being applied to people at all.

He slumped down in the chair by the desk. "What would my parents think about this," he whispered to himself. Like him, they had been driven by the urge to help people. Wouldn't they have wanted to cure diseases? But he was missing something. There was danger. What did Dayelle know that Ven's parents hadn't?

The answers wouldn't come tonight. What he really needed now was sleep.

***

Ven slept horribly. His mind hadn't stopped racing, but even worse than that was the rock hard bed he'd slept in. It had been Doctor Brogerman's. "Apparently the man not only lacked emotions, but lacked physical feelings as well," Ven said to Tem who stood beside him.

Tem laughed and said, "Shall I find a new mattress?"

"Yes, if possible, but I'll want you to come with me this morning as we work with Mia." They stood on the second floor of the inner courtyard. The cool, morning air was calming as it filled his lungs. They'd already eaten breakfast and looked through Mia's usual routine.

Mia sat at a table below with two other subjects, a boy and a girl.

"What are their names?" Ven asked.

"Ambrose is the shiny girl," Tem said. "The imperviousness impacted her appearance a little differently." Indeed, Ven noted how her hair and skin glimmered like metal in the light. "And Dami's the name of the boy. The three of them have ranked in the top five rather consistently. The subjects tend to group together like that."

Ven found that every subject was equally a physical marvel like Mia, though not all of them were as naturally pretty in the face. The subjects had no extreme physique, but they had an athletic build. No hulking muscles, no deathly thinness, no extra weight. It was peak physical health. He'd be surprised if they couldn't all run for miles at a full sprint.

Mia and most of the other subjects avoided looking up at the staff on the second floor. Ven never once caught her glancing up at them. Dami, however, ventured so far as to smile and wave on occasion.

"Do you think they hate it here?" Ven asked.

"Certainly not. They don't know anything different than life inside the facility."

Ven doubted that. "Despite that, I wouldn't be surprised if they hold some kind of resentment for being stuck here. They wouldn't like or trust us, and they clearly haven't been trusted either. This would make them feel like we're against them."

Tem folded his arms. "I suppose that could be true. "

"Let's head down," Ven said. He was interested in meeting other subjects, but wasn't sure they'd be open to interacting with him. Dami seemed approachable though. Tem followed him down the stairs and out into the enclosure.

"Good morning," Ven said as they neared Mia's table.

"Good morning," Dami said with a nod, though Mia merely looked at Ven with an impassive expression. Ambrose gave him a quick look before pointedly turning away. Ambrose's light gold hair and brass skin easily made her the most unique looking subject.

Ven cleared his throat. "I was reviewing your schedule this morning, Mia. I'd like to do things a little differently if you don't mind."

"Do I have a choice?" Mia asked.

Ven smiled. Providing a person with options was a basic method from one of his psychology books to help them establish a sense of control. "Well, yes actually. To some degree. Your paperwork did mention that there are certain activities you enjoy. I'd like you to pick one to do." This earned him another glance from Ambrose. He could hardly believe that they were the same age as him. If he had to guess, they looked more like they were all in their early twenties.

"Climbing," Mia said without hesitation.

"Very well," Ven said, then addressed Mia's friends. "By the way, I'm Doctor Yashke. It's good to meet you."

The three subjects stood from their seats, and Ven noted that Dami was an inch taller than him. Dami offered another small nod before leaving, Ambrose at his side.

"Tem, if you'd show us where this climbing is," Ven said. Tem led the way to the far end of the courtyard. They went through a door and down a long hallway. "What kind of climbing is it that you do?" Ven asked.

"We climb the cliff face," Mia said. "Are there other ways to climb?"

Ven shrugged. "I don't know. You can tell I'm not a climber."

Tem eventually led them out a door on the southeast end of the building. It was outdoor, and a massive black rock stood before them, rising well over four stories. It had a steep surface, etched with cracks. The area was fenced in by a tall brick wall.

There was only one other subject currently attempting a climb while his doctor stood by. Four other staff members roamed the perimeter. They seemed like guards except for the fact that they weren't armed.

"This is it? You climb that?" Ven's jaw hung open.

"They're quite able climbers," Tem said.

"And you enjoy it?" Ven said

"You asked me to pick, so I did." Mia removed her shoes and approached the rock at a jog, her steps bouncing.

Mia jumped at the rock, catching a small lip with a single hand. Both her feet found purchase on a sideways crack. She moved fluidly, as though she were climbing a ladder. Ven watched with mouth agape, entranced. In a matter of seconds, she had quickly passed the other subject who was only halfway up the rock. Mia reached the top in less than a minute.

Then she jumped off the rock. Ven's heart lurched, and he screamed as he sprinted over. "No, no!" She crashed face-first into stony ground in front of him with a fleshy crack.

He dropped to his knees, heart pounding furiously. "Why," he said, trembling hands held out, unsure what to do.

Mia rolled over. She took one look at his face and burst into fitful laughter. Even Tem chuckled from behind. She struggled to get the words out between her laughing as she said, "I'm impervious, remember?"

Part of him wanted to be mad, but her pure, unfiltered laughter was contagious, and his own laugh erupted.

"That will be the highlight of my year," Mia said as she stood.

"Wow," Ven said. There wasn't even a single mark on her face. "I suppose that puts my understanding into perspective. Whatever your condition is, you truly are remarkable. Any other human would likely have died from that just now."

Mia's smile vanished. "Yes, well, I suppose I'm less human then."

"That's not what I meant," Ven said. Then he thought of the dragonblood. *Did* that make her less human? Certainly not. "Do you know where your unique trait originates from?" He wasn't sure if he was supposed to ask that, but the question merely slipped from his mouth.

Mia's eyes were hard as they scanned his face. "They didn't tell you, did they?" Her voice was barely a whisper. Tem still stood near the door of the building, several feet away. Perhaps he wouldn't be able to hear.

Ven glanced at the others in the area, also far enough away. Her whispering set him on edge. Was she saying something she shouldn't? He lowered his own voice. "No. No, they haven't told me anything, nor was it contained in any of the paperwork I've been given."

"Then you know as much as I do." She folded her arms and turned back to face the giant rock.

Of course they wouldn't have told her. How old could she have been when they did this to her? She'd probably been too young to remember any of it.

"It must be difficult," Ven said. "Not knowing why you are different. Do you know why they study you?" He'd used the word "they" even though that essentially included himself.

Mia breathed a laugh. "Yes, apparently they want to find a way to heal others by seeing how my body recovers from things that you *normal* humans struggle to overcome. They've spent seventeen years trying to figure that out. I think they have all the answers they're going to get, they just want to keep us here."

Her continued use of the "they" meant his tactic was successful. Ven wasn't about to explain how some research could indeed take many decades to truly learn the deeper answers. Instead, he said, "Yeah, that sucks—I mean, can see how that would be frustrating." He had to force himself to remember to use more professional language. Dad always tried to correct him on that while they worked with patients. "Perhaps not knowing when or if it will end makes it even harder."

"Precisely," she said. He found her word choice interesting. It reminded him that she was raised by doctors.

She was in pain. Every day was suffering. He could see it. Even that fleeting moment of laughter earlier was likely a rare occurrence. Or perhaps it wasn't as bad as he thought. After all, she didn't seem to be despairing. One thing was certain, however. She didn't deserve to be here.

He went and stood beside her. "It *will* end, Mia. Of that much I'm sure. Have hope in that." In just a few weeks, in fact.

Her deep, untrusting eyes scrutinized him. He expected that pleading look again, but it didn't return.

"We'll see," she said, then went to climb the rock again.

# Chapter 8

## The Job

Zein walked outside the facility and headed west. He'd been dreading this inevitable moment for weeks. His feet crunched on dry grass. There hadn't been much rain for the last month. Patches of clouds dotted the sky, surrounded by bright blues.

Ahead of him, hands clasped behind her back, Sitena Rosars looked off to the north. Today she wore a tight, white dress, loose just past the hips. She had a golden shawl about her shoulders. Her appearance was a stark contrast to the dark stone cliff rising behind her. She did not turn to look at him. She seemed intent on proving that the empty land ahead of her was more interesting.

Was she evil for what she wanted to do? No. Ambitious perhaps, and most certainly naive. Like her, most of the investors lacked vision of the consequences their actions would take. Money was all that mattered.

"We've got a job for them," Sitena said in her low voice.

Zein sighed. "I was hoping you weren't serious about that."

She turned to look at him, offering an amused smile. "Come now, Doctor Huan, you know me well enough to understand that I don't merely speculate."

"Indeed. That doesn't mean I can't hope."

"You are wise, doctor, but you lack vision at times." She started walking off, parallel to the dark cliff beside her, clearly expecting him to follow.

*Always the theatrics with these nobility.* Zein kept pace beside her.

"I knew from the beginning, you see," Sitena said. "I always considered the possibility that the subjects would be capable not only of surviving more, but of *doing* more. Your concern about their psychological state can also be helped by giving them a deeper purpose to their lives. Allowing them to take action will help them."

"Yes, ma'am, this can be true, but I fear for other consequences."

"Speak frankly, doctor."

"Very well." He stopped walking, and she turned to face him. "Most of the subjects do not have reasonably sufficient mental capacities to be exposed to true warfare. The only fighting they've done is sparring with each other. If we were to allow them any level of violence against somebody who does not have the same physical resilience, people could die. Killing someone can have multiple effects on the killer, and with the subjects, they have developed a culture of superiority among them.

"If allowed to fight against those without the impervious trait, it allows them to compare themselves to *us*. They already have a sense of distaste towards the facility staff. I wouldn't want them to feel like they can express that distaste. Fear of going to the isolation room would dissipate if they realize they could overpower anybody who tried to force them there."

Sitena folded her arms. "You worry they'd become uncontrollable?"

"Yes."

"But you have other means of security in place, do you not? You know what I'm referring to."

"Of course we do, as a last resort."

"Then it's simple. If any of them rebel, you must ensure that a public display is made of them. Reinstill the fear. But also—" She paused and looked back to the north. "You can win them over with loyalty as well. Less dependable at first, but be sure that your new doctors help to sway the subjects towards loyalty or devotion. Let them feel that *you* give them purpose."

"Yes, this will take time though. When are they expected to fulfill this job you've gotten them?"

"Two days."

"My word! That's not at all the time they would need." Zein fiddled with a button on his suit.

"This requires a small team, doctor," she said. "You only need four subjects. You can select those who are more mentally stable and perhaps more adept at combat. If it helps you feel better, you can send a doctor along with them."

"Send a doctor into battle?"

Sitena laughed.

Perhaps she thought it would calm him, but it frustrated him more. Another thought occurred to him. A frightening one. "What is the job? Where are they going?"

"They wouldn't tell me the exact location, but it's supposed to be a farm and refinement plant. They apparently stole some rare product from our sponsor and have been trying to replicate it for themselves. They want to steal the stockpile and burn the crop. They didn't make it sound like it's a heavily guarded operation, so it should be relatively simple."

"I didn't realize you had such experience in banditry." Zein couldn't look at her as he said the words. People would die. The job was so vile his stomach turned.

"Don't pretend you're so gallant and honorable. This is going to fund your continued research. That is our real objective. We still want to cure the world of malady, doctor. This is a means to making it possible."

What she said was true. Zein wished it didn't resonate with him, but he knew they needed funding to continue operating. Paying several doctors was expensive, even though they'd managed to lower wages with the new ones, all of their income came from donations and sponsorships.

Something about the place they were targeting sounded familiar though. "You mentioned burning a crop?" Zein said.

"Yes, and that doesn't involve killing anyone."

Unless the owners were intent on protecting it. The subjects wouldn't know how to restrain themselves.

"A crop involved in manufacturing a rare good? Something that seems to involve proprietary knowledge?"

Sitena's brown eyebrows rose as she regarded him. "Yes, that seems to be the implication. Why so curious about those details?"

Sitana was an intelligent person, no doubt, and he was wary of her withholding information for her own advantage. Zein was determined not to share anything with her that he didn't have to. "Oh, I didn't excel at psychological studies as a student, or in practice, but I understand the value of convincing myself of the morality of the task. You say these proprietary goods were stolen? Very well, I can sympathize with the desire to return them to the proper owner."

"Very good," Sitena said. "Make a selection of the team and inform me tomorrow afternoon."

Zein dipped his head in a bow. "I will do so." He turned on his heels and went back inside, his pace quickening with each step.

He had suspicions. This wasn't a random job. It was calculated. That refinement plant sounded like the same place from which *he* purchased a rare poison. Did Sitena know that already? For all he knew, Sitena herself was the sponsor.

A voice broke him from reverie.

"Doctor Huan," Taye said. "Your latest meeting didn't go the way you wanted, I'm assuming?" She stood across from him in the hallway, just beside a door that led down into the cellar.

"It went as we'd assumed," Zein said, "and we have less time to prepare than I wanted."

"But something else troubles you?"

"Yes." He lowered his voice. "Come with me to the cellar. I'd like to check on our stock of dragonsbane."

# Chapter 9

## Departure

Mia stared at the ranking board. Her name was only on rank four. Dami was in first, then Ambrose in second, and another subject named Baze came in third. Baze was arrogant and annoying. She hated coming in behind him. And even though Ambrose was her friend, that didn't mean she wanted to be behind her either. Mia wanted another competition so she could rank back up.

Staff told her to wait out here in the enclosure, and she knew she should do something besides stare at the ranking board. There was a plant in one of the quadrants in the courtyard that was showing little flower buds that she wanted to take a closer look at. She didn't get the chance.

Footsteps came from behind her. The staff didn't know how well she could hear. Possibly all the subjects had the same hearing, but she'd never heard the others talk about it. Her old doctor was a testament that normal humans had hearing deficiencies. She recognized these steps as Ven's. He walked as though worried the ground was too soft to be tread on, or maybe he felt like he was sneaking. Nobody else she knew walked so quietly. They seemed like the kind of steps someone took when they were treading somewhere they didn't belong. Interestingly enough, the steps became louder and more confident as he drew near.

"Mia," Ven said, his voice gentle. "The administrator wants to meet with both of us now. Would you follow me?"

There it was again. An invitation to follow rather than a command. "I'll just sit here, thanks."

Ven smiled with a breathy laugh.

Why did he think these things were funny? She'd expected him to get upset and start threatening her with the isolation room.

"Come on," he said. "I know you're as curious as I am to see what the administrator wants."

True enough. Mia didn't really want to sit there, she wanted to test Ven's reaction. In fact, he probably knew that, and that's why it had been amusing to him. It had only been three days since he'd arrived and he knew her too well. That was why he knew she wasn't serious about staying seated.

She stood with a sigh.

He wisely said nothing else and led her inside to a small office room that contained only a bookshelf and a moderate sized desk facing the door. Behind the desk sat Taye Mansen, and beside her stood the administrator, Doctor Zein Huan. She'd seen him only a handful of times. It was interesting that subjects only had one name and everybody else had at least two, if not more.

Three other subjects were led into the room as well, including Ambrose, Dami, and Baze. Dami gave her a warm smile that tickled her chest. He was clearly excited about whatever this was.

Doctor Huan spoke first. "As part of the ongoing training, the five of you will be sent on an exclusive mission."

"The five of us?" Ven interjected.

Huan's blank expression did not change. "Yes, it includes you, Doctor Yashke. This will be much different from the previous examinations we've done. We've mentioned how our research here with you is critical to providing lifesaving treatments for other people across the globe. That is still something we can accomplish, but this mission will help you be prepared to take a more active role in that initiative.

"I understand that this will be a new experience for all of you. Your mission is to enter a potentially hostile facility and retrieve a set of materials from inside." He rested his eyes on Ven as if Ven would know what he was talking about. "Some people will attempt to prevent you from removing this material, but you will remove it anyway. You four subjects were selected because you've proven that your sparring skills are adept as well as your resilience in case anybody on this mission tries to harm you. You are free to ask questions for clarification."

"So," Dami said, "we go inside this place, take the material, and then leave. We will have to push people out of the way to do it. Is that all?"

"That's simply put," Doctor Huan said, "but yes. That's all you have to do."

Ven's face paled.

Doctor Huan seemed to notice as well. "And Doctor Yashke will be there to both analyze the results and follow up with each of you to see how you mentally process this kind of activity. It will be fine, doctor. Tem has reported your methods already. They will prove helpful for all four of them."

"We'll be leaving the facility?" Ambrose asked.

"Yes," Doctor Huan said. "Immediately. I have transportation awaiting as we speak. Everything is already prepared. It will take over a day for you to reach the mission site. Now, exit the door and staff will escort you. Doctor Yashke, stay a moment."

Mia led the way out of the office. She couldn't help but smile and look at the other subjects. Even Ambrose was smiling, but Dami had a far-off look in his eyes. Two members of staff directed them through the facility all the way out the front doors. Mia had never been out here. An open expanse stretched before her. It was like a breeze of air electrified its way across her skin. Her mouth gaped.

"Look at those," Dami whispered, pointing at the small buildings lining the road.

Mia nodded absently, noting how the buildings were so tiny and built of something entirely different than the facility.

"Board the carriage," said one of the staff. Their team was ushered to some large box atop four wheels. "Doctor Yashke will join you shortly and you'll be on your way."

In front of the carriage, seated on some built-in chairs, an gruff woman sat with her arms gripping a cloth-covered wheel. Other staff and people she didn't recognize stood around the area, watching as if this were some kind of spectacle. *It is though, isn't it? We're leaving. For the first time.*

Mia climbed into the carriage. There appeared to be six seats that awkwardly faced each other. She sat on one side, hoping Dami would sit beside her, but Ambrose came in and took the spot, then Dami sat beside Ambrose. Baze sat across from Dami, but he merely stared out the open door. For a brief moment, they were left without staff watching them.

"Can you believe we're leaving?" Mia ventured to ask.

"Only to come right back," Ambrose said.

True. Mia sat back in her chair.

"But still," Dami said, "this does present something new. It will be a performance test rather than merely a resilience test. This could be the kind of thing they've been preparing us for the whole time. I'm at least curious to see what it is."

Ven entered the carriage and they grew silent. He sat across from Mia, the door closing behind him. He'd regained his normal color. "This machine is awesome," he said. "I've never seen anything like it. Powered by…" He glanced across at them all and said nothing more.

The carriage moved. Slow at first, but then it lurched quickly. Mia bent to look out the window, watching the small buildings roll past until there was nothing but the plain landscape of small, scattered bushes, dead grass, and blackened rocks.

"I'm curious what your thoughts are regarding this mission," Ven said to none of them in particular. "It's something very different for you all."

"What does it matter?" Baze said. "Our thoughts are meaningless."

"No, Baze," Dami said. "Our thoughts matter. Thoughts offer individuality, and nobody can take your thoughts away. You own them." There was passion in Dami's words. Mia wished she'd been sitting next to him. She could just imagine heat emanating from his body.

"Whatever," Baze said, leaning back in his seat, arms folded.

"But why do you care what our thoughts are?" Mia asked. "What does it matter to you?"

Ven nodded. "Thoughts are important. It helps to see your perspective on things. My interpretation for instance is that this mission sounds a little scary, but that's probably because I don't share your impervious trait, and I've never done anything like this."

"It doesn't sound very smart to have sent you, then," Mia said.

Ven laughed. He did that a lot. More than anybody else she knew.

"You make a good point," Ven said. "I think it's because they know I want to help you. Genuinely. But speaking personally, this isn't just a job for me. I don't like to see people hurting."

"We don't hurt, so this is a stupid place for you to work," Baze said.

"And we don't need your help," Ambrose added.

"Pain is experienced by more than our bodies," Ven said, but he leaned back, letting the conversation drift into silence.

He was a curious thing, and she found herself wondering what Dami thought of him. Normally, Dami would have been the one doing most of the talking, but his silence was almost eerie. He only stared out the window.

# Chapter 10

## Names

Zein Huan watched from a third story window as the carriage depart-
ed, arms folded. Tem stood beside him, fidgeting.

"It could just be a coincidence," Tem said.

"It's not," Zein said with finality. "How many other people do you know
with the Yashke family name?"

Tem crossed his arms and rocked from one leg to the other. "Do you
think he knows, then?"

"That remains unclear, though I'd find it hard to believe he'd come here
under such conditions if he did."

"Was it a good idea to send him off with the subjects, then?"

"A very good idea, yes." Zein spared Tem a glance. "I will play whatever
card we're handed. If young Doctor Yashke had ulterior motives, I would
expect this mission to shed light. Also, if he has even a scrap of the com-
passion and intelligence of his predecessors, then he might be exactly what
the subjects need. You've noted it yourself—his approach with the subjects
is different from other doctors. He's almost relatable with them. This can
be advantageous."

"But what if he is here to cause problems? What if there's an issue on the mission?"

"Rebelie is the one leading the carriage," Zein said. "She is adequately equipped to handle any such issue. Besides, I believe the subjects will be more interested in proving themselves than anything else. All four subjects have consistently been in the top ranks. There's a reason for that. They are competitive. This is the only life they know. Though we may not trust them completely, we can trust that they enjoy their ranks. That can only be maintained by leading a successful mission."

Tem nodded with a grunt. "Alright, then. Forgive me for my nervousness. I know you are very strategic with every move you make."

"It's alright. I only hope I'm enough steps ahead." The carriage disappeared out of sight as Zein's thoughts turned inward. Something still seemed off. He didn't know what it was, but there were other gears in motion. He wondered if he should approach Doctor Yashke about his relatives. Could this be their son? They didn't seem to have any family. Perhaps he'd been wrong about them.

Time would tell.

# Chapter 11

## Fire and Blood

The dark sky splayed out above them in a wide, glorious view. All Mia could do was stare. Stars stretched out all across her view. She'd rarely gotten the chance to see the stars so clearly. Her life was so miniscule in comparison to the expanse. Ven was already stretched out on the ground, sleeping. If her body was superior to his, why did she struggle sleeping? Maybe her body felt like it needed less rest. That was probably it.

Baze stood over Ven's body.

Mia leapt to her feet. "Baze, what're you doing?" her voice was a quiet whisper.

"I could kill him right now."

Dami and Ambrose gathered around.

"Now isn't the time, Baze," Dami said. He placed a hand on the back of his neck where his metal insert was. The doctors wouldn't ever tell them what it was, but maybe Dami knew something she didn't. He grabbed hold of Baze's arm and glanced toward the carriage. The driver was there somewhere.

"You know something about them?" Mia ventured to ask.

Dami gave a nod that was barely perceivable.

"Then when is the time?" Baze said, shrugging the hand off.

"Later," Dami said. "We should finish this mission. Trust me."

"Trust?"

"If not me, then who?" Dami said.

Baze sighed. "Whatever." He went back to his spot and laid down.

Dami nodded to both Ambrose and Mia. He was always planning something.

Mia laid back down and it still took her a while to fall asleep. After all, the stars were so *bright*.

That morning, they all woke up just as the sky began to lighten, hues of yellow and orange pushing into the blue sky. Mia sat up and watched the sun's slow ascent. It was amazing. How had she never seen this before? She gripped a fistful of rocks and dirt. All of them were staring at it.

"It's beautiful isn't it?" Ven said. Nobody responded. "I'm sorry you've been deprived of such a thing, but I intend to change all that if I can."

"You intend to get us free from the facility?" Mia asked. She glanced over at the driver who was coming back from a copse of trees, eyes keen, observant.

Ven looked down. "I mean to help change things though I don't know what that looks like yet." He took a sharp breath and looked back up. "We should eat and get going. Our destination is fairly close."

No answers, of course. This would be Ven's way of stringing them along. They boarded the carriage and resumed the journey. The land turned into rolling hills, the trail winding between them. Mia tried not to stare too hard at the occasional wildflower.

They'd been riding for about two hours when the carriage came to a stop. They hopped out. The landscape here was different. The hills were greener with big trees sprouting up between them. It was all she could do to not stare at them. All this time she never knew that the world could look so different. Maybe that mountainous flowery place Ven talked about actually existed.

The carriage driver pointed, her other hand hidden in the folds of her coat. "Should be just over those hills. I'll be waiting here when you get back."

Baze took off running. It looked fun, and Mia raced after him. They moved faster than the carriage. Wind blew through her hair, and she laughed despite herself. There was so much *space*.

"Wait," Ven called distantly.

Mia stopped, her feet digging into the soft dirt, and looked back.

Ven was sprinting after them, still close to the carriage.

"Oh my, he's slow," Ambrose said.

Dami laughed. "Or we're just fast."

"This will take ages. Maybe we should carry him," Mia said.

Ambrose raised a golden eyebrow at her. "Not a bad idea, but he's *your* doctor."

Mia set her jaw. "I can do it." She hoped she sounded more confident than she felt. She loped down the hill, trying not to think about touching Ven. *But I am going to touch him. How do I not think about it?*

"Wow," Ven said as she got close, "I figured you all could run fast, but not—"

Ven's words got cut off as Mia scooped him up and threw him across her shoulder. She wanted to make it look easy to the other subjects, but it was harder to keep balance at first than she thought. Instead of moving at a full sprint, she jogged, Ven's stomach bouncing on her shoulder. At least he was lighter than she'd thought.

"Mia," Ven said, voice panicked.

"It's faster this way," Mia said. They reached the top of the hill twice as fast as Ven would have. The other subjects looked like they were trying not to laugh.

"Mia, put me down. Please."

"Fine," Mia stopped at the top of the hill and swung Ven to his feet. He immediately dropped to his knees and clutched his stomach. He wheezed and took a few gasping breaths.

The subjects all gave each other the same open-mouthed expression.

"What's happening, doctor?" Mia said.

Ven laughed. "I'm not impervious, Mia. Bouncing around on your shoulders actually hurt me. My body doesn't then adapt to the pain. It just keeps hurting."

"So, I shouldn't carry you?"

"Not like that, no," Ven said. He stood up. "We don't have very far to go anyway. That should be the spot right there by the windmill." He pointed over the next hill where a large windmill peeked over the top. "Let's proceed to the next hill and then plan things out. Doctor Huan described the location of the goods we're looking for."

When they proceeded at a slow walk, Ven rolled his eyes at them and said, "Oh come on. Don't drag your feet so much. It's not like I'm asking you to stare at the floor for an hour." This earned a few chuckles, even from Ambrose. Once they reached the next hill over, they went and stood under the cover of a couple trees clinging to its side. It offered a decent enough vantage to look at the buildings ahead.

Mia hadn't expected there to be so many individual buildings. How many people were there? Not just at this location, but everywhere. How vast was the world?

"There," Ven said, pointing. "It's in that walled section. There should be a greenhouse of sorts. It's a place for growing plants. We'll want to... set that on fire, and then remove the product from inside the neighboring building. There's a locked room with a locked chest inside. Hopefully one of you can bash those open."

"Can I do the fire?" Baze asked.

Ven shrugged. "I don't see why not." He handed over a tool and explained how to start the fire with it.

"The rest of us can go with you inside the building," Dami said.

Mia laughed. "Yes, if you're as squishy as you've seemed so far, you'll need any protection you can get."

"It's probably true," Ven said. He sighed. "Let's get this over with." He started out at a light jog. Mia went out in front of Ven just in case, and he made no objection.

"I used to think I was fast, you know," Ven said.

"You tend to be optimistic," Mia said.

He didn't respond but she could almost feel him smiling.

Ahead of them, people paused in the street as they noticed Mia and the others approaching. Some seemed confused, simply staring, but others started to run away as if they knew it was no ordinary group.

"I don't think they like visitors," Ven said.

By the time they neared the first building, everyone had caught on and started taking cover. A bell rang out across the small town in warning.

"Head straight for the walled building, Mia," Ven said.

The street had emptied as they jogged down it. Dami came beside Mia as they approached the gate. It slammed shut with a clatter. Four men stood out front holding strange contraptions in their hands. One of them shouted a word. The contraptions triggered, launching sticks with metal ends at them. One stick bounced off Mia's chest, and two of them bounced off Dami.

The four men gasped in alarm, threw down the contraptions and drew out metal weapons instead.

Mia considered that they were squishy like Ven. No problem. She sprinted the remaining distance, ducked under a swinging weapon and stretched out her arms, pushing two of the men. Both men soared across the ground. Their bodies crashed into the gate behind them. Dami did the same thing to the two other men, their bodies joining the heap. They lay there, motionless.

Dami laughed and flexed his arms, but all Mia could do was stare. One of the men had blood dripping from his mouth. He was dead. She killed him. Her breath went shallow. A wave of euphoria washed over her, but it felt dark at the same time.

Ambrose, Dami, and Baze took a charge at the gate, breaking it down as they rammed it with their shoulders. Baze took off, clearly eager to start burning things down.

Ven stood beside Mia, looked down at the bodies, then back to Mia. "Are you okay?" Ven's expression was unreadable, like a mask had been fitted over his face.

Dami frowned at her.

"Of course," Mia said. "Just surprised."

Ven's eyes narrowed. "Me too, but we can talk about this later, okay," he said, voice quiet, though Ambrose and Dami would certainly have heard him.

"Alright, let's find this stuff and get out of here," Ven said. He pointed toward the closed door of a stone building. Dami and Ambrose made quick work of that, and inside was a hallway guarded by a few more people. Dami and Ambrose took off at the people, giggling as they started throwing them around like paperweights.

"You don't have to," Ven said, clearly agitated. "You don't need to hurt everyone! You could just shove them into a room!"

Dami and Ambrose ignored him. They were lost in their frenzy. The euphoria of killing humans must have affected them as well, though they seemed to revel in it.

Mia walked beside Ven as he stomped through the hall, face covered in shear distress.

Ambrose had taken one of the people's weapons and was impaling everyone she could find, even some of those who'd already fallen. Blood spattered across the floor and walls. The whole scene was a nightmare.

"Leave them be!" Ven screamed, face twisted in agony.

Mia felt the same urge to join them, to take out her years of frustration for being holed up. For once, violence against non-subjects was acceptable, yet she couldn't bring herself to look at the gore left behind by Ambrose and Dami. Instinct told her to stick beside Ven. He was just as vulnerable as these other people. He would die just as easily, and she wanted to keep him safe.

Ven sprinted down the hall and tapped on a door. Mia shoved the door open. Inside, the room was empty save for a few chests on the floor.

"Break these open," Ven said. "I'm not sure which one has what we came for."

Mia did so easily. All she had to do was grab the locks and yank them off.

"This one," Ven said, looking in at the contents of a small chest. It contained small vials of a purplish green liquid. "Can you carry it?"

"Looks easy enough." Mia closed the chest and picked it up.

"Alright, let's go," Ven said, then strode back into the hall. "Let's leave! Dami! Ambrose! Come on. We need to get Baze and get out of here."

They listened this time, and they were silent. Ambrose's maniacal giggling had stopped, but their bodies were speckled red with blood.

They found Baze outside, crouched in front of the burning greenhouse. He watched a body as it warped in the flames.

Mia blinked her eyes away. Her throat dried. The smell of burned flesh stung her nose. Her lungs were heavy, the air thick like sludge, and her stomach seemed like it had twisted into knots.

Baze joined them and they passed the dead bodies at the gate again. Mia didn't want to look, but she did. The blank stares. The mangled limbs.

They'd killed people today, and Mia was certain she'd never be the same again.

# Chapter 12

## Trauma

Ven sat in the hallway outside Doctor Zein Huan's office. His leg bounced up and down. The white light overhead blared. He'd been thinking about the conversation they would have ever since he left the manufacturing facility. He'd seen horrors in his life, but nothing compared to what he witnessed two days ago. Nothing like that should happen again. Ven wasn't a real doctor, but he'd still spent most of his life out in the world trying to *heal* people. Would Zein listen? Would he throw him out? Dayelle was right. He knew more than ever that this place needed to go down.

The doorknob to Zein's office twisted with a rattle and a shiver ran down Ven's spine. Taye Mansen stepped out into the hall. "Doctor Huan will see you now."

Ven bounced to his feet. Taye held the door open for him, but she did not follow him inside. Instead, the door clicked shut behind him.

"Have a seat, Doctor Yashke," Zein said. The office was immaculately clean, save for a small stack of paperwork at the end of the desk. He sat in the chair opposite Zein.

"So," Zein said, folding his hands in front of him on the desk, "tell me how the job went. Specifically, what's your analysis of the subjects? What did they do?"

"The subjects," Ven said. He remembered their frightening speed. He remembered Ambrose with the sword. He remembered the look of horror written on Mia's face. His leg was bouncing again. "Well, the important details start once we got to the gate. There were four guards. They fired crossbows at Mia and Dami, but they bounced right off. Mia and Dami charged them. The subjects are extremely fast and strong. The guards went soaring when the subjects made contact. All four of them died as their bodies crashed against the gate.

"Responses from the subjects varied at this point. Mia looked surprised. One of the guards she'd hit was bleeding from the mouth. I don't know if the subjects have ever seen someone bleed before, and they all stared. Mia was transfixed a little more, but not in an amused way. I tried talking to her about it on the way back here, but I don't think she wanted to engage in that conversation with the other subjects around.

"Dami and Ambrose seemed a bit..." Ven paused. The word he wanted to use seemed sickeningly accurate. "They seemed excited. They broke down the gate, and Baze ran in to start the fire on the greenhouse. I wasn't with him as much, but he killed somebody in the fire.

"The worst part is when we got inside the building. Dami and Ambrose killed everybody in sight and wouldn't listen when I told them to stop. I've heard this can happen with soldiers sometimes. Mia didn't attack anybody else though. She stuck with me as we found the chest and left. She seemed more oriented towards our objective."

Zein said nothing, but merely bit his lower lip and stared at his fingers. He took a deep breath. "I anticipated as much. Mia's reaction is encouraging, but the other three subjects are concerning."

"I've read studies about this before," Ven ventured to say. There were several books that addressed the psychological effects of killing. He'd only read a few things about it, but the information seemed relevant. "I've heard the subjects refer to other people and themselves differently. Almost as if they view themselves as something different than humans. The more distinct they make themselves from other people, the easier it is to kill them."

Doctor Huan nodded. "This is astute. I have made similar assumptions, worrying that the subjects will consider themselves superior to others. Perhaps Mia's connection with you has made her feel that we are more alike, and thus her impulses were more controlled. We should share this information with their doctors as well. It may be vital in helping pacify their animosity."

Ven shrugged. "All I can say is that these missions will not be good for them. Or us, apparently, if it only exacerbates a feeling of superiority."

"Speaking frankly, Doctor Yashke, that may not be the last of such missions we'll have to send them on, due to forces outside my control. I will use the information you've shared to further dissuade it though. Thank you for your help. I'll be speaking with the doctors of the other three subjects, but I need you to focus on helping Mia process everything. Can you do that?"

"Of course."

"One more thing." Zein leaned forward. "How did you learn about the job here at the facility?"

Ven's mouth hung open as his heart shot up. He had not been prepared for such a question. "Referral, actually," Ven said, coming up with the quickest answer. "Another student from university mentioned it to me. I don't know where he got the details."

Zein nodded slowly as he leaned back in his seat. "Very well. Good day."

Ven let himself out. He strode down the hall, his cheeks burning with anger, and his heart still thundered in fear. There was no way they should let the subjects go on another mission. His hands trembled. This was no doubt the evil that Dayelle referred to. Sending the subjects on these missions would turn them into monsters.

He tried to imagine if a subject got on Earth somehow. Would they be bulletproof? How would somebody be able to stop such a force? Whatever information Dayelle needed, he only hoped he could find it fast.

He headed straight to the cafeteria, a wide room with rows of tables. Most of the other staff were there eating lunch. After getting a tray of food, he went to find the nearest seat without paying much attention.

"Sorry, this table is reserved for adults." It was Doctor Makarr.

Ven almost forgot the arrogant doctor altogether. Fortunately they hadn't crossed paths very often, except for here during lunch.

"No worry," Ven said. "I still have some work to do." Ven continued walking with his lunch right out the door of the cafeteria.

"Sir," Tem said, popping up from his own seat. He came out the door a second behind Ven. "Sir, it's good to have you back."

"I'm glad somebody thinks so," Ven said.

"How're the subjects?" Tem asked.

"Physically unharmed as predicted, but possibly traumatized. I'm probably traumatized too, speaking frankly."

"Do you want to talk about it?"

"I thought we were."

Tem breathed a laugh. "I meant in the emotional processing kind of way."

"I know, I apologize for being facetious. But it was scary, Tem. It was scary to see the kinds of things that they can do. I understand they're subjects, but I feel like they are..." He paused. He realized that Tem likely reported everything directly back to Doctor Huan. What he'd wanted to say is that he felt like the subjects were victims, but realized he couldn't say that without sounding like he was against the facility. He needed to keep up the illusion long enough for his true employer to bring down the whole operation. Something was very wrong with the research here.

"Like what?" Tem said.

"Like they're frightened," Ven said, making up a quick answer. They went out a door leading to the main outdoor enclosure where all the subjects were eating lunch.

"You know we aren't supposed to eat with them, doctor?"

"I do," Ven said, "but sometimes we have to be a little unconventional to get optimal results. I'm sure that's not a foreign concept here."

"True indeed," Tem said, pausing a safe distance away from the subjects as Ven continued.

Ven scanned the tables. He primarily wanted to speak with Dami and Ambrose, but their table was jammed with other subjects, speaking to each other with unusual energy. Their voices quieted as Ven passed, many eying him with varying expressions.

He found Mia seated by herself at the far end of the enclosure and made his way there.

She glared at him as he came and sat across from her.

Ven ignored it. "This seems like an uncommon place for you."

"There's clearly nowhere else to sit." She shifted her dark glare over to Dami's table.

"Is there some hostility there? Were you forced away from sitting with them?"

Mia gave a slight shake of her head. "No, not really. There were just a lot of people eager to ask about the mission, and I don't feel much like talking about it."

"I can understand why. Would you say that the others are eager?"

"More than I am, at least," Mia said. She glanced at the nearest table where a group of three subjects quickly turned their heads away. "You know we have very good hearing, right doctor?"

"It wasn't stated in your paperwork, but I suppose that makes sense," Ven said, lowering his voice to a whisper.

Mia placed her elbows on the table and leaned forward. "Much better," she said in her own whisper. He could barely hear it over the echoing chatter that filled the enclosure.

"How *do* you feel about the mission? I noticed you'd experienced a bit of shock after the first... encounter."

Mia shook her head and placed a spoonful of potatoes in her mouth. "Shock is a good word for it. I didn't think they'd... I didn't think that would happen. I knew you were squishy after carrying you, but I didn't think you were all *that* squishy. It didn't feel right. The others didn't seem to care as much. Was my reaction odd?"

"No, not at all. It was normal, in fact. A very human response."

"What about their reaction then? Why was it different?"

"Also very human, but they're different people, aren't they? All people react to things differently. In fact, your response seemed like the more mature one. It showed an awareness for the experience of others. As humans progress through adolescence, that becomes more common." A fact that he hated having to acknowledge as he too was still in adolescence.

Mia nodded. Her reactions were interesting. She'd trust whenever he shared information, but she'd mistrust him if he sought information from her.

"I didn't like it though," Mia said. "Did I do something wrong to those people?"

Ven sighed. "I think it's hard to say, Mia. You acted in ignorance, just like when you picked me up, you didn't know that it would hurt me. The other subjects however, I'm sure they were curious about doing something different or having a unique experience. Killing can sometimes feel exciting or empowering, and people will react differently to that. It's sometimes hard to judge what another person is going through. Not all of us have the same level of empathy."

"Your opinions are very objective."

Ven smiled. "It comes from how my parents taught me. I think I occasionally talk more objectively than I feel, but it does help to view things from a more optimistic perspective at times."

Dami abruptly stood from his table and approached them. "I've never seen any staff come in here and eat with us before." He sat next to Ven.

Ven shrugged. "I know. I'm probably throwing things off."

Dami laughed. "No, it's fine. It just shows that you're different. But look," he dropped his voice, "I know we didn't talk about it much on the way back. I was still trying to process what had happened. Doctor, outside these doors, do people kill each other? Does that happen often?"

Ven immediately thought of his parents. "Unfortunately, yes. There are murders and wars all the time. It's horrible."

Dami shook his head. "And people like us, we're very effective at it, aren't we? Do you think they'll make us do it again?"

Ven shivered. He toyed with a bit of food in his mouth before answering. Dami's curiosity was certainly genuine, but what for? Did he *want* to kill again? "It's possible. Nothing has been confirmed to me."

"I don't want to kill for them, doctor," Dami said.

"Well, it's not really my choice to make," Ven said. This was an unexpected response from Dami.

"I know," Dami said, "but maybe you can help us sometime." With that, Dami got up and returned to his previous table.

Ven felt Mia's eyes on him as he focused down at his food and shoveled it in. Sure, Ven wanted to help them. Clearly the subjects didn't want to be sent on missions to kill people, and he didn't want them to do that either.

He also wanted to bring down this facility, but what could he do? It wasn't like he could just let all the subjects out somehow. Could he?

He still needed to locate information for Dayelle, but perhaps he could expedite things.

"I do what I can," Ven mumbled to himself.

# Chapter 13

## Defensive Measures

Zein folded his arms as he stared out toward the setting sun. He stood on a balcony at the top floor of the facility. A few birds chirped from their hiding place in the rafters. The door behind him opened and closed.

Tem joined him, leaning his elbows on the edge of the iron railing, head peeking over the edge to look at the ground. "It was as we suspected," Tem said. "The subjects noticed that we can't hear as well as they do, so they've been communicating with whispers a lot of the time. Even with the echoing of the enclosure, we wouldn't be able to hear them."

"So what have they been saying?" Zein said. Despite his resolve, anxiety tightened in his chest.

"Well, from what we can hear." Tem pulled a small device from his pocket. It could be placed in the ear to easily hear even better than the subjects. "They mostly talk about kissing and such. They are 17 after all."

"The important details, Tem."

"Of course. Well, the subjects seem to have generally agreed that they don't like to kill for us, but they certainly don't insinuate that they don't like killing. Mia doesn't speak about it at all. Baze seems less enthusiastic about it than Dami and Ambrose. I suspect he's still a little in shock. His doctor said he has a hard time relating the details of watching somebody burn to death. Dami has also implored Doctor Yashke to help them. To what degree, I'm not sure, but he said it under the context of not wanting to kill for the facility."

Zein took a deep breath and let it out slowly as he scanned the horizon. Dark clouds rolled in gradually from the north. It had been a hot, dry season so far, but the clouds hinted at a coming summer storm. "When you say the subjects don't insinuate that they don't like killing, what do you mean?"

Tem popped his neck. "They've bragged. Especially Ambrose. Baze freely shares that he shoved somebody into a fire."

"Have you spoken with Ambrose's or Dami's doctors?"

"Once we finish here, certainly," Tem said.

"And what was Rebelie's assessment?"

Tem nodded. "She confirmed the details we've gotten from everyone. Doctor Yashke did say something about changing the facility one night, but he also seemed to intentionally hold back on how he communicated with the subjects. I don't know if he suspected Rebelie's ability to overhear all their conversations, but perhaps he's just cautious."

"So nothing poignantly incriminating," Zein said.

Tem nodded.

"And the subjects are keener than they let on. If we could determine Doctor Yashke was holding back, they most certainly did. Dami in particular. He's intelligent. Calculating."

Tem let out a long breath. "Dami concerns me the most.

Zein had thought the same thing. Dami was different than the other subjects. He interacted charismatically with everyone, even the staff. The thing that concerned him, he realized, was Dami's intelligence. "What makes you worry about Dami?"

"He's been more excitable, I'd say. Moving from different groups or individuals. He hasn't been saying anything explicitly. I wonder if he suspects that we can hear more than we let on. He's maintaining relationships as usual, but more so than usual."

"Indeed. You must keep a close watch on him. He thinks himself a leader. If any of them are capable of stirring up trouble, it's him. His behavior during the mission concerns me, and I'm feeling that I made the wrong choice by sending him."

"Hard to know those kinds of things without data," Tem said. "Do they have another mission coming up?"

Zein's brows creased. "I meet with our gracious Lady Rosars tomorrow morning," he said, trying to keep the sarcasm from his voice. "I'm sure that will be our topic of discussion. I hate to admit it, but that last job paid very well. No doubt our investors will think of nothing else now that they've seen us generate some revenue."

"Isn't profit what you want?"

"Yes, of course, but not in this way. I wanted to cure diseases, not kill people."

"But you'd tolerate it?"

"With hesitation, yes. As long as the subjects don't get any bad ideas." He turned to face Tem. "You see what we're doing here, don't you? Many of these subjects were born with deficiencies or had diseases when we acquired them. They would have been cast off by their parents. Now look at them. We've saved their lives, and we can save others. We just need to figure out how to do it without making them so impervious to *everything*.

"So yes, if these missions pay well enough to continue funding our research, then I'm willing to allow it. My concern is merely regarding the willingness of the subjects to remain if they are given enough room to explore or even to realize the fragility of a normal human."

Tem pushed back from the railing, realization dawning on him as his eyes widened. "You mean to suggest that they could rise up against the facility? Would they attack the staff?"

"It's a possibility," Zein said, trying to sound frank and objective, though he hated to think what might happen to the facility if they did. "There's no real risk to the staff though, if that's what you're concerned about. Not you, at least. Guards should be able to respond in time before anything serious happens."

Zein pulled back his sleeve to check the wristwatch he wore. "Continue your observations. We'll speak again tomorrow."

Tem took that as a dismissal. He nodded to Zein and said, "Goodnight, doctor," then left the balcony.

Not a minute later, his guard captain came through the door. "Sir, the guards have been fully equipped as requested. We'll be placing additional guards tomorrow morning with the shift adjustment."

"Why not immediately?"

"Shift changes are usually done in the morning, but we can implement it immediately if needed."

"Do it now."

"Right away, sir." The captain ran and disappeared through the door.

Had Zein's voice been that urgent? He held out his hands and noticed a slight shaking in the fingers. Yes. He was nervous. He could feel his quickened heartbeat. An uprising was what he feared, but why did it feel so immediate? He pulled a weapon from his belt where it hid beneath his doctor's suit. Well, it wasn't technically a weapon. Only the subjects were at risk from its use. It was little more than a small black mechanism with a trigger. All one had to do was aim it at the intended target, then press the trigger. It would connect with the dragonsbane release capsule inside the subject's neck.

They'd be safe, certainly, but he still didn't like the idea of killing his subjects.

# Chapter 14

## Theft

*E*verything will be fine. It'll be just like stealing from my teacher. Ven tried to ignore his sweaty palms as he strode down the hall. Why did they sweat so much? He felt calm about his decision. His breathing was even. This was going to be easy. He planned it out as well as he could for a spur-of-the-moment decision. But still, his hands were sweating. The telltale sign of his anxiety.

His confidence had been firm up until this moment. Pretending to be a doctor was second nature, but stealing was not something he was proud of.

Would he feel guilty afterwards? Was that what was making him nervous? Nonsense. He was doing the right thing. The subjects deserved a chance to make decisions for themselves. They were people too. *I must have a chronic issue of helping people whenever they ask, even if it's insane.*

Besides, this would be the perfect way to expedite the mission. He still had no idea how all of this was connected to his parents, but he did not want any further involvement with killing. That was not what he signed up for, and this facility needed to go down as soon as possible.

Dami was about to receive the help he asked for. All Ven had to do was steal a key.

He first saw the key when Tem gave him a quick tour of the facility. It hung on the wall outside a guard room. Such an odd place to keep a key. Of course, only staff would have access to this area of the facility, but still, that put a lot of trust in everyone.

Ven came up to a door at the end of the hall that separated the guard's quarters from the rest of the facility. A square window in the door allowed him to peek through just in time to see three guards running off down the hall.

That was the first time he'd *ever* seen staff run. *What's got them riled up?* He wiped his hands on his pants. Now he needed to walk in, grab the key, and walk out. Simple enough, right? He stared through the window for a solid ten minutes, but there was no other movement. Where had all the guards gone?

After one more glance behind him, he opened the door, took a few quick steps towards the key, snatched it off the hook, and then went back out the door just as easily as he'd entered. He hurried back down the hall.

Too easy.

Something *must* have gone wrong.

He looked behind again just in case, but the hall was empty. When he turned back, he bumped right into Doctor Makarr.

"What are you doing here? This is a research sector," Makarr said.

*Uh oh.* Should he make something up? No, he didn't have to lie. "I'm not restricted from coming here," he said, dodging around him.

"That didn't answer my question."

"Fortunately, I don't have to answer your questions either. Have a good night, Doctor Makarr." Ven hurried away, unable to hide the smile that crept onto his face. Though he didn't like being at odds with anybody, controlling his own situation sent a thrill through his chest.

Now he needed to find Dami before the subjects went to bed. By this time, the subjects would either be finishing up with their doctors or ending their free time. Many doctors escorted their subjects directly to the rooms. By pattern, Ven could assume that Dami was at the enclosure talking to other subjects.

When Ven reached the enclosure and stepped outside he already noticed something different. More staff lined the second floor walkway than usual. He knew they were guards, but other than the occasional knife looped into a belt, they scarcely appeared armed.

Dami was there with a few other subjects. Mia sat at her table by herself, staring at a patch of plants under the fading sunlight. A few dragonlights added light to the enclosure.

He hesitated a moment. Should he give the key to Mia? He doubted she'd have the determination to lead everybody out. Dami was the most sensible choice, but how would he safely pass the key with all these people watching? He wiped his palms on his pants. He groaned and made his way toward Dami. Sometimes more eyes and ears could help hide something in plain sight. He just hoped it would work.

Dami looked up at him, the whites of his eyes almost glowing. Did he already know what Ven was planning?

"Good evening, everyone," Ven said.

"Hello, doctor," Dami said, "how can we help you?"

"Dami," Ven said. He glanced up at the staff on the walkway. Many eyes glared down at him. He thought he caught a glimpse of Tem walking around among them. "Dami, I want to make sure that you aren't planning on hurting anyone."

"Is that what this is about?" Dami looked around at the staff on the walkways as well. Both their voices were loud enough that many of them could easily hear.

Ven shrugged. "I don't know what it's about. Increasing the staffing isn't part of a doctor's responsibilities here. I've been thinking about you and the others since the mission. I want to make sure that you wouldn't try to hurt anyone." He spared a look at Ambrose who also stood among the small crowd.

"You know I'm friends with most of the staff and subjects, right? I wouldn't plan on hurting *any*body here. Believe me." Dami shook his head for effect.

"Alright." From inside his coat pocket, Ven palmed the key into his sweaty hand. It fit under his thumb. "Well, I wish you a good night." He reached out to shake Dami's hand, passing the key along in the same motion. "And the same goes for everyone. It's better to build others up than to break them down."

Dami nodded to him as Ven stepped away and went over to Mia. She didn't look up as he sat beside her.

"It has felt like a long day, hasn't it?" Ven asked. Mia said nothing, only stared down at the few budding plants beside their larger companions. "You're troubled."

Mia let out a soft sigh. "He's planning something," she said, voice barely more than a whisper, not through an effort to be quiet, but more from exhaustion.

"Who?"

"Dami." She looked up at him then.

Her brown eyes carried a hint of green he'd never noticed before, but they seemed tired. Strange. For some reason this surprised him. He never really thought of the subjects getting tired.

"What do you mean?" Ven said.

"I don't know, but he's acting different somehow. You can tell it too, can't you? You're different from other doctors. Even though you've only known us for a couple weeks, you understand us better."

Ven only shrugged.

"That's why you told him not to hurt anybody, right?"

"I've been concerned about him and the others since the mission. I don't want him getting any ideas."

Mia grunted and got to her feet. "Well, he's got ideas already."

"Do you know something I don't?"

"'Know' isn't the right word," Mia said as she started off towards her room and Ven followed, "but something about him has already changed." Her voice had come almost shaky on that last word.

Realization settled in, but Ven said nothing until the door to the building closed behind them. A guard nodded at them from the stairway. It was unusual to have somebody posted there. Mia pointedly ignored him, and turned her head away.

They paused outside the door to her room. Being this close to her private space evoked a rising sense of awkwardness, but he pushed past it and said, "Mia, you were attracted to Dami, weren't you? And something about this change in him has also changed the way you've felt. Is that what has you troubled?"

Mia blinked at him. "What does it mean to be attracted?"

Now it was Ven's turn to blink as his cheeks warmed. "I've never had to describe that before... I suppose it means you like him, enjoy his company, think he looks handsome." These halls echoed. He became even more aware of the guard further down the hall who could probably hear some of what they were saying. "You think about him when you're not together, and you get a thrill of excitement just being near." A chill went up Ven's arms as he locked eyes with Mia. "Or like, maybe you'd want to kiss him. That kind of thing." He inadvertently looked at her lips before blinking rapidly and turning his head to the side.

"What's a kiss?"

Ven scratched his head. "Uh, when people touch lips together I guess."

Mia laughed, startling Ven. "I know what kissing is, doctor," Mia said, laughing again. "And what attraction is. We're not completely ignorant."

"Very funny. I seem to catch everything except for when you're teasing me," Ven said as Mia opened her door. He got that strange feeling again as he looked into her room. He realized that this might be the last time he'd see her if Dami was successful. "Well, whatever happens, stay safe, Mia."

She raised her eyebrow at him. "I've never been cautioned to stay safe before. Sort of comes with being impenetrable to everything."

"Right." What else could he even say at such a moment? He couldn't reveal too much with the guard nearby. "Good evening." He strode away before her door closed, surprised to find that his cheeks burned with a sense of... anger. Angry that he couldn't say anything else. Angry that he hadn't felt like he could give her the key. Angry that he still hadn't acquired any information regarding the subjects' operation.

This could serve both objectives. He'd free the subjects, yes, but in the ensuing chaos, perhaps he'd find the opportunity to hunt for data.

He passed the guard and went upstairs to his room. It took a while for him to fall asleep, but it wasn't very long before he was awakened by loud noises.

The escape had started, and by the sound of it, he'd made a terrible mistake.

# Chapter 15

## The Getaway

Screaming jolted Mia awake. This was it. The moment she'd feared. She could tell by the dim light that shone through the bottom of her door that it was still night. Her heart pounded. She sat up and placed her feet on the floor.

The screaming persisted, as well as crashing and yelling. It was as if the whole building would come tumbling down. She expected her door to explode any minute, but she only sat there, paralyzed with anticipation.

But her door never opened.

The horrible sounds continued for what felt like hours, but she knew it was only a few brief minutes. She waited and listened, but a haunting silence settled across the building.

Her stillness became annoying. *I'm impervious. What am I afraid of?* She threw her blanket to the side and got to her feet. The doors were locked from the other side, though with her strength, that wouldn't prevent her from being able to open it. Besides, who would come let her out if everyone was... dead.

She placed her hand on the doorknob and was about to give it a hard twist when she heard footsteps and whispers from outside.

"Hers is the only door that hasn't been opened," a voice said before cutting off.

Mia waited as the footsteps approached. Was it staff or subjects? Perhaps Dami succeeded in getting them all free.

She stepped back from the door and the knob turned. When the door swung inward, two staff members stepped inside. Her stomach tightened, but she couldn't tell if she was relieved or disappointed.

Their postures warned her. They stood at a distance from the door and they took a step back when they saw her, holding up some black device toward her as though it might ward her off. By their widened eyes, she could tell they were afraid.

She played cautious, saying nothing, hoping they would say something, but they only stared as if unsure what to do.

More footsteps from the stairs drew their attention. They took a couple steps back and ushered Mia into the hall where she saw Doctor Yashke come down the stairs, followed by Tem and a couple other members of staff. The tightness in her stomach loosened at seeing him. Relieved to see her doctor alive? Nonsense.

Ven's tired eyes lightened as he looked at Mia, but his tall shoulders drooped and his light hair stuck up in the back. He somehow seemed even paler than usual, and she suspected he hadn't slept at all.

"We're going to see Doctor Huan," Tem said to Doctor Yashke.

"Are you sure about that? With her?" said another staff member, indicating her head at Mia.

"Of course," Tem snapped. They were all on edge, their air of professionalism seemingly vanished. "He requested it."

Mia had known Tem for a while, but hadn't heard him talk much around her. This was the first time she'd ever seen him snappy.

"Come along now everyone," Tem said, leading them down the hall. "Something terrible has happened. You won't like what you see."

When they went out the door, she beheld a massacre. Bodies littered the enclosure, a more dreadful scene than what occurred on their mission. Fellow subjects lay among the dead, though their bodies were not mangled.

Mia clapped her hands over her face and dropped to her knees, but strong arms gripped her beneath her armpits and lifted her back to her feet. She couldn't look—didn't dare open her eyes.

"I have no words of comfort for you, Mia," said Ven, voice close to her ears. He spoke with quiet solemnity. "What happened here is horrible, but we must keep walking. Walk with me, one step at a time."

His arms held her up. She'd never thought of him as strong, but as he moved forward, she found her footing, still clasping her eyes shut as he led her along. She continued that way for a few steps before she realized how weak she must seem. After a sharp breath, she pushed Ven's arms away and opened her eyes, staring straight ahead to avoid the scene around her. She kept it together enough to follow a staff member across the courtyard until they got back inside. This area of the building looked thrashed, but at least there were no bodies.

What she still couldn't grasp was that other subjects were dead. Sure, she'd heard of a subject failing to pass a test before, but that had been years ago, before they'd all built up more resilience. How had that happened? This meant that she too was somehow more vulnerable than she'd ever thought.

Dami had done this. And the doctors had driven them to the brink. Anger and confusion roiled inside her brain.

Shards of Doctor Huan's office door lay scattered about. It had been completely ripped from its hinges, bits of stone and white plaster littered the hall. Doctor Huan himself looked completely unfazed, seated behind a desk that had been crippled into halves, tidying a stack of papers that he set on the floor as the group entered his office.

Mia had never been escorted and flanked by so many staff members before, not even when they'd take her to the box. They looked more on edge now that they were in the presence of Doctor Huan, watching her so closely she could almost feel the strain on their eyes.

"I'm going to be very straightforward about the situation here," Doctor Huan said. "Several subjects led by Dami attempted a forceful escape. Most of the subjects died, as well as many staff members. All other subjects besides Mia either forcibly exited their rooms or were released by other subjects. Only Dami and Ambrose successfully left the facility."

"How did the subjects die?" Ven asked.

Mia thought the same thing. Why did Dami help everyone else get out except for her? Perhaps it was a good thing she'd been left behind. If he had freed her, she'd probably be dead with the others.

Doctor Huan nodded toward a staff member holding one of those strange weapons. "Those trigger a device that was installed inside the subjects years ago, prior to their change, activating a toxin to which they are not able to build resistance. Dami's doctor somehow managed to remove his and Ambrose's. It's a very quick death otherwise."

Mia's breath left her lungs. All they needed to kill her was a switch.

A frown crossed Doctor Huan's face as he leaned back in his seat, the first expression he'd made since they entered. "As you can both guess, Dami and Ambrose are not the type of people you want to have running amok. We know that they've already killed a few people just outside the facility, and their rampage is sure to continue."

Mia rubbed at her forehead. She felt as sick as if she'd just drank some poison for a test. Her stomach boiled and her throat was sticky. "What about me? Why am I here?"

"Mia, we—" Doctor Huan started and paused. She couldn't ever remember him pausing to collect his thoughts before. "We need you to subdue Dami and Ambrose. There are other methods... but we do not have the time nor means to pursue those right now. You're the only one who would be able to get close enough to them to apply the toxin."

"You want me to try and kill them?"

"It's the only way," he said. "Their power cannot be diminished, and I'm not confident they will mend their ways enough to be trusted. They will hurt more people. Many years ago, the dragons themselves had to be slain for the same reason. They pursued reckless murder and enslavement without any fear of repercussion. That kind of power often lends itself to a sense of superiority that is difficult to overcome once acquired."

Mia squirmed uncomfortably. "What does that mean for me?"

"Doctor Yashke and the rest of us have concluded that you at least connect with humanity well enough to consider the lives of other people as meaningful. You were not alone in this. I believe Baze would have successfully passed this test as well if we'd had enough time to help him through his emotions. Dami and Ambrose released every single subject except for you, and in the terrible confusion, all subjects who ran for the door were exterminated." Doctor Huan paused, jaw clenched. "Staff was instructed not to eliminate those subjects who remained passive, but those instructions were not carried out correctly."

Mia bit her lip, holding back the sob that pulsed within her chest. All of them were dead. She blinked rapidly, afraid to show the tears that threatened to explode.

"How did that happen?" Mia managed to say.

Doctor Huan let out an angry breath. "I... am afraid to admit that we were likely infiltrated when we had new staff arrive. Some of the guards who were equipped with triggers were deliberately not following orders, but they have since been detained. We did not stop them in time."

Ven's eyes widened, and he placed a hand over his chest.

Doctor Huan lifted his hands. "After last night, our research here is ruined. I'm truly sorry if you've felt yourself a captive here, Mia. We should have been more honest with you all from the beginning." He quickly rifled through some papers on the floor and picked up a small, aged sheet before reading from it. "Subject is two years of age. Name is Mia Fendwen. Father deceased. Mother has an illness of the mind, recently lost employment as a launderer. Subject is severely malnourished with some lung damage from an incident where she nearly drowned only a month ago. Several sores found on torso and arms. Possible illness derived from chemical exposure worsened by the lack of nutrition. Life expectancy is less than two months. Mother offered to turn over the subject. Accepted full compensation."

"What is that?" Mia asked.

"It documents you and your condition when we purchased you from your mother," Doctor Huan said.

Mia swallowed the lump in her throat. "May I have the paper?" Feeling bold, she held her hand out.

Doctor Huan didn't hesitate to hand it over.

Mia ran her fingers over the smooth surface of the paper, softened with age. Her fingers trembled. She *had* existed outside the facility once, though she still wasn't sure what that even meant to her.

"We saved your life, Mia," Doctor Huan said, "not as a way to force you into indentured servitude, but that we might discover a way to help others. You've seen it. You know how frail people are. We're doctors here, our lives devoted to improving the human condition. We've been unsuccessful in finding a way to isolate treatments. I'm afraid there *isn't* a way to isolate individual mutations. Our research here is over, but we can't let Dami and Ambrose cause further harm. I'm *asking* you to help, not commanding."

Mia tried to swallow but her dry throat prevented it. The roiling pain in her stomach didn't stop.

Ven leaned forward and asked, "And what about me?"

"Your value as Mia's physician is critical," Doctor Huan said. "Her greatest chance of success is with your help."

"Why?" Ven rubbed at his chin in thought.

Doctor Huan gave Ven a blank stare. "Can you imagine her unprecedented level of trauma? Any therapy she could get would be a great help. You've already shown devotion to her well-being. She needs somebody she can trust."

Mia eyed Ven. Trust was a strong word.

"If I do this, then what?" Mia said.

"Then you may do as you please. We won't withhold you here."

"I'll help her," Ven said.

"You'll help me kill my friends?" Mia said, voice tinged with anger. "Didn't you say just yesterday that it's better to build others up than to break them down?"

Ven cringed. "These are unfortunate circumstances, but look at all the harm they cause. If... killing them means saving many, many others, then it seems like the only way to get the best outcome. It's a compromise."

Mia rubbed her forehead again. "I don't want to do it."

"I know," Ven said, his voice soft, eyes sad. "But Doctor Huan's right. You're probably the only one who could get close enough to them without being torn apart. What you've seen them do is horrible. We can't let that happen again."

*He's right.* She didn't want him to be. But would they really just go on some killing rampage? Could Dami really do such a thing? She'd never truly know unless she had the chance to confront him. Her jaw clenched and unclenched until she mustered enough courage to say, "Fine. The box, let's do it."

"The box?" Ven said, raising an eyebrow.

"An adopted expletive the subjects have used," Doctor Huan explained. "She's saying she'll help."

"Oh, right," Ven said. "So do we know where to find them?"

Doctor Huan rose from his seat. "We have a suspicion. You'll leave immediately."

# Chapter Sixteen

## Chapter 16

### Morality

"We're heading there based on a suspicion?" Mia asked.

She stood behind Ven trying to look at the map in his hands. Her proximity made it hard for him to concentrate.

"Yes," Ven said. "Though it seems a strong suspicion. Where would rampaging murderers go if they escape their so-called captors? Killing those who funded their imprisonment might be a start." He looked over his shoulder at Mia's frowning face. "Sorry, I don't use those words as a means of describing your own experience. Not that I have a full grasp of how they're thinking, but it could be something along that line. Also, they have reason to believe that they are receiving help from someone."

Ven looked back at the map, mostly to hide his own shame. All of this could have been his fault. He'd given Dami the key to the door. Would that have made much difference anyway? Dami could have broken down that reinforced door eventually. There was only one thought that comforted him. *Somebody removed the poison from Dami's neck, and it sure wasn't me. That's the real reason he got away.*

But who could have known about the poison in the first place? Ven hadn't known about it until now, and even knowing about it didn't give him the knowledge of how to remove it. Whoever else had helped Dami must have been much more informed. Could it have been his secret employers? But no, he couldn't see them removing the one failsafe against such a dangerous person. They would have been smarter than Ven.

Frustrated, he thrust the map into Mia's hands and paced across the gravel. Aware that he could cause Mia anxiety, he tried to appear as calm as possible but knew he was failing.

His saving grace was the arrival of their carriage that functioned like a wooden car with horrible suspension.

"You'll need speed to get there in time," Zein said as he walked up to them from behind. "This should help you travel a little faster than a subject's running speed."

"Remind me how we know where they're going?" Mia asked.

Zein sighed. "Truthfully, we believe he's after the investors—those who funded the research to begin with. One of them was here at the time all of this started. Dami targeted him specifically, like he knew exactly where to find him and what he looked like. Any unaided subject would have no such knowledge. If someone has instilled an interest in him to seek revenge on the investors, then there are two of them he'd target first due to their particular resources. We're sending you to the more likely of the two."

"I don't suppose we get to know the names," Ven said.

"It would be better if you didn't."

"Alright, so we get to this place, Dami and Ambrose show up, then what?" Ven said. He imagined Ambrose and her almost glowing visage coming and ripping his arms off like an angry angel.

Zein withdrew a few syringes from the inner pocket of his suit and handed two to Ven, and two to Mia. "Mia will need to get one of these syringes inserted and released into the device in the back of their neck.

The poison capsule is removed, but the cavity and metal chamber that held it will still be in place. The subject's bodies have healed around the device there and their current imperviousness would prevent it from being removed."

Mia lifted a hand, eyebrows raised. "I have to stick this in their necks while fighting both of them at the same time?"

"You'll find a way," Zein said. "You were first rank in fighting."

"Yes, but I always choked against Dami."

"Then don't choke."

Ven ventured to put a reassuring hand on Mia's shoulder. They *would* figure it out. They had to. He didn't want anybody else to die—especially not Mia.

"Very well, off you go," Zein said, nodding at the carriage. "Your driver knows where to take you. And don't break any of those vials on yourself, Mia. It would cause severe pain if the contents came in contact with your skin."

"I'll try not to drink one if I get thirsty," she said.

Ven held back a smile as he waited for Mia to enter the carriage first. He came in right after, and the carriage moved with a jolt before he could even sit. Mia steadied him before he almost fell on her, gripping one of his hips and his arm until he got his footing back. He sat across from her, trying to ignore the heat flushing to his face. These things needed seatbelts.

"I don't think this is going to work, Doctor Yashke," Mia said, wringing her hands as if nothing had happened. She leaned forward so that her dark hair framed her face on either side, the whites of her eyes nearly glowing between her black lashes.

It actually annoyed him how striking she was.

Ven cleared his throat. Now wasn't the best time to be contemplating her beauty. "I've already got an idea. And please, you can just call me Ven."

Mia shrugged. "Alright, *Ven*. What's your idea?"

"Well, we have to separate them."

"What do you mean 'we?'"

"I'll help. I have to distract one of them while you fight the other."

"Ven, getting ripped apart will only take a few seconds. I'm not sure that's worth it."

The nightmare image of Ambrose pulling his arms off returned and he shook his head to clear the thought. "That won't happen. I'll talk to Dami. He likes to talk."

"No, he likes to *pretend* he likes to talk. He'd rather rip you apart. You saw what he did to everyone else." Mia leaned back in her seat, lips curled in disgust.

"I'll make him talk. He doesn't want revenge against me. He knows I'm not an enemy and wouldn't need revenge." Ven didn't voice the idea that he hoped Dami would see him as an ally. He gave Dami the key after all. Wouldn't that be enough to buy him a few words? He worried that Mia would hate him for helping free Dami. Who would do such a thing? Was he really that much of a fool? He was too trusting. Oliver told him that right before he got in the car with Dayelle.

"Alright, if you want to get yourself killed, why not? But let's say they come frolicking up holding hands, how do we separate them?"

Ven ran a hand across the back of his neck. "I haven't finalized the wording quite yet, but I can do it."

"And what about me?"

"Lay low until I separate them."

"We're about to die." She slumped in her seat and looked across at him with her dark eyes.

He was distracted again. "We're not going to die."

"Can you get this thing out of my neck?"

"I don't know, I honestly haven't even heard about it until today."

"Maybe you could look at it?" Her voice was earnest.

Ven shrugged. "Couldn't hurt. Well, I guess... maybe it could, but I'll be careful. Can you sit here in front of me?" He pointed at the floor of the carriage.

Mia rose from her seat and drew back the curtain to let in more light before she sat on the floor between Ven's legs, her back facing him. She leaned forward and pulled her hair in front of her, revealing a round, metal contraption at the edge of her hairline.

Ven placed a hand on her shoulder to help steady them against the bouncing of the carriage, then bent down to inspect the device. It was flat, barely protruding from the skin. He traced its small outline with his fingers. Mia's skin was warm, but she shivered as if he'd tickled her. He pressed lightly against the metal. "Does it ever hurt at all?"

"Never," she said. Her voice was soft.

He tried stretching the skin around it, but it held tight as if stuck to the metal. There were four small recesses in the metal, the only sign that something could be done with it. "Well, I don't have much insight to offer, unfortunately," he said. "I assume a specific four-pronged tool is needed in order to remove anything. I've never seen such a tool though, so it's unfamiliar to me."

She grunted. "Some secret tool that's probably impossible to find. Of course." She still lingered on the floor in front of him.

"We could find one eventually," Ven said.

"Are you sure you could trust me without it?"

"I trusted you before knowing it was there."

Mia got up and returned to her seat. "You trusted Dami too though, didn't you?"

Ven shrugged. "Well, yes, I know I tend to expect the best out of people, but I trust you a lot more than I did him."

"Seems like a dangerous approach to things."

"It could be, but I'd rather expect the best and help people achieve their potential than to avoid them or let them struggle on their own. Besides, I'm right *most* of the time."

Mia shifted her gaze out the window. "Well, I'm not sure how trustworthy I really am."

Ven chewed his cheek, trying to understand what she was feeling. "You're afraid. Maybe you feel like you haven't been able to make a lot of your own choices so you question your character, but you're a good person, Mia. The fact that you're even considering things like that shows that you have more morality than Dami or Ambrose. I don't think you can compare yourself to them."

"And yet we'd kill them." Mia bowed her head.

"Yes, but we'd kill them in order to preserve other lives." Ven rubbed his temples. "If there was another way, we'd do that instead, but I don't think they can be contained."

"Still, it doesn't feel good."

"I know what you mean." Ven looked out the window as well, the carriage frequently jolting uncomfortably. He wondered how the whole thing didn't just break apart, but there was a reason he wanted to study medicine, not engineering.

They continued in silence for a while, and Ven even managed to doze off a couple times before the carriage came to a halt.

"We're here," the driver shouted from outside. Then they heard her footsteps racing across the gravel as she ran away.

"I guess she doesn't want to be around in case they're here," Ven said.

Mia gave a short nod, eyes wide. They exited the carriage together.

# Chapter 17

## Drowning

Mia took the lead, striding towards the silent manor that lay ahead of them, its gate hung ajar, slightly crooked. Their driver had taken off in the opposite direction.

"Box," Ven whispered. "We might be too late."

"Don't use my expletive," Mia whispered back, giving him a fresh look, hesitant to admit her amusement that he wanted to fit in with her. "Maybe everyone's already dead."

"They could be sleeping. In the middle of the afternoon." Always presenting the improbable optimistic possibility.

The manor's short, stone wall was mostly obscured by tall trees that surrounded the whole property. Their feet crunched over thin gravel as they entered the open gate. Nothing moved. A neatly aligned garden to one side of the property burst with vegetation, and it smelled like crushed leaves. Mia expected the front door to be hanging as limply as the gate, but it was closed. Her fingers tingled with anticipation. The two-story brick home appeared otherwise unharmed.

"Maybe we're not too late," Ven said as he approached the door.

"Or maybe you are." It was Dami's voice, coming from behind a clump of thick bushes. "I guess it depends on whether you were coming to kill *Lord* Haelon or save him."

A shiver went up Mia's spine.

Blood sprinkled Dami's arms. Even his gray, athletic clothes were decorated with it. "He is dead, just to verify," he said.

Mia tensed, but Ven's shoulders dropped and he sighed almost as if he was relieved. She scanned the bushes and trees, wondering where Ambrose was hiding as well.

"Dami, I'm glad to see you're well," Ven said.

*Is he lying? Was this some setup to bring me here?* Surely Ven didn't mean it. Mia clenched her fist.

Ven sighed. "I didn't know about the poison in your necks. I'm so sad about the other subjects. I didn't expect things to go that way."

Dami shrugged. "I did, and I'm the one that let them out, so don't torture yourself over it. I knew they'd die and that only Ambrose and I would make it out." He sat on a decorative boulder and crossed his legs casually. "How did you get out, Mia?"

Mia didn't answer immediately. She held back a gasp with the revelation that all those deaths were Dami's fault. Her blood pounded through her body, exercising her all-too-practiced skill of hiding her emotions as her anger simmered. "I waited until everything went silent." She didn't want to offer too much information while she couldn't exactly tell what Ven was trying to do. And where was Ambrose?

"Ah." Dami laughed. "You were too afraid to come out. It's because you lack the fighting spirit, Mia. This is why I selected Ambrose to come with me instead of you. I could tell after the mission that you wouldn't have it in you to do what needed to be done. She's better-looking than you too, so I guess that worked in my favor."

Mia's cheeks burned. She wanted to spit in Dami's face, but Ven spoke before she could do anything. He really was good at hiding. All this time, everything he'd done at the facility just seemed like a lie. All a farce to win favor so he could break out.

Clever indeed.

"Where is Ambrose?" Ven said.

"Probably dragging your driver back here," Dami said. "She ran outside and watched as your carriage pulled up. We could hear that machine coming from quite a ways out. Did the investors send you here to find me? Maybe try and kill me? They already failed at that."

They were about to die. Mia could feel it. Dami somehow knew everything.

Ven laughed this time. A short laugh. Mia could tell it was fake, but hoped Dami didn't know Ven well enough to tell. "No, Dami," Ven said. "Let's just say I've had a secret employer this whole time. Not the doctors, not the investors."

Ven glanced back as Ambrose approached the manor, dragging their driver by the collar of her shirt. The woman kept trying to stand on her feet and walk, but Ambrose moved too fast to allow it.

"They had some information to share with you," Ven said. "Though not with Mia or Ambrose."

Dami smiled, his white teeth gleaming behind brown lips. "You want to talk to me, just the two of us in other words. Separate me from Ambrose." He grunted an amused laugh. "You know what, sure. I have nothing to worry about from you. Let's go take a walk around back." He winked at Mia before leading Ven around the other side of the building.

Mia couldn't shake the feeling that Dami somehow knew their whole plan. He'd take Ven back there just to bury him in the ground.

"I didn't expect to see you alive," Ambrose said as she dropped the driver to the ground. The middle-aged woman groaned before rising back to her feet. Her arms and face were scraped, and her clothes scuffed and torn at the knees.

"I have my ways," Mia said. Was Ambrose really better looking-than her? Mia ground her teeth at the mere question. Why would such a question even matter? She didn't need to care what Dami thought. Ambrose was about to die anyway. Her friend. Her sister. She gulped. Her enemy. Mia felt the vials hidden in her shirt, held against the skin of her chest by the tight clothing.

"Frankly, I figured you'd be too weak or stupid," Ambrose said, tying her shoulder-length golden hair back with a strip of cloth. "How did you learn about the poison and get it out?" She tapped the back of her neck.

Mia clenched her fists. "I can be persuasive when I need to," she bluffed. Ambrose must've thought Mia's had also been removed. If only. "You shouldn't underestimate me."

Ambrose shrugged. "To be honest, I was hoping it would just be me and Dami left alive, but oh well. We're going to build a whole nation of superior people together. Our impervious trait can pass on to children we have, did you know that? And our bodies won't decay like other people, so we'll outlive generations of humans."

"That's grandiose," Mia said. She'd wondered about such possibilities, but never trusted the staff enough to ask them. Dami's false friendliness towards the staff had allowed him to learn things that most subjects probably never had.

If there was a time to attack Ambrose, it was now. Ven did his part by luring Dami away, but she didn't know how much time she had. Would she be *able* to attack Ambrose? Her friend?

"It's inevitable," Ambrose said, raising an eyebrow at Mia. "Nobody can hurt us now without the poison in our necks. It's just a shame I can't kill you."

That was all the motivation Mia needed. She sprang forward, covering the distance to Ambrose in a flash. She didn't need to spar with Ambrose, just grapple her into a position to insert the poison.

Ambrose kicked at Mia, aiming high, but Mia jumped over Ambrose's leg and flipped through the air before her shoulder collided with Ambrose's chest. Together, they rolled to the ground, stopping with Mia on top as Ambrose's back was to the ground.

Ambrose jabbed Mia's face with her elbows, the blows feeling like little more than pressure on her flesh. This position wouldn't work. She needed to get at Ambrose's back. She also needed to make sure Ambrose didn't break the vials against Mia's skin.

Mia kicked up her feet and rotated on her hands to land on the ground by Ambrose's head. Ambrose attempted to rise, but Mia yanked her hair towards her with one hand and pulled a vial out with another.

Ambrose tried to twist around, but Mia lifted them both up to their feet before jumping onto Ambrose's back, a knee jabbing her down, and one leg wrapping around Ambrose's thighs. Ambrose screamed and fell to her face, head still held up as Mia kept a tight grip of her hair. Mia fumbled with the vial, struggling to get it inserted until it finally slid into place. She clicked the small lever on the vial just as Dami came running around the side of the manor.

"What have you done?" he bellowed.

Mia stepped back from Ambrose's already limp body. She hadn't made a sound after the toxin was released. It simply ended her.

Dami charged over to Ambrose's body, and Mia backed away further. She was subtly aware that Dami would probably attack her, but her mind couldn't focus. And where was Ven? Perhaps Dami had already killed him. She'd just killed her friend. This was what the doctors had done to her. They'd saved her life when she was younger, but they'd turned her into a killer.

After Dami pulled the empty vial from Ambrose's neck, he turned and snarled at Mia. "You betrayed us."

"I have to," Mia said. "You'll keep killing people if I don't stop you."

Dami stood and hurled the empty vial at Mia. She swatted it away. "I kill my captors," he said. "There's nothing wrong with that." He approached her in large strides.

Mia readied herself. She'd beat him this time. She had to.

When he came into range, she swung at his face but he didn't even bother blocking. It didn't matter. Nobody was keeping score. This wasn't a competition. What was it she had to do again? How did she beat Ambrose? The anger on Dami's face was disorienting, his teeth bared in rage. She didn't *want* him to be angry with her.

"How dare you fight for them, Mia," Dami said, shaking his head slowly.

"And who are you fighting for?"

"Me!"

"But if they don't stand a chance, is it really even a fight?"

Dami breathed a laugh. "No. Not really. They're insects to you and me, but you can't look past your own humanity. We're more than them. What does it matter if I kill a few bugs? They should know their place."

"We're still human too, Dami."

"Maybe we were, but not any more." He shook his head. "I was six when they tore me from my father's arms. I remember his screams as they left him in the street. He was sick. Dying. Weak. Pathetic. I remember exactly what he looked like." He let out a huff. "And I am nothing like him."

The box. Dami actually remembered something from his life before the facility?

But his way of thinking was off. *Superiority. It was just like Doctor Huan described.* "We might be impervious, but that doesn't mean we aren't human. That doesn't justify killing them."

"You're wrong. I'm going to make things better." He shrugged. "Too bad you won't be around to see it all come to fruition."

Dami lunged at her midsection, and she skipped back to avoid it, but he grabbed her around the waist before she could get away. He lifted her up and carried her over his shoulder as he ran, but this would work to her advantage. She could easily insert the poison from here. She fumbled to retrieve the vial from beneath her shirt, but just as she pulled it free, he slammed her into the ground. He'd run them all the way to a river that flowed behind the manor. When he slammed her down, it loosed the vial from her grip.

"Do you remember our drown testing?" Dami said as he maneuvered around Mia's arms, apparently unaware of what he'd just avoided.

Mia had enough sense to recognize that he was going to try and get her into a locked choke hold. Without being able to breathe for a long enough time, even impervious subjects could die.

She went into a panic, kicking away to avoid Dami getting behind her, but he had a firm grip on her upper arm. They twisted around each other. They struggled for what seemed like several minutes, neither of them gaining the advantage.

"You'll choke like you always do, Mia," Dami said. "You could never beat me."

At that moment they locked grips on each other's right forearms. He started to twist her arm and she knew the best thing to do was twist his the same way. They came shoulder to shoulder with his arm over his head. She had the advantage and spun to get behind him, but he ducked low before jumping up, smashing her face with his head before he flipped backwards through the air. He landed directly behind her. His other arm instantly snapped around her neck.

She was in the choke hold. Her right arm stuck straight up while her left arm was free, but there was nothing she'd be able to do to get more air. She kicked back at him, elbowed him, tried to wriggle free, but nothing would work. Eventually, stars popped into her vision, and she attempted to lean forward and hoist him onto her back. She dove toward the water. They splashed down together. His grip remained firm. She'd run out of breath before him anyway.

An eternity of time passed as she kicked and squirmed. Being underwater made it feel as though everything moved in slow motion. Eventually, it all went black.

# Chapter 18

## Revival

Ven peered out from his hiding place behind thick bushes. He knelt at the edge of the slow-flowing river, water soaking into his pants.

He couldn't help the tears that gradually formed at the edges of his eyes as he watched Dami and Mia struggle. He knew he'd die if he went out there to confront Dami. As soon as they got around to the other side of the manor, he realized Dami's only intention was to torture him. It had started with his fingers, two of which were likely broken.

"So who's your employer, then, doctor?" He asked, gripping another finger, but Ambrose's screams led Dami away. He backhanded Ven's jaw before running off. The blow hit with enough force to leave Ven unconscious for a few seconds.

But now he had to wait. He'd come out if he needed to, but he read Mia's entire file and the statistics on all the testing she experienced over the years. Her body had a stunning ability to survive without fresh breath for fifty-five minutes. It would enter a sort of frozen state, most organs slowing their function.

Ven always had a good sense of time, but wished he had his phone to check how long had passed. Dami held Mia underwater for somewhere around thirty minutes, just staring down at her beneath the water, sometimes shaking his head, before he resorted to finding a couple large rocks which he placed on her chest to keep her head submerged. Once he did that, he looked around the area for another ten minutes as if to try and locate Ven or perhaps the driver.

Ven ducked even lower, laying down beneath the bushes, water soaking into the rest of his clothes. A great crashing sound echoed from the other side of the manor, but afterwards was a long stillness.

It was approaching the fifty-minute mark when Ven dared to come out of hiding. He approached Mia by walking up the edges of the river where it was only knee-deep. One thing he suspected was that the subjects had never swum before, so if Dami came after him, he could possibly get away by swimming across the river.

He ground his teeth at the great splashing he made as he walked upriver. Not the most subtle approach. He reached Mia with no sign of Dami. With great difficulty, he managed to push two large rocks off Mia's body, then he heaved her to the surface. He placed her head on his shoulder and wrapped his injured hand under one of her armpits, then pushed out into the river. He used his feet and free hand to swim downstream to the other side of the river.

Once on the other side, he dragged Mia behind the trees and bushes until they were hidden from view.

He turned his full attention to her condition. She was still alive, but there were likely only a couple minutes left. Since her lungs stopped working, he would need to return them to function. He immediately started CPR.

It only took one blow before Mia suddenly coughed up into his face.

She looked up at him with wide eyes. With one great inhalation, her body unstiffened. "Where's Dami?"

Ven shook his head. "I don't know. I'm just glad you're alive."

Mia nodded then looked down at Ven's right hand which still rested on her sternum. "If you wanted to kiss me, you picked a weird time to do it."

Ven withdrew his hand with a snap. His body burned from chest to face. "Mia, that's not at all what this is. It was part of resuscitation. I had to get air back into your lungs."

"Of course." Mia sprang to her feet and took a few steps towards the bank of the river.

Was she offended? Ven didn't know what to make of her reaction.

"I killed Ambrose," she said.

"I'm sorry. I know that must not have been an easy decision to make," Ven said, rising to his feet. He looked at his fingers, the pain throbbing.

"It was easier to do when I got mad at her." Mia clenched her fists. "I wish there was another way."

"I can understand that. I just wish we'd been here in time to save some of the people. Do you think our driver is alive?"

"I remember her running away again when Ambrose and I started fighting." She glanced back at him and then stepped down toward the river. "We should go find her. We should also check the building to see if anybody survived."

"Good thinking," Ven said. "But I'll check the building, and you can search for the driver. Do you know how to swim?"

Mia shook her head and tucked her hair into the back of her shirt.

"I'll help you across." He led her down into the water and showed her how to lay on her back and float. "Alright, now keep your head here on my shoulder. I'll keep one arm under you while I swim across. It's how I got you here."

Mia nodded and allowed Ven to help her get her head on his shoulder. The skin of their cheeks brushed as she got in place and an electrifying shiver ran down Ven's neck. Their faces were so close, and she looked up at him with her big, beautiful eyes, her lips slightly parted.

"Are we going?" she asked, casting her eyes around.

Ven stuttered. "Y-yes, of course." He pushed off into the river, leading them back across. Mia kept instructions well and remained still the whole way. They reached the other side and walked through the foliage back to the manor.

"What about Dami? Do you think he's still here?" Mia asked.

"Possibly. Let's hope not. Unless you're ready for a second round." Ven patted the inner pocket of his coat. "I've still got my vials."

"Give me one in case he is," Mia said, holding out a hand.

Ven handed one over. The pain in his fingers was magnifying with the passing of time. They were already getting swollen. He checked to make sure they were properly set. The bones seemed fine as far as he could tell. He gathered a few sturdy twigs from the ground before they came out into the manor's yard.

"I'll check inside," Ven whispered.

Mia gave a short nod and jogged toward the front.

Ven wished Dami was gone. *But why? Isn't that why we're here?* He doubted Mia's abilities. She had seemed to panic a bit in their fight earlier while Dami appeared level. If only Ven knew more about fighting. Or at least had enough confidence in himself to run out and try to use the poison on Dami.

He turned the knob to the back door of the manor. It was as eerily quiet as the outside, but he checked every room and called out to see if anybody would answer. Nobody did, but he found one room with a few lifeless bodies, throats torn out. He quickly ducked away. He'd never seen anything so brutal, and a deep sadness gripped his chest. After a depressing search of each room, he returned to the pantry and scavenged for food. The residents wouldn't need it anyway.

After finding some bread, carrots, and a strip of cloth, he went out front.

Mia wasn't there. His pace quickened. Maybe she'd been dragged off by Dami. They should've stuck together. He hurried to the front gate and sighed with relief as he found Mia trying to help their driver push the carriage into an upright position. Dami or Ambrose must have tipped it over.

Ven let out a gasp of relief. "I'm glad you're okay," he said to the driver as he hurried over to help.

"I'm surprised to be alive, to say the least," the woman said.

Ven placed the food on the grass and went to one end of the carriage. "I'm sorry I never even caught your name before."

"It's Rebelie," she grunted. "Let's lift on three, eh?" Rebelie counted to three, and they all heaved.

Mia wedged herself underneath and pushed up with her legs, giving Ven and Rebelie enough space to push it over the rest of the way.

When they were done, Mia shivered and flexed her hands.

"Are you okay?" Ven asked. He hadn't seen her do that before.

Mia frowned, but then her features softened. "Oh, it just feels tingly when my body readapts. No survivors inside I'm assuming?"

Ven shook his head. "But I did find lunch."

"Toss me one of them carrots, if you would," Rebelie said. Her accent was like a mix between Canadian and southern Louisiana. "We'd best be off. I had instructions to take us to the next location if we were either too late or unsuccessful here."

Amused at Rebelie's dialect, Ven held back a smile and tossed a carrot over.

"Where to?" Mia asked.

"Next house," Rebelie said. "Get in, quick. I seen how fast that man runs."

When they climbed inside, Ven handed some food over to Mia, but she didn't eat. He wrapped his broken fingers with the sticks and cloth he'd gathered. It wasn't the nicest splint he'd ever made, but it would at least keep his fingers from shifting out of place.

"I don't know if I can do it, Ven," Mia said.

"Of course you can. You're a better fighter than he is. You just panicked."

"Why did I panic? How do I not do it again? It was easy with Ambrose." Her voice pitched higher than usual, and she bit her lip.

Ven thought around a bite of bread. "You aren't convinced he needs to die." It was a guess, but he wanted to see how Mia reacted to the idea.

Mia leaned forward in her seat and held her face in her hands. "I don't know."

"Well, I'm not sure I can solve it for you, Mia. You're more capable than you think. Caring about life—caring about people—it doesn't make you weak. But when you face him again, I need you to try your best. If you lose, he's not going to give you another chance like he did today. He'll stay there until you're dead. I don't want you to die. I'd be very sad if that happened. So please, if only for my sake, don't lose."

She looked up at him. "You want me to win so that you don't get sad?"

"Yes."

"Very motivating."

"I know, I should have brought it up before. You probably would have beaten him already."

"Oh, certainly. I wouldn't want you to cry or anything."

"Definitely not. I look horrible when I cry."

Mia smiled. "I'll do my best to spare you of that embarrassment then."

"You're very generous."

She leaned back in her seat, looking more relaxed.

Ven really did want her to win. Dami was nothing short of a monster. The facility had done this to him. Tortured him. Twisted him. Ven could only imagine the resentment Dami felt. And though Mia possessed the same power, she was compassionate and sympathetic. She was beautiful, not just in the sense of having a flawless body, but beautiful because of who she was. He found her actions and thoughts intriguing, and her reactions to difficulties compelling and inspiring.

She glanced over at him, and he realized he'd just been staring at her. He turned to look back out the window, but not before he caught the hint of a smile at the edge of her mouth.

# Chapter Nineteen

# Chapter 19

## Value

"It's empty. He already came through here," Rebelie said from outside the carriage.

Mia opened the door and looked out anyway. She burned with so much energy that her fingers tingled with it. Though still nervous, she'd been ready for a fight.

"Maybe he runs faster than I thought," Rebelie mumbled.

A few people stood outside the establishment. Half of the brick building had crumbled. They were in a small town by the looks of it. Several other buildings lined the street, built close together. She'd never seen anything like it. There were so many people. She stared, awed at the variety.

Ven got out and asked a few questions.

Mia vaguely heard the details. Some man ran in. Tons of screaming. Building collapsed. Same man ran out. They'd tried to find survivors, but with no success.

"What do we do now?" Ven asked the driver.

"Head back to the facility from here," Rebelie said. "I didn't have no more instruction than this."

Mia groaned and sat back down inside the carriage. She clenched her fists. *I need to end him. I'm going to get away from the facility. I'm going to see the mountains and the flowers.* She'd been holed up in a building her whole life, but she knew if she let Dami run around freely, then that subtle pain in her gut that something was wrong would never leave her.

Ven stared at her again, this time with a frown of concern. Why was he so worried about her, anyway? Such a weird doctor. She could have sworn he thought her attractive or something, but he'd said his interactions with her were completely professional. Could it be that he genuinely cared about her? *That would be a first.* She *did* want to trust him though.

They traveled the rest of the day in silence. By the time they arrived back at the facility, the sun was setting. The place had been cleaned up somewhat in their absence. At least Mia didn't see any dead bodies as they gave her a meal and sent her to bed. As the only subject left, she didn't have anybody to talk to. The staff was barebones anyway. She only saw perhaps five members of staff the whole evening. Ven gave her some space until escorting her to her room.

"We tried our best today," he said, "and tomorrow we'll try our best again."

She resisted rolling her eyes and instead looked away, not wanting to think about the softness in the look he gave her.

"Hey," he said, giving her a light touch on the chin so that she'd look back at him. "I'm serious. I believe in you. You can beat him. We'll make this work."

His touch seemed like such an intimate thing to do. Nobody had ever touched her like that. She glanced down the hall. No other members of staff had even accompanied them here. Ven was doing it again. Acting like he cared. Why did he have to make her feel things? She wanted to shove him away.

"I guess we'll find out, won't we?" she said. "I'll see you tomorrow." She stepped away from him, toward her door.

Ven nodded and headed for the stairs then paused and turned back to her. "Mia. My parents always taught me to use positive affirmations, especially at moments where I feel inadequate. I'll share a few with you. You are important. You are beautiful. You are good, and smart, and caring. You have value. You have the ability to do great things."

The words sent a shiver across Mia's skin.

"You are wonderful," he said at last with a smile. "Just thought I'd let you know." He then retreated out of sight up the stairs.

A semblance of peace washed over her. Once she had her door closed, her shoulders dropped. Her muscles relaxed. Had Ven's words really made that much of a difference in how her body felt? She hadn't realized how tense she'd been ever since they got back here, but being in her own room helped lighten her mood. Maybe she was important. Maybe she was valuable and wonderful. And what did he mean by beautiful? She let out a sigh, knowing she was thinking too much of it. Under the yellow light of a dragonlight lantern protruding from the wall, she changed into a clean set of clothes and laid down. Sleep came quickly.

# Chapter 20

## Old Research

Ven wasted no time. From the second floor, he walked to the other side of the building. The hallway was eerily barren. This area was sleeping quarters for other subject doctors. *Where are they? Had they all been killed in the uprising?* Maybe they'd been sent home.

He wouldn't mind the chance to go home, but he still needed his answers. What was he even doing out here? Curiosity. It was all some crazy idea to learn more about his parents. For all he knew, Dayelle might not even have the answers he was looking for. Yet somehow he was here, in a place that shouldn't exist.

He missed sitting by the fireplace, leisurely reading a book while Oliver brought him a cup of hot cocoa. All they had here was bitter coffee.

But his thoughts returned to Mia. He couldn't abandon her, of course, but he also didn't want to die. *I'm not going to die. Mia will win.* Even as Dami was breaking his fingers, he'd still imagined Mia charging over and defeating Dami in a heartbeat. It hadn't happened that way, but he didn't like to question his optimism. Better to have joy and high hopes.

The muted sound of his boots echoed hollowly as he turned the corner. He hoped this area would be empty as well, but he heard voices as he got near the next turn.

The voices were both female and unfamiliar. He mainly didn't want to come across Doctor Makarr.

"... should reconsider our situation," said one of the voices. Judging by their attire, it was two research doctors. They looked at him as he turned the corner.

"Hm, I'm surprised to see you back here," said one of them, her hair a graying red.

"I doubt he's even aware of the situation, Monia," said the other doctor. They leaned against the wall on opposite sides.

"What do you mean?" Ven said.

"Well, after that little massacre," Monia said, "you can imagine that none of us wanted to remain here, but they won't let us leave. Said it was in our contract. The audacity!"

"Nobody signs a contract like that expecting that their research subjects are invincible monsters," said the other doctor. Her suit was surprisingly crumpled and her black hair was pulled up into a messy bun. "I do remember reading about how staff would be provided with adequate protection, but that certainly didn't work. I should think that makes our contract invalid. My name's Keja by the way."

"If only I could get my lawspeaker involved," Monia said. "What brought you back here, anyway? You're the only staff member who's been allowed to leave, you know. I would have thought you'd run off as soon as you were outside these walls."

Ven shrugged. "I'm just doing what I can to prevent others from getting hurt."

Monia scowled while Keja smiled.

"It's called sympathy, Monia," Keja said. "Probably why they assigned him as a personal physician and kept us on research."

"Sim-puh-thee," Monia said, sounding out the syllables. "Never heard of it."

"I should get going," Ven said, walking past them. "Do you keep old records in the lab? I no longer seem to have an assistant, so I'm needing to collect information myself."

"I'll help you," Keja said. "Your cause seems noble enough and perhaps it'll mean us getting out of here a little sooner." She pushed away from the wall. "There are three rooms stuffed with old paperwork. Filtering through that on your own would be a pain. Care to join us, Monia?"

"I'm going to find some more coffee," Monia said. "You run along."

"This way," Keja said to Ven, leading him to the stairs. She took him up to the third floor, passing a guard. There weren't many of those left.

"What sort of information are you looking for, anyway?" Keja asked.

Ven wasn't sure how much he should tell her. "Well, origination information ideally. Anything there might be from when they first arrived here. I'm hoping it will help me work through some things with my patient. Trauma treatment."

"Finding the source, certainly," Keja said. "I only took one course on psychological treatment and knew it wasn't for me, but I at least remember something about finding the source."

It wasn't quite like that, but Ven said nothing. He wondered what courses or schooling looked like on Orund.

"This should be the room you're looking for," Keja said, opening a door.

Inside were a few rows of shelves stacked with papers, wooden boxes, and old trinkets.

"Wow," Ven said. "Is there any order to it?"

"Sure," Keja said. "Old junk over here, papers here, and oh, boxes filled with random items. Who's pocket watch?" She reached into a box and pulled out a watch hanging from a dull, iron chain.

Ven started with the papers. Some of them really were quite old, documenting many of the first experiments or commenting on the behavioral patterns of the subjects. A lot of them were attempts at essays. Apparently they actually tried to educate the subjects for a while, which he hadn't been aware of, like basic math and reading.

"They really don't mind us looking through all of this?" Ven asked.

Keja dug through the boxes. "I suppose not. It doesn't matter what we know since we can't leave anyway. Well, except you. Perhaps I should have you contact my lawspeaker."

Ven kept looking until he found a dusty box filled with papers from an early date. There were even a few records written by Doctor Zein Huan himself. One paper noted the necessity for termination measures should a subject prove to be dangerous or not useful with copious documentation regarding the use of a plant called dragonsbane.

That was the poison. He suspected it was the same substance they must have retrieved from the factory on the first mission. He set those papers aside and kept digging until he found another sheet mentioning something to do with drilling into the young subjects' bones, particularly the legs and skulls, but these "additional transfusions" were mentioned as unsuccessful or even lethal. The sheet even included some diagrams of where the drilling on the bones occurred. Gruesome as it seemed, Ven set that sheet aside as well. How many children might not have made it? He cringed at the thought.

A jolt of energy rushed through his body as he found another paper documenting the installation of the "security measure." The poison-delivering mechanism was apparently coated in dragon's blood before getting inserted into a drilled recess on the lowest point of the skull where it was then fitted to the bone itself. This procedure was explained in great detail which extended through several sheets. Most importantly, it contained drawings of the implements and tools used for installation, including a four-pronged tool for installing the cap with a poison-release valve linked to the trigger devices used by the guards.

He took that one page, folded it up, and stuck it into a coat pocket, making sure Keja wouldn't see. Now he'd just have to find one of those tools. It looked vaguely familiar, like some kind of powertool back on Earth.

His breath caught and his vision spun for a moment as he again realized where he was. Another planet. Another world. How did that work? Was this a different dimension? His vision blurred and he grabbed the shelf to steady himself. A dull pain grew in his chest which he instantly recognized as anxiety. He took a sharp breath through his nose and let it out gradually. He inhaled again, slowly this time, noting the scent of dust and metal, the cold touch of the iron shelving against his hand, and the sound of Keja digging through a box.

Wherever he was, it was real. He shook his head and checked the other boxes but couldn't locate any of the tools that could remove the poison valve.

"Well, I have an idea of what I want to know," Ven said. "You don't think they'll mind if I take some of these papers with me?"

Keja stood with a groan. "Depends on who you ask, but I don't see anybody stopping you."

"Thanks for your help," Ven said.

"Don't mention it. I just have no enthusiasm to continue researching under these conditions."

Ven walked out the door. "I can understand that. I should hurry and get some sleep tonight."

"It is past the optimal sleep time," Keja said. "These dragonlights mess with our natural sleep patterns."

"Good night," Ven said to her before rushing back down the stairs. He returned to his room the same way he'd come and stashed the papers under his bed. He wasn't sure if he'd be able to get the information over to Dayelle. They needed to prevent this kind of thing from happening in the future. That was his real task. But what was it she'd told him to do? Say something about grapes while getting his food? What if their agent had died during the massacre?

He took off his coat and transferred the paper with the tool information under his pillow. One way or another, he'd get his answers.

# Chapter 21

## The Village

The next morning, Mia sat at the table with Ven eating a simple breakfast of salted eggs. The walkway on the second floor was completely
empty. Nobody stared down at her. A single staff member stood at the far
end of the enclosure.

A door opened and closed from the west wing and Doctor Zein Huan
approached their table with Tem just behind him.

"Good morning," Doctor Huan said, a brief smile flashing across his
face. "I hope you both slept well."

Mia blinked up at him. The man was both savior and captor, but his
good intentions felt hollow. His smile seemed more acted than sincere. She
was still just an experiment to him. This whole task of taking down Dami
was probably just so he could cover up his mistakes. She put her head down
and took another bite of eggs.

"Good morning," Ven said.

"Mia, I'd like to show you something today," Doctor Huan said. "Tem
will show you out front when you're done eating."

"Very well." She hadn't referred to him as 'doctor.' Would he notice?

Doctor Huan merely turned on his heels and strode back the way he'd come, leaving Tem to sit beside them, watching as they finished up.

Mia shoveled the rest of her food down just to avoid Tem staring at them.

Tem smiled. "Follow me, then."

When Ven stood to join them, Tem held out a hand. "Just Mia will be coming, Doctor Yashke. She should be returning by the afternoon at the latest."

Ven looked at Mia and gave her a short nod.

It was odd for her to recognize that she felt nervous getting separated from Ven. What could they be showing her that they didn't want Ven to know? She followed Tem silently through the halls of the facility. She'd only been down it three times now, but this route to the front of the building was familiar to her now. Their shoes echoed through the empty halls until they exited out a pair of double doors to the loading and unloading area just behind a large gate, a crisp blue sky greeting them overhead.

"Join me here," said Doctor Huan before entering the carriage door. The gates ahead swung open. They were taking her away.

Mia bit her lip. Tem only nodded at her when she glanced his way so she approached the carriage and entered with a precision leap. She closed the door and sat across from Doctor Huan. The vehicle moved immediately.

"You know, I haven't traveled very far from the facility in quite some time," he said.

"Where are you taking me, Doctor Huan?" Mia responded coolly. She glanced out the window.

Doctor Huan raised an eyebrow. "We're visiting a nearby village. You may skip the formal title now, Mia. Please call me Zein."

An odd proposal. Ven was the only other doctor who'd asked her to do that. It could be a way for people to gain trust with each other and maybe

Doctor Huan was employing the same tactics as Ven. "I don't see anybody else call you 'Zein.'"

"Yes, well everyone else you've seen talk to me has been one of my employees. It's appropriate to use titles in such scenarios."

Mia paused. "Am I not an employee?"

"No, Mia. You are under no agreement to serve me as they are. Yes, I purchased you from your mother, but that only relinquished rights of guardianship, which, according to local law, expire when the child reaches the age of sixteen. What you do with your life at this time is completely up to you."

Mia considered for a moment, brow furrowed. "So, I could jump out of the carriage right now, and you wouldn't try to stop me."

Zein clasped his hands before him, body bouncing with the movement of the carriage, and yet he looked as comfortable as if he were seated behind his desk. "I would be disappointed, certainly, especially with so much riding on your success with the current task. There are many lives at stake. But to respond, yes, I would."

"What would become of Doctor Yashke and the others?" She carried little sympathy for the other staff, but she was curious what the owner of the facility had to say.

"He would be released, as we'd previously discussed before sending you out to find Dami. We'd prefer Dami neutralized of course, but Ven would stand no chance of succeeding without your assistance. You're the key to Dami's capture. In all likelihood, the information Dami receives is specific enough that I would be surprised if he didn't return to hunt down and kill all staff who have knowledge of our research."

"Did you send some of them away already? Could he really track them all?"

Zein frowned. "For the same reasons, I can't send them away, unfortunately. Not until there are certain measures in place to secure their confidence. The confidentiality of the procedure that you and the other subjects experienced is of utmost importance. We wouldn't want anybody else like Dami on the loose."

"Like Dami? In other words, a fiendish, unstoppable killer?"

"Naturally."

"Which I have proven not to be. This is why you've trusted me."

"Indeed." Zein's hands were still clasped before him.

"But if I complete this task and kill Dami, you'll let me go free?"

"Yes."

"Would you remove the poison from my neck?"

"No. It's a necessary precaution should you ever take a turn for the worse. You can't deny the logic behind that."

Mia squirmed a bit in her seat. "I'm not sure I'm comfortable living with the idea that somebody could suddenly end my life at any moment."

Zein gave her a solemn smile. "Mia, such is the experience of all humans. If I were you, I'd consider that sense of mortality a blessing."

Mia leaned back, struck by the idea. It was true. Normal humans could easily be killed by any number of things, and yet they somehow all lived on as if nothing was wrong. "Why are you taking me to the village?"

Zein sat back as well and folded his arms. "A wiser question. I want you to see how people live. I know you were denied a true childhood and that you were raised outside of normal conditions. You are considerably more educated than most, but I want you to see the ways and lifestyle you are working to preserve."

Whatever that meant. The carriage came to a stop.

Zein led the way out of the carriage. They'd stopped in the middle of a village. Or maybe it was a town? Mia wasn't sure what the difference was. This village was not unlike the one she and Ven visited yesterday when trying to stop Dami.

The dirt street was lined with a few small buildings, few of them rising above two floors, mostly built of painted wood, though some of the larger buildings were made of stone on the first floor. The road was just wide enough to turn a carriage around. A few people walked the road, mainly steering clear of the carriage. There was only one other carriage which passed them on the other side, pulled by two large, furry animals with hoofed feet.

"Walk with me," Zein said.

Mia silently complied, taking stride beside Zein.

The clothing everyone wore was interesting, mostly simple cloth, not the athletic clothes worn by subjects, the crisp suits worn by doctors, or the pressed uniforms of the other staff. Several women wore dresses, and most of the people wore boots and hats.

Two couples stood off to the side of the road, chatting amiably. They burst into laughter at some reference to a cousin.

A girl walked along beside her mother. "What about Marray's dog? We can have it."

"No," said the mother, "we can't have Marray's dog, that's hers. I don't think she'd want us to take it."

One man had a canopy setup in front of his building, an assortment of vegetables arrayed on tables. A few others would come and sort through the products, making some kind of exchange of coins before walking away with vegetables.

Zein paused at a table and made a purchase for a round, mostly white vegetable with a small root dangling from the bottom and tinged red near the top where a few green leaves sprouted.

"You could try this, if you want," Zein said. "It's called a turnip. My parents used to grow some on their property when I was a child. I used to dig some up and eat them when the season was right." He handed the vegetable to her.

Mia had a hard time picturing Zein as a child. He had wrinkles around his eyes and forehead, sure, but he seemed ageless. She looked down at the turnip, turning it in her hands. She wasn't really hungry, but she did want to try it. Tasting something in its raw form was an uncommon practice when all of her food was normally prepared for her. Avoiding the dangly root at the bottom, she took a bite, her teeth breaking the surface easily. The flesh was crisp and wet with a mild sweetness to it.

"What was that exchange for?" Mia asked before taking another bite.

"Money," Zein said. "In the outside world, people work to create goods or services in order to receive money, which can then be traded for other goods or services that they do not produce on their own. Take that field for instance." He pointed to a large, open field behind a small building. "That field is planted with vegetables. The owner of the field must maintain the land. It's hard work, and most of their time is spent maintaining it. They might have additional time for mending clothes, repairing their home or shoes, but not enough time to do other necessary things. Additionally, vegetables take time to grow and become ready to eat, so how does this person continue to eat when the vegetables are not ready? Once harvested, the vegetables are exchanged for money, which the owner can trade for other foods or supplies when needed."

"I get it," Mia said. "But you don't produce anything. Where did you get money?"

Zein grunted. "Truthfully, I have received money in exchange for research. Research is focused on creating a future product. Like farming, there is lots of maintenance and waiting involved, but unlike farming, I have been paid before the vegetable was prepared to eat essentially."

"Why would anybody do that?"

"Otherwise, that particular vegetable would not be produced," Zein said. "It's expensive to grow and maintain, but the payoff and value of it would exceed the investment."

Mia got it. Some things were worth more. Higher value would mean higher investment. "I'm not the vegetable in this analogy, am I?"

"No, Mia. The subjects were the ground. The end product was essentially never produced."

"This product was supposed to be some kind of cure, right?"

"That's correct."

"And you messed up."

Zein gave her a solemn glance. "Instead, I created a disease. An unexpected outcome. Research always has its risks, but I didn't imagine the immediate risk of a dangerous subject removing their only human vulnerability. It was considered an unlikely possibility." He waved an arm toward the town. "This freedom these people experience is at risk. Dami would ruin them."

Mia looked across the village. She realized she didn't care much if they were ruined. Did that make her evil? Then she noticed the little girl and her mother just before they entered a building. It did make her heart hurt to think of Dami harming the girl. She thought of her own mother, sick and poor, unable to help.

"I think I understand," Mia said.

"Good," Zein said. "I wanted you to understand the gravity of what we must do."

Mia nodded, thinking again about how much she didn't care about the rest of this village. What would it matter if it was destroyed? Would she even feel sad? All of her friends were already dead besides Dami. Would she be sad if Dami was dead? *What about Ven?* She ground her teeth at the thought. That reaction alone told her the truth. She wouldn't want Ven to get hurt.

"Can we head back now?" she asked.

"Certainly," Zein said, eyeing her carefully before turning back down the street.

# Chapter 22

## Fire

Ven paced outside. He walked around the walled recreation area where the dark, monolithic climbing stone stood. The air burned today, and he wished he could take off his lab coat. What he wouldn't give to wear a t-shirt and gym shorts.

It would be time for lunch soon and Mia wasn't back yet, which only added to his anxiety.

He carried his small bag in one hand, the stolen papers tucked inside. How was he supposed to notify staff that he had valuable information? He tried to remember the details, but his brain felt muddled.

There was only one other staff member outside, monitoring the wall. This one was armed with a crossbow and mace, but his eyes looked to the land outside the building, not at Ven. Here was the only place Ven saw staff who bore the actual appearance of guards.

*Enough pacing.* He went back inside and took the long route to the cafeteria. Instead of crossing the large enclosure, he stuck to the halls. He could hear his own breathing as he twalked. The noise of it bothered him, and he focused on the floor, observing the white tiles as they passed beneath him. What a boring building. Leaving here must have been such a shock for Mia, Dami, Ambrose, and Baze. The only place with any color was the enclosure where at least a few plants grew. No wonder Mia liked plants.

He reached a short line of staff waiting for food. Among them he recognized Monia and Keja. He gave them a small nod in greeting. *Grapes. I was supposed to say that I wish I had grapes.*

"Grapes!" said one doctor returning to his table with his plate. He had a small pile of grapes in a bowl as well. "Wow. Never thought I'd see the day."

Ven's mouth hung open. Of course. The one day he needed to say that was the day they actually had some. He prepared himself for the awkwardness. "I wish I had grapes," he said loudly.

A couple other doctors laughed and one looked at him with a shake of her head. Ven shrugged it off. He could certainly handle a little bit of social awkwardness.

After getting his food, he sat by himself, which was much easier to do now that there were much fewer staff. Despite the urge, Ven resisted getting up and talking to other staff. He knew it would help distract him from some of his nervousness.

Keja approached him anyway. "You look tired. Did you sleep much last night?"

Ven gulped down his bite of bread. "No. I woke up at the same time as usual, despite the exciting late night venture."

Keja smiled. "Yes, you sure know how to entertain a woman."

"I wish it was my own idea. I've heard that searching through old junk in storage rooms is the way to a woman's heart. Figured I'd give it a try."

Ven was only joking, but Keja's smile broadened and her eyes softened as if she were taking his jest as flirtatious. She wasn't unattractive, but she was also easily twice his age.

"Well, was your experiment with women's hearts successful?" she asked.

He hastily took another bite of bread, shoving it into his mouth so he couldn't say anything for a moment. A shrug was all he offered. *Was* it successful? Apparently Keja thought so. *Maybe I should've searched through there with Mia.* He tried to swallow, but the bread was dry and he instantly started choking.

Keja's eyes widened and she rounded the table as if to help him dislodge the food from his throat, but Ven managed to cough it up before she could wrap her arms around his chest.

"Got it," he said through his mouthful of bread. He took swigs of water to help the bread move down.

She still moved to place a hand on his shoulder, a smile returning to her face.

"You've reminded me of my need to get some rest," Ven said. "I haven't had much time away from my patient for a while, so I think I'll go catch a nap."

Keja stepped back so Ven could stand. "Glad I could be of assistance."

"Thank you," Ven said.

He returned his tray and rushed back to his room. Catching up on sleep was not a bad idea. Perhaps tiredness contributed to his nervousness. He dropped his bag beside the bed and laid down after taking off his lab coat.

He'd never been good at taking naps, but soon enough his thoughts drifted.

He awoke perhaps an hour or two later. Instead of feeling rested, he felt groggy and wanted to sleep more, but he needed to check if Mia had gotten back. If anything, perhaps he could find Tem and see if he knew anything about how long they'd be gone.

Halfway down the hall, he heard the first shout.

"Bar the doors!"

Two staff members sprinted down an intersecting hall.

"What's wrong?" Ven shouted after them, but they paid him no mind. Ven flew down the stairs. He burst out into the enclosure, hoping to find more people there who knew what was happening.

"He's here!" someone screamed from across the way. "He's here!"

He only saw a couple other people, but gauging by the sheer horror and panic he saw, they could only be referring to Dami.

Ven shivered as fear washed over him. Mia was gone. She was the only real protection they had. He still had one vial of poison tucked away in his suit, but he knew he wouldn't get a chance to poison Dami without her. His thoughts raced. The best he could do was survive and find Mia.

He had to get away.

The first thought that came to mind was the exercise yard. He dashed across the enclosure, passing someone else running the opposite direction. Distant screaming echoed down the halls. A deep rumble shook the building as if it had been hit by something massive. Maybe dragons themselves were coming to punish them for their research.

Ven burst through the door, crashing into the guard who'd been outside. They both tumbled.

"Watch it!" the guard said. Ven had never heard the guards speak harshly to doctors. "Where are you going?"

"Hiding," Ven admitted.

"You'll be exposed out here," the guard said, straightening his uniform, "but good luck." He hurried inside.

Ven got back to his feet. He wasn't planning on hiding in the exercise yard. A clouded midday sky greeted him overhead as he ran across the yard, straight to the outer wall. Would Dami come looking specifically for him? Undoubtedly. He imagined it would take maybe two hours for Dami to scour the building by himself. That would be plenty of time.

As Ven reached the wall at a sprint, he leapt and barely grasped the edge of the upper walkway. He slowly pulled himself up. The dull, red brick was a rough surface, but it made it easy for his shoes to grip. It got easier once he got an elbow over, then the other. When he finally stepped onto the top of it, he was panting. *I'm out of shape.*

Looking down the other side of the wall, he estimated it was a twenty foot drop with a downward sloping hill. The wall had apparently been built on a small, natural plateau.

"That complicates things," he said aloud. He wanted to get to safety, but wasn't interested in breaking a leg in the process. He walked the wall, searching for a safe place to get down until he identified a location where a rocky section of the cliff jutted out from beneath the wall. He could land on that, then jump down the rest of the way, cutting the fall in half.

After gripping the edge of the wall and gritting his teeth against the pain in his fingers, Ven shimmied down until he was dangling from the wall, hanging just a couple feet from the ground. He let go, feet slipping on the uneven surface of the rocks beneath. A rock cut his hand as he grasped for it, trying to keep from falling backwards off the small cliff. It steadied him just long enough to get his ankle unwedged from between a couple rocks, but then he lost his grip and slid down the dark gray rockface.

The ground at the bottom was covered in deadened grasses and thick dirt, but the slope of the hill and the force of his fall made it so he started tumbling. After a few flips, he drew to a stop on his hands and knees, a cloud of dust floating in his wake. An involuntary cough barked from his throat, and he shook dirt from his hair. The makeshift splint on his hand was still in place.

He took the last few steps to the base of the hill and looked back up at the wall. It seemed much higher now than it had from above. His guess on height must've been off. He kept walking around the hill, further from the facility, patting and brushing the dust from his clothes as he went. It might've made for a bit of camouflage, but filthy clothes made him too uncomfortable.

At one point, he heard a window shatter from the facility and something crashed into the ground. Ven ducked, laying flat. His only hope of survival was not to be seen. He stayed there for a while until he heard another shattering window, followed by a scream and another thud. He tried not to imagine what that was. Dami was probably making his way from room to room.

Ven got back to his feet and hurried on. The ground ahead evened out as he climbed a slight incline. He got some distance from the facility and crouched down behind a few blackened rocks.

He imagined Dami interrogating the other staff, finding out he'd been there. The guard would tell Dami that he'd seen Ven. Somehow Dami would trace his steps. *No, this'll work out. I'll just wait until he leaves and Mia comes back.*

He peeked out from behind the rocks. The facility was large, and he couldn't pick out any movement until he saw a bit of smoke rising from a corner. How well could subjects see? He knew they had sharp senses, but he couldn't remember details about their sight capabilities. He ducked back behind the rocks, wary of exposing himself.

Despite the fear, he kept looking back at the building and the path he'd taken to get here, thoughts of Dami sprinting towards him constantly invading his mind. More smoke rose, black and billowy. Flames licked out from a window.

At least his secret employers would be happy to see that. But what about the information they'd wanted? They'd wanted to know about the operation the subjects had undergone in order to become impervious, and Ven had acquired at least a bit of that. The papers were still stuffed in his bag in his room, far from the location of the fire. If he wanted answers about his parents, didn't he need to supply that data?

He chewed his tongue in thought, considering the possibility of the papers being burned up in the fire. Anxiety rippled through his chest. He could destroy the information without giving it over to the secret employ-ers. It was suspicious that they wanted the information to begin with. They didn't need to know how the operation was done in order to prevent it later, did they? Probably not. But who was he to judge? What he really needed was the truth, and Dayelle could offer that. Hypothetically.

Ven thought he heard his name being shouted in the air. He gulped, trying to wet his dry throat.

Another hour passed before Ven felt comfortable enough to emerge. A third of the building had been engulfed in flames. The papers. He could potentially still retrieve them. *Did anybody else make it?* Every step he took felt like he was trudging through water. Despite watering, his eyes felt dry. He doubted Dami left anybody alive, but Ven had to check.

The front entrance was untouched by the flames, and it looked like the fire was dying down and had stopped spreading at least in one direction. He made his way through a shattered gate. Every door he passed was either open or destroyed. The air was thick enough with smoke that Ven started coughing. He covered his mouth and nose with the front of his shirt, but his eyes watered.

The only sound was that of his own shuffling feet and of the distant, crackling flame. The halls were deserted. The once immaculate building was in unrecognizable disarray, debris scattered everywhere.

He hurried down the halls, wondering if he should be stealthier. He still wasn't sure if Dami had left. The second floor is where he saw the first body. He checked for a pulse. Dead. Every person he came across was the same. The heat intensified. Turning the corner, he found the hallway with his room was already burning with fresh flames.

The papers would be destroyed. Would Dayelle still tell him about his parents? He turned around. Dami left no survivors. Best to get as far away from here as he could. Breathing was hard enough. A deep groaning rent the air just before a thunderous crash rumbled the ground.

The building was collapsing. This fire must've been worse than he'd thought. He sprinted even faster, coughing as he ran. He fumbled down the stairs, ankle twisting when he missed a step. His stinging, watery eyes made it hard to see small details. It wasn't until he took a wrong turn that he became really concerned about his safety. He scolded himself for entering the building to begin with. It was on fire! Why had he come in at all? Did he really think the papers would have survived?

When he got back in the right direction, it felt abnormally hot, but he didn't see any immediate flames. He kept running but realized his danger when he noticed that the ceiling's normally white paint had taken on a yellowish hue. In a few places, it was burned all the way through.

The floor above him was on fire.

Another deep groaning echoed through the hall, this time filling him with dread. His muscles screamed as he sprinted further, dropping the hand that had held his shirt over his face so he could pump both arms. Something crashed nearby as the groaning intensified. A glance back revealed a smoldering beam of wood that fell through the ceiling.

The wall beside him collapsed completely, a spray of bricks bursting around him as the ceiling sloped to one side and fell around him as if in slow motion. A thundering of burning rubble rained from above but Ven never stopped sprinting, his eyes focused on the white hall in front of him.

A mere four seconds must have passed by the time everything crashed down, but not before Ven made it through a broken doorway marking the separation of the hallway from a waiting area near the entrance of the building. A cloud of smoke and ash exploded around him as the flaming debris came down just behind him. Broken shards of brick and wood pelted him in the back, and he stumbled to the ground. He coughed and dragged himself forward on hands and knees.

Across the room was a door that would take him outside, but as smoke filled his lungs, he couldn't bring himself to stand. He kept crawling, eyes bleary as if he was bawling. Perhaps he was. His body certainly felt battered. The pain of his broken fingers was only a dim sensation. But he'd make it. Of course he would.

He fell to his face just in front of the door, blackness enveloping his consciousness.

# Chapter Twenty-Three

# Chapter 23

## Truth

Mia leapt from the carriage before it stopped. She hit the ground at a full sprint, gravel spraying out behind her with each step. At full speed, she ran faster than the carriage. No wonder Dami had gotten everywhere before them.

The facility before her had either collapsed or was blackened by the fire. Some areas still burned, and a couple patches seemed untouched.

"Don't get caught in the rubble," Zein shouted after her.

She didn't care what Zein had to say. Mia faced death hundreds of times in just seventeen years of life, many of them at his order. This risk was one she was taking of her own volition.

Ven was inside. She'd left him here. Maybe that was why she'd felt anxious leaving him behind. She hadn't been here to keep him safe. If only she'd held her ground and insisted Ven come with them. *But I didn't want to seem attached.* It was petty.

She ground her teeth. It was too hard to know if she was ever making the right choice. Her indecision was probably one of the reasons she wasn't like Dami. He at least had conviction behind his choices.

Saving Ven was right, though. She knew how fragile he was.

The smell of smoke hit her like a wall when she came within a few steps of the facility. A familiar smell. They'd done burn testing on the subjects a couple years ago, holding their arms over open fires. Mia had reached such a level of resilience that she could grasp a coal in her hand without any damage, though it would feel hot.

Mia reached the first door she could find on the building and pushed it open, accidentally ripping it from its hinges. It flew across the room and smashed into a pile of rubble on the other side. A cloud of smoke puffed out across her head and she ducked down to see beneath it.

There, lying on the floor with arms outstretched, was Ven.

Mia gasped and took hold of Ven's arms, pulling him outside. Once they were a few feet from the building, she turned him around and checked to see if he was alive. The carriage came to a stop.

Ven's light hair was singed on one side, a cheek was blackened with soot and bleeding, and his clothes had burns in several places. A vein on his neck pulsed with life.

"He's alive," Mia said as Zein got out of the carriage.

Zein only nodded and walked a little back down the graveled street, pointedly not looking at the burning facility.

Mia wondered if he'd simply given up now that the building was gone, but he stopped a few paces up at a well and pulled up some water. He brought the whole bucket over and splashed some across Ven's forehead.

Ven blinked his eyes and immediately started coughing.

"Sit up," Zein said. "Try to drink some water."

Ven sat up, still coughing, and took the bucket of water Zein handed him. He took a few gulps as soon as he could stop coughing long enough to allow it. After a few more fits of coughing and drinking, he finally spoke. "That was wild."

"What happened?" Zein asked.

Ven related Dami's attack, his escape, and his return to the building. His voice had a slight rasp to it.

"Did you see Dami at all yourself?" Zein asked.

"No," Ven said, "but I'm sure it was him. His... handiwork was familiar." His expression was grim.

"Why did you even come back?" Mia said.

Ven bowed and shook his head. "Because I'm an idiot. I'd thought perhaps I could find some survivors. Help others escape. I was too late anyway. Everyone I came across was already dead." He avoided her eyes as he'd said it, suggesting a lack of confidence. Was he lying?

"You almost died by going back in?" Mia raised her eyebrow at him.

"It would appear so," Ven said, gingerly touching the singed hairs on his head.

"It's my fault," Zein said, gaze now firmly resting on the ruined building. Sweat glistened on his bald head. Mia hadn't realized it was hot. "Though I hadn't fully anticipated his return to the facility, I understood the possibility. I should have had everyone relocated. I considered the means of transporting them all to be too difficult."

"Oh well," Mia said spitefully. "What's a little more death on your hands?" Her quick shift to anger alarmed her.

Zein was expressionless as he responded. "What's done is done. From here it's best we look to the future."

"What do you recommend? Do you know where else Dami might have gone?" Ven croaked.

"I have suspicions," Zein said. "But the true concern is the method to kill him. Do either of you still have the vials of poison I gave you?"

"We have two remaining," Ven said, pulling one out from his tattered coat. "I have one and Mia has the other."

"I used one on Ambrose and lost one while fighting Dami," Mia said.

"Those are the only ones remaining," Zein said. "The rest were stored here at the facility. I assume that's why he came here once he discovered that we have a way to kill him. There's also an additional method that may work. One that was used in more ancient times against the dragons of old. It may help to have both methods available should you need them."

"What method is that?" Mia said, wary of yet another way she might die.

"And why didn't we try this other option before?" Ven added.

"We needed to respond to the emergent need," Zein said. "This method would not have been needed had you been able to effectively apprehend Dami at your first confrontation. I do know of Mia's loss record when fighting Dami, and I recognize she may have some psychological difficulty when facing him."

Mia ground her teeth.

"This method involves a specific weapon," Zein said. "Few exist, and the location of most of them is unknown, though I do have a suspicion on where one may be found."

"Why is everything only based on suspicions?" Mia asked.

Zein raised an eyebrow at her. "I haven't seen it for myself, but I'm at least 90 percent certain in this case if that helps provide more assurance."

Mia folded her arms.

"This one belongs to a nobleman in the city of Peskan," Zein said. "It has been passed down for generations. They likely have two or three such weapons in fact, but there's one in particular you will want."

"Why just the one?" Ven asked. "Are the other two not as effective?"

Zein shook his head slightly. "They are all equally effective, but this one is smaller. The other two are of a more common design fitting that of a broadsword. That would ordinarily be fine if Mia were wielding it, but unfortunately she will not be able to hold the weapon."

Ven and Mia shared a look.

"Why is that?" Mia said.

"The weapon was crafted using the same poison that you have in those vials. It's very touch would cause her great pain. It will need to be you that wields it, Doctor Yashke."

Ven frowned. "And... I can't wield a broadsword?"

"Your smaller musculature would make it difficult. It's a fairly heavy weapon."

"I'm lean," Ven said, looking down at himself.

"Yes," Zein said. "The weapon I'm proposing you retrieve is more of a dagger. It will be easier for you to maneuver, and you should have an easier time concealing it."

Mia stood back up. "I'm assuming we can't just ask this nobleman if we can borrow the dagger, can we?"

"I'm afraid not," Zein said. "He can't know what we're needing to do, and I don't believe he'd be willing to part with it. He'd probably enlist his own crew to eliminate Dami in that case."

"And that's a bad thing?" Ven said.

Zein folded his arms. "Yes. We don't want anyone to know that humans have existed with such impervious qualities. Nobody should get the idea that such a thing is possible, so utter discretion is necessary."

"Won't some people already know about Dami?" Ven said. "I mean, he was seen yesterday doing things that were not ordinary."

"Seeing someone run fast is different than knowing why they run fast," Zein explained.

Ven gritted his teeth. He wouldn't mind if somebody else took care of this issue. He was not qualified to hunt and kill anything, let alone a person that was practically superman. He gulped down some water then said, "Alright, so we borrow this man's dagger, then how do we find Dami?"

"I'm not sure where Dami will be, but he has targets in Peskan," Zein said. "He'd end up there eventually. I will be there as well. Once you have the dagger, you should meet me at a place called Juns Hall. It will be easy to find if you ask around. You will want to retrieve the dagger and meet me there as soon as possible. I would suggest using subtler means to accomplish this. I don't believe barging in would be most effective."

Mia barely restrained the venom in her voice. "And what will you be doing while we take care of the difficult tasks?"

"I have several things to get done as well," Zein said. "I have contacts in Peskan that I'll need to touch base with. I should have some additional resources at my disposal by the time we meet at Juns Hall."

Ven placed the empty bucket aside and got to his feet. "Well, I would feel more confident using a dagger than trying to insert a vial in Dami's neck. Is the dagger effective?"

"Stabbing him anywhere along the torso, neck, or head would work."

"Alright," Ven said. "Are we taking the carriage?"

"Yes," Zein said. "Rebelie has already been given instructions. When you arrive in Peskan, she will take you to meet Jalett Fon. She will help you find a way into the nobleman's home. The nobleman's name is Yubo Huan. I will travel separately. I have a couple things to wrap up here locally."

"Huan?" Mia asked.

"Yes," Zein said with a sigh. "We are very distant relatives. Not on good terms either. Shall we go?"

"Of course," Ven said. He looked to Mia. "Ready?" He walked to the carriage before she could respond.

He was acting strange. Almost terse in his responses. Mia felt as though he didn't want to talk to Zein anymore. She followed him wordlessly, ignoring the nod Zein gave her as she left.

"What's wrong?" She asked as she sat across from Ven. The carriage took off, wheels grinding on the gravel before launching.

Ven heaved a sigh. "I don't like having another method for killing you."

Mia shook her head. "Me neither, but I must admit that I like the idea of you being more useful in a fight."

"I was a very helpful distraction that first time."

"Yes, but where were you when Dami and I were fighting?"

Ven frowned at the floor. "Hiding. Like a coward."

"It was the right thing to do at the time, given the circumstances. You're alive right now because you hid. And I'm alive right now because you hid. If you hadn't survived, I would have drowned. All I mean is that next time, if you don't have to hide, maybe we'll win."

"True enough," Ven said with a smile.

"Always quick to embrace the positive."

"Of course."

"Is there anything else bothering you?" Mia asked.

Ven leaned back in his seat, smile broadening. "Look at you, all concerned about my feelings. When we first met, you were all procedural."

Mia grunted. "It's still procedural. I've just gotten better at sounding more human. I don't want my companion to be unstable before a mission."

He seemed to take her words more seriously than she'd intended and looked out the window for a moment. "I don't like secrets. I think all the secrecy is what got my parents killed. I don't like lying either. It makes me uncomfortable." He squirmed in his seat. Folded his arms. Unfolded his arms. Squirmed some more.

Mia wanted to ask about Ven's parents, but she let the silence linger until he spoke again.

"I'm only seventeen," he said.

"I knew it!"

"You did?"

"Well, no," Mia shrugged, "but you do look young even though you're tall. Much younger than any other staff, and especially younger than the doctors."

Ven nodded. "I'm also not officially a doctor."

Mia cocked her head at him. What did this mean about him? Why come to the facility at all? "Then what are you?"

"I don't know," Ven said, throwing up his hands. "A spy or something. I've been studying to be a doctor though, and both my parents were doctors, and I worked with them all growing up. I'm sure I have just as many hours as a newly licensed practitioner. If that's even a thing here."

"I don't understand," Mia said. "How did you end up at the facility? I thought all the doctors had to meet certain criteria."

"I had some help creating false credentials. I wanted to learn more about my parents. They both died recently, and I'm pretty sure it's because they were meddling in something that dealt with dragonblood research."

"What's that?"

"It's you." Ven's blue eyes looked crystalline in the light filtering through the window. "Well, not exclusively you, but the reason you're impervious has something to do with dragonblood research. It's a whole field of study that's supposed to be illegal, but nobody seems to follow the rules. Everyone knows it can be extremely dangerous, but nobody is willing to give up the use of lights that don't require a flame for example."

"That makes me illegal?" Mia asked. This must have been what Dami was referring to. The blood of dragons ran in her veins, and that was somehow illegal?

Ven looked up in thought before saying, "No. Well, I don't know what the laws are. I was told your operation was illegal though. The one that made you impervious."

"I see." Mia rubbed her lower lip. "So what happened to your parents? Were they caught?"

Ven shook his head. "I don't know, but I'm pretty sure they got murdered. I have no way to prove it though, and that's part of why I came to the facility. Somebody told me that I could learn more about my parents if I helped them take down the facility."

"Well, it looks like you succeeded without even trying."

"Right," he looked away again. There was something he wasn't telling her. "Oh, before I forget, I did find something out that can help." He rifled through his pockets until he pulled out a paper. "I found out what we need in order to remove the poison from your neck." He leaned forward in his seat, holding the paper out to her and pointing at a drawing. "We need one of these. I'm hoping we can find one in Peskan."

Mia smiled. Ven really was trying to help her.

# Chapter Twenty-Four

## Chapter 24

### Peskan

T hey spent two days on the road when the city of Peskan came into view. It nestled up near the base of a small mountain range. Ven loved the mountains. He wondered how Mia felt, seeing them for the first time.

The landscape changed. No longer were they in some barren desert. Not far from the road, a river wound through the flatlands, several farms stretching out from the opposite bank. A wide variety of trees and vegetation grew in the area. It reminded him of Montana.

The road was wide and in very good condition. Rebelie let Mia sit with her up front, and Ven opened the carriage door, opting to hang out of the opening to watch the changing scenery. It seemed a wild thing to do, especially with how fast they were going, but the road was smooth enough that he barely noticed. He also got a good enough view to see Mia's widened eyes sparkling as she looked from left to right, soaking it all in.

They passed several slower moving travelers on their way. Most people walked, some rode horses, some rode in carriages pulled by oxen or horses.

Ven only saw one other dragonblood-powered carriage like their own, passing them on the opposite side of the wide road.

"You might want to go back inside," Rebelie said as they neared the walls of the city. "A vehicle like this catches enough attention." Rebelie halved their speed.

Ven ducked back inside and Mia came in after him, easily climbing around the side of the carriage. Her black hair was askew. She smoothed it out with her fingers and tied it back.

"I've never seen so many people," Mia said. She looked back out the window. "Are there many cities like this?"

"Maybe," Ven said. He had no idea how many people lived in this world, and he wasn't sure he was ready to explain to Mia that he'd come from a whole different world. Where would he even start to make sense of that?

She tilted her head at his response but said nothing.

The carriage slowed to a crawl, matching the speed of the general masses coming and going beneath the gates of the city.

Ven and Mia looked out opposite windows. The people here dressed much like those they'd seen in other villages, though wide-brimmed hats seemed like a common trend, some made of grasses, and others decorated with feathers, pins, and colored fabric. There were a few buildings outside the walls. Several guards around the gates wore shiny breastplates and plumed helmets.

Once through the gates, the road got bumpy with brick pavement. All the buildings were at least two stories tall, the first floor always made of gray stones. Traffic thinned out after only a couple blocks once they passed a few market stalls. Mia openly gawked at everything. Here in the early afternoon, the sun was still high, but the arching roofs stretched a bit over the roads, making it feel like they were traveling through a forest.

They turned the corner into a residential area. Here, the road was not kept as well, and it was interspersed with patches of crumbled pavement, many holes filled with dirt as a quick means of repair. The traffic here was thinnest. Everybody else walked.

In front of an open doorway, a familiar woman with a tanned face and dark hair looked directly at him. Once their eyes met, she inclined her head and retreated through the door behind her.

It was Dayelle.

Ven flung the door of the carriage open. "Stop here for just a moment, Rebelie."

"Aye," Rebelie said, stopping the vehicle. "I don't recommend lingering too long, doctor."

When Ven jumped down, Mia made as if to follow him. He lifted a hand up. "Best if you wait here. I don't think we want very many people to see you. I'll be back in just a moment."

Mia frowned at him but sat down, eyes narrowing. He was pushing her trust.

Ven closed the carriage door and made his way back down to the building Dayelle entered. The door was open. He went inside to a room that was empty save for a couple wooden barrels in the corner. A hallway stretched out ahead of him, firelight flickering from a distant room. He left the door open behind him and proceeded down the hall, pausing in front of the door.

A candle rested on a small table beside the window with the curtains pulled back, offering additional light. Dayelle stood in front of the window, arms folded as she gazed outside. She looked over her shoulder at him as he entered. "There's my handsome young doctor," she said in her low, accented voice. "Congratulations. The facility is mere rubble. I know you had some part in Dami causing such a ruckus. It wasn't quite the subtle approach I was expecting from you, but it worked nonetheless. We need to apprehend him."

She wore a fashionable brown and red dress and a black corset. It looked like she was ready for a renaissance fair.

"How did you find me?" he asked.

"We have a listening device in the carriage." Her smile revealed white teeth.

"Oh." He tried not to seem alarmed. "I didn't think your organization would be the type to use dragonblood technology."

"On the contrary," Dayelle said. "We certainly don't appreciate the development of such technology nor the means required to create them, but we've seized a lot of equipment in our time. It would be a waste not to use them, and we're doing it in a way that's not fueling the industry."

"I see." His cheeks reddened. That meant she'd heard his admissions to Mia. "I tried to get you some information I'd stolen from the facility before it burned down, but when I went to retrieve my bag, it was too late."

"Don't worry about that," she said. She turned and leaned back against the plaster wall behind her. "Our other agent got your message at the cafeteria. He snuck into your room, got the papers from your bag, and smuggled them out before Dami arrived. They didn't provide any information we didn't already suspect, but it certainly confirmed a few helpful details. It was a bold move for Zein to attempt dragonblood infusions on humans. Such methods were used several years ago but always resulted in death within a few hours. We're not sure how he succeeded, but he goes to great lengths to keep that detail secret. Hopefully it dies with him."

Ven shuffled his feet and gulped. They were some sort of spy organization. Of course they knew everything he'd been up to.

Dayelle smiled. "Don't be so nervous, Ven. You've done well, given the circumstances."

"But I haven't really done much of anything."

"Sure you have. You're from Earth. You've been raised and trained to have greater emotional awareness and have a better understanding of psychology than any of the doctors here on Orund. This allowed you to develop a closer relationship with Mia, where she has been able to see you as a fellow human. If not for that, she'd most likely be with Dami. Together, without the dragonsbane in their necks, they would have been unstoppable."

"And that was... part of the plan?" Ven said.

"Crucial. We made your paperwork good enough that we expected you to be placed with one of the top performing subjects. And I do have your first payment." She bent down and retrieved a small sack from under the table that jingled with coins. She placed it on the table but kept her hand on it. "There is one thing I'm concerned about though."

Ven gulped. "And what is that?"

"All your talk about releasing Mia when this is done." She frowned, her red lips curving. "I hope such conversation was said as a means of earning her trust. You know that she cannot live. Her very existence is a threat to present stability. Once Dami is taken care of, Mia must come next."

"She is a good person. Innocent," Ven said, standing up straight.

"Certainly true. It is indeed quite a shame, but as long as she lives, there's the threat of others duplicating her condition. That cannot be allowed. Do you disagree?"

Ven chewed his cheek. He clenched and unclenched his fists. What he said might determine whether or not Dayelle would hold up her end. But also, even if they managed to bury the whole thing, that didn't guarantee that the operation couldn't be discovered by somebody else. He breathed out slowly. "I admit the risk, yes, but at the cost of an innocent life? I've told her I'd help her get free."

"She's one soul. Ending her life would ensure the security of countless others. Such a balance cannot be measured, darling. And though it may be honorable to keep a promise, it's more honorable to do what is right."

It was wrong. So wrong. What was he to do? *It's not like I'm holding a knife to Mia's throat right now. I don't have to kill her. I can find another way.* Ven shook his head. "I see your point," he lied.

Dayelle nodded at him and pushed the money across the table toward him. She placed another item on the table, a black trigger device. "You will need it eventually. Only after Dami has been subdued."

Ven had never earned his own money before, and the weight of the sack in his hands gave him a surge of satisfaction. He was curious what kind of value their currency had. How strange would it be to bring some back to Earth? He quickly tucked the trigger device into a pocket. His skin burned where he touched it, and he resisted curling his lips in disgust.

Dayelle looked directly in his eyes. "It's standard practice for doctors to be taught about maintaining the collective health of a society over the health of an individual. When one becomes subjective to the situation is when such insight gets clouded. Maintain professionalism with Mia."

"I understand," Ven said, peeking into the bag to see what looked like gold and silver coins and a few gems. He didn't dare argue. His parents had not taught him such a philosophy at all. They once stayed with a sick neighbor all night as she lay on her deathbed with a horribly contagious disease. His parents had risked getting sick themselves just to comfort a friend. Wasn't that *more* noble?

"I'm glad we see eye to eye," Dayelle said, her beautiful smile returning. "Now run on back. Mia will be getting anxious."

Ven turned to leave with a nod, tucking the sack of money into a pocket on the lower end of his lab coat where the bulge would be less noticeable. His parents had left him with considerable wealth after their passing. If they were really gold and silver coins, he assumed he held a small fortune.

He blinked against the sunlight as he stepped back out onto the street.

Rebelie, who'd been peering over the edge of the carriage, plopped back down on her seat.

A man sitting on a step from across the street stared at Ven with raised eyebrows. Ven realized he still looked like he'd just walked out of a burning building.

He hurried inside the carriage and sat across from Mia, not daring to meet her eyes.

"What was that about?" she asked as the carriage lurched forward.

Dayelle could somehow hear everything they said in here. He looked around at the corners of their compartment. "I... saw somebody I knew. I hadn't expected to see her here. It was quite a shock." No lies there. "I explained a bit of our situation, and she offered to help us out." He showed her the bag of coins, loosening the drawstring to show the glittering metal inside.

Mia frowned. "That was nice, but money? How does that help?"

Ven shrugged. "Not sure exactly, but money can do a lot of things. The little I had from Zein would only get us a bit of food."

"Zein explained money to me. I guess I still don't understand."

Ven forced a laugh, trying to push past the unease in his stomach.

Mia leaned forward, scrutinizing him even closer, but he couldn't bring himself to meet her eyes. "Are you well?"

"I'm not sure. Medical training suggests I could use a lot more water and good sleep."

The carriage stopped. Rebelie knocked on the wall of the carriage as a sign for them to exit.

"Probably best you walk the rest of the way from here," Rebelie said as Ven and Mia came out. "Just keep walking straight down this road, then take a left and it's the first building on the right. Should have a broken owl statue on a wooden post by the door."

"That'll work," Ven said. "Thanks, Rebelie."

"Good luck," Rebelie said, then steered the carriage away as Ven and Mia proceeded down the road.

After two days of sitting, walking felt great. Ven resisted the urge to start jogging. They caught a lot of attention. Everyone they passed stared at them unabashedly. One young man even tripped on a crumbled brick as he gawked at Mia.

Did Mia really draw so much attention? Then again, Ven remembered the first time he'd seen her as well. Though she didn't have that glowing aura like Ambrose, Mia bore a unique, majestic beauty like nothing he'd ever seen before.

Mia pressed her lips into a thin line and untied her hair so that it dropped down. "Why do they stare at me so much?" she whispered to him. "Do they know?"

Ven shook his head. "No, but a person as beautiful as you is extremely rare. It catches a lot of attention. And somebody as burnt as me." Ven chuckled. "We may as well be a pair of dragons walking down the street."

A bit of red colored Mia's light brown cheeks. He'd never seen her blush.

"We need to get you one of those brimmed hats I saw all the women wearing," he said. He glanced at her form-fitting athletic attire. "And probably a cloak or something."

Mia kept her head down and folded her arms as they turned the corner. This street was narrower, and the brick pavement was little more than gravel. There was a quick movement further down the way as someone disappeared into a dark, wooden structure.

Ven led them to the first building on the right, as instructed. There was indeed a post with some kind of bird statue on top, but its head had long since crumbled away. They walked up three steps to a wooden door. Ven knocked on the thick surface. The door was so heavy that it hardly made a sound. He may as well have knocked on a tree.

"Ouch," Ven said. "Maybe you should try."

Mia raised an eyebrow at him, then briskly knocked. The door rattled on its hinges.

Ven loosed a breathy laugh. "That'll probably work."

The door swung open two seconds later. "Hoy, keep it down!" A short woman in her fifties peered up at them from the doorway. "I heard you the first time." She looked them over, eyes flicking across them like a fly trying to find somewhere to land. Her dark gray hair was fashionably done, wrapped and held up with a sparkling chain tiara and two silver pins. She wore a plain dress of dark green.

"Are you Jalett Fon?" Ven asked.

"I am. What brings you here, strangers?" she said. Her words were dictated carefully, much the way Ven was used to hearing from queens in British films.

"Zein Huan sent us," Mia said.

Jalett held a finger up to her lips to shush them. "Don't mention that name in this city." She glanced up and down the street. "Come in." She opened the door wider and stood to the side so they could enter.

Once inside, she closed the door and led them down a wide hall until they came to a sitting room with soft couches lining the walls. Elaborate decorations covered the walls, and a fireplace glowed under a stone mantel. There were several original paintings, mostly portraits, but one of a glimmering ocean under a setting sun caught Ven's attention.

"My father painted that," Jalett said. "Most of these in fact." She waved her hand across the room. "Please, make yourselves comfortable."

"They're very well done," Ven said. "Was he an artist?"

"Hardly," Jalett said. She rang a small bell in the corner of the room. A well dressed man appeared at the door a moment later.

"Refreshments for our guests, please," Jalett said. The man inclined his head and disappeared as quickly as he'd arrived. "So that mad doctor is still alive, is he? I figured he'd have gotten himself killed by now. Never was good at making friends."

"He's still alive, as far as we know," Ven said.

"How did you two get wrapped up in his affairs?"

The servant returned and placed a tray of biscuits on a small table. He poured a steaming drink into three small cups.

Ven glanced at Mia. "We're not sure what details are necessary," he said. "He gave us your name as someone who might be able to help us."

Jalett's eyes narrowed, but she lifted a cup to her lips and sipped slowly.

Ven burned his tongue on the first sip, but stared as Mia, completely unaffected by the heat, drained her cup in three gulps.

"Who are you?" Jalett asked.

"I'm Ven Yashke. This is Mia."

Jalett looked at Mia. "Just Mia?"

"Yes," Mia said. "Do most people have two names?"

"Two or three, yes," Jalett said. "What do you need help with?"

"We need to borrow a weapon from Yubo Huan," Ven said.

"My word." Jalett placed her cup down, expression darkening with disappointment. "Lord Huan? Zein's truly as mad as I remember. How could he possibly have thought that you two could steal one of those from his castle?"

"We have to get into a castle?" Ven asked.

"Yes," Jalett said. "Yubo Huan is lord of Peskan. That castle on the upper hill is where he resides. I'm assuming you're after one of the legendary dragonsbane swords. That's the only place he'd be keeping them. What use could Zein have with a dragonsbane sword?" She tapped her chin in thought.

"We're not sure," Ven answered, wondering if he'd spoken too quickly. "But he's not after one of the swords. It's a dagger."

"Oh." Jalett was silent for a moment as she considered the new detail. A smile slowly lifted the edge of her lips. "That certainly doesn't make the task ahead of you any easier, but it does make it more worth it. And it would be very entertaining to see how Lord Huan would react."

"Why's that?" Mia asked.

Jalett shook her head. "Zein was always good at luring away the ignorant." She took a deep breath. "Those dragonsbane weapons have been handed down for generations. The Huans were one of the primary families responsible for organizing the dragon hunters in order to eradicate the dragons. At the time, nearly 700 years ago, dragons formed the ruling class of intelligent society while humans functioned as workers, slaves, and warriors."

"Wait, so do dragons look like people?" Ven said. "I thought they were giant lizards."

"Both true," Jalett said. "They can assume the image of a human, but the process is supposedly complicated and temporary. The Huans helped forge the original dragonsbane weapons, and they were one of the first to assassinate their dragon lords. They then helped other cities and nations find freedom as well. Since then, dragons have been exterminated. Anything related to dragons has been deemed evil, as it is a sign of our oppression.

"However, as you may have noticed, dragonblood research and technology is thriving. Supposedly, the Huans amassed large amounts of dragonblood which they secretly sell off, all the while enforcing very strict anti-dragonblood laws. I'm not sure where you're from, but that's why you won't find much dragonblood tech here in Peskan. Despite its magical quality, most of us suspect that dragonblood can't be held in storage very long before spoiling, certainly not hundreds of years. We assume they keep a dragon in the castle and they bleed it out to maintain a supply. It would be quite a scandal, though nobody could ever prove it to be true. The dagger you mentioned is rumored to be the weapon they use to bleed the dragon. It would be closely guarded."

"Then how do we get to it?" Ven asked.

Jalett somehow managed to straighten her posture even more. "I was once employed there. I have a good understanding of the layout and a strong suspicion of the location where the weapon might be kept, but first, tell me of your skills. Mia looks like she's built to assassinate people. Do you have any particular talents?"

Ven and Mia shared another look.

Ven cleared his throat. "I have experience as a doctor. Mia does have certain combat proficiency. She can also run really fast and jump high." He rubbed his chin. "Overall, she can physically do just about anything better than anybody."

Jalett raised her eyebrows at Mia. "And she's stunning. We could work with that. What about you, Ven? Any special talents aside from medical treatment?"

Ven shrugged. "I can... get through doors. I have experience in stealing things, though nothing high profile." He glanced over at Mia then looked away. He hadn't told her about his past with stealing.

Jalett blinked at Ven then said, "You might honestly have better luck sending Mia in alone. I have a good option for her."

"We have to go together," Mia said. "I'm not leaving you alone again," she said to Ven when he cast her a questioning look.

"Very well," Jalett said. She folded her arms and thought in silence for a moment. "I have an idea that could work, but it will depend on a hasty exit. Do you have money?"

Ven felt at the bulge in his coat pocket. "Yes."

"Then the first thing you need is a change of clothes," Jalett said. "Fortunately, we are at a time where Yubo Huan's eldest son, Siwen, is open to courting and will soon seek marriage. He has quite possibly made his selection already, but the door isn't closed." She rang the little bell again. "I will forge a letter using an Endellan seal to his lordship stating that you should be arriving tomorrow. Mia will pose as Nesua, the daughter of Kan Demora of Lota. Lota is a small village in Endel with very little renown. The ruling family there should most likely be unknown here in Peskan."

The servant came through the door.

"I'll be writing a letter," Jalett said to the servant.

He nodded and disappeared, returning only seconds later with writing materials which he placed on a small table at her side.

"Lota's lack of fame should easily be overridden by Mia's startling beauty. Siwen wouldn't dream of turning down a meeting with you. It would be wise to discuss an interest in the dragonsbane weapons. Peskan is famous for them, particularly among the nobility. Be charming. You must ask about the dagger, and hopefully Siwen would like to please you. That should get them to show you the dagger."

"What about me?" Ven asked.

Jalett smiled. "You must pose as her guard. It's customary for dignitaries to have their own guard in attendance, especially for courting visits. Siwen will likely have a couple of his own that will accompany you as well. Once the dagger is in sight, if Mia is as skilled as you say she is, you must seize the weapon and make a run for it. I'll map an escape route for you so you can flee the city."

"A small problem," Ven said. "Once we have the dagger, we still have some business here in the city."

Jalett considered this for a moment. "Then you must hire decoys. I see no other way of buying you enough time than to have the Huans believe you've fled. Your remaining business needs to be handled quickly after that. I wouldn't recommend staying more than a day."

"We can do that. Do you know where we can purchase all the things we need?" Ven asked.

Jalett smiled. "Of course I do, but all the transactions must be made by Mia whilst you accompany her. There should be no connection made back to me. The first thing I need to do is write the letter announcing your arrival and draft up instructions for you, the stables, and the hirelings who will act as decoys, but you two need new clothes immediately. Were you seen on your way here?"

Mia sighed. "Yes. A few people saw us as we walked here after we got out of our carriage. I caught some attention."

"That could be a problem," Jalett said. "You are easily distinguishable. We'll need to get everything done quickly." She stood. "Come. I've a cloak for you, Mia. You must keep your face hidden until we get you in a suitable dress. I will give you instructions to find an excellent tailor who will likely have some things already drafted up for fitting. Who's ready to practice their acting?"

Ven smiled. He'd already been doing that.

# Chapter Twenty-Five

# Chapter 25

## Lady Nesua

Ven tugged at the sleeves of the dark green uniform Jalett told him to wear. The sleeve didn't quite reach his wrists, and the material was more firm than he liked. He imagined suits from the 1800's would have looked similar.

He pushed the door open to the waiting room where Jalett was training Mia on how to act like a lady.

"Ven, just in time," Jalett said. "I was explaining societal classes. You'll need to be deferential to Mia and refer to her only as Lady Demora. Also, do not speak at all in the castle unless you are spoken to directly."

"Easy," Ven said. "I'm good at not talking."

Mia rolled her eyes.

"Mia, more important than being ladylike is being flirtatious and coy," Jalett said.

"How does that work?" Mia asked.

"Ven, come stand here and face Mia." Jalett stood back as Ven moved over. "Now say something to compliment her."

"Uh," Ven stammered and looked Mia in the eyes as he said, "Mia, you are brave and have outstanding emotional intelligence."

Mia looked down, shook her head, and failed to hold back a smile. When she looked back up, her eyes sent a warm shiver down his spine.

"I have nothing to teach you there, apparently," Jalett said. "One thing you can try, and don't overdo it, is to lean toward him when you speak. I'll demonstrate." Jalett faced Ven, leaned toward him slightly. "Then make a comment or ask a question and return to your original position. Based on what we've discussed, say something to Ven as if he were Siwen Huan."

Mia stepped up to Ven and took a deep breath before saying, "I hear you have quite the collection of weapons." She leaned in a little closer and lowered her voice, staring him straight in the eyes as she said, "I'd love to see them up close."

Ven's skin tingled at the mere proximity of her body. He smiled. Whether from amusement or pleasure, he couldn't say.

Mia leaned away and laughed. "Did I do it right?"

"You're a natural," Ven said, glancing at Jalett's knowing look. "I wish I had a collection of weapons to show you."

"You'll have one," Jalett said, hefting an iron mace and handing it over. It was lighter than Ven expected, and weighted similarly to a hammer. "Now go on—time to get your dress." She handed him a paper. "These are instructions for where to go and what to buy. You'll be the one providing direction to Lady Nesua and escorting her. She will follow."

Ven nodded as Mia pulled a deep hood over her head. "Let's go shopping."

***

Mia stared at herself in the mirror and tried not to seem too stunned at her appearance. She wore a dress, the color of which she could only describe as reddish brown. It fit snug around her chest and torso and then loosened right at her hips so that she could easily bend her legs. Two skirt layers stretched down to her ankles and left a bit of skin exposed just before her shoes.

"Are you sure you wouldn't like some heels, madam?" Kitena, the shop owner asked. She was a middle-aged woman with a kind smile. All of her curtsies, bows, and deferential appellations were so foreign.

"Quite sure," Mia said. She'd tried the heeled shoes on and found them far too restricting.

"As requested, I added the extra fabric to the legs so that you'd have more freedom of movement," Kitena said.

Ven and Mia had already finished most other tasks, including hiring the decoys. They came by the dress shop earlier to get measurements for Mia, and now the fittings had been completed.

The building was three stories tall, but this dress shop only occupied the bottom floor. Its walls were completely covered in satin red fabrics, draped from the ceiling. Several dresses were displayed, as well as sections that showed off various lacing textures, fabric types, and color selections. The shop was empty save for two dressing maids that stood off to one side of the large room, waiting patiently with hands folded in front of them. Ven waited outside the building with an armed shop guard.

Mia turned her eyes away from the mirror and strode across the floor of the shop at a quick pace. Sure enough, the extra fabric did make it easier to maneuver and raising the skirt up her hip meant she'd be able to run. She paused and bent to a crouch, which also worked well enough. If the dress truly did become an impediment, she could always rip the skirt part off before they ran. She wore a set of knee length pants beneath it. "This will suit my needs," Mia said as she returned to the mirror. "Never know if I might need to run away if things don't go well at the Huans."

Kitena laughed. "I'm sure it won't come to that. Yubo and Siwen are both very gentlemanly."

Mia had openly told Kitena about the intent to visit Siwen at the castle tomorrow. It was all part of her cover as the young Lady Nesua Demora.

"I'm sure they've rarely seen a woman of such beauty," Kitena said. "And I mean this in the most complimentary fashion, good lady, but you move with the finest grace I've ever seen. Like you were raised by cats."

Mia wasn't sure what cats were and didn't know how to respond. She smiled and pretended to be distracted by looking in the mirror. The dress was quite beautiful. Lace embellishments decorated the entire front and back of the torso. The design made them look like little flowers and leaves, which Mia secretly adored. A soft white fabric filled the space between her shoulder straps and also formed a silky collar at the base of her neck.

"I know a hair specialist you could see as well. You could stop by there tomorrow morning before your visit, unless you have other arrangements already."

Mia recalled the hair style most of the ladies wore. It typically involved putting the hair up, which would risk revealing the strange metal device installed on the back of her neck. "I have recommendations for that already, thank you."

Kitena curtsied in response.

"I'm satisfied with the dress," Mia said. "My escort will make payment."

Kitena curtsied again. "I'm happy you are pleased." She waved a hand at the dressing maids and one of them hurried to the door to fetch Ven, running as if on tiptoes.

As Ven came inside, his wide eyes swept across the room, audibly gasping as he saw Mia. "Perhaps I'll need a second weapon, Lady Demora." He inclined his head to her. "I may need it to hold back the hosts of men who will swoon at your feet."

Mia rolled her eyes and smiled nervously. She had to admit, Ven was far too good at acting like her servant, and he clearly enjoyed it.

Ven dug out a few coins as payment and handed them over to Kitena.

"Come along," Mia said to Ven as she headed for the door.

"Thank you, Lady Nesua," Kitena said. "Good luck tomorrow."

Mia nodded back to Kitena as Ven hurried over to open the door. The sun was getting low as they stepped out onto the cobbled street. This area of the city was well kept, without a sign of debris, and there were still several well-dressed people wandering about, finishing their last-minute shopping.

Ven pulled the paper list from his pocket and looked through it again. He'd checked it so many times, Mia was surprised he hadn't memorized it by now. She pulled the hood of her cloak fully over her head.

"That's everything," Ven said. He knew how to talk quietly enough that only Mia's enhanced hearing could pick it up. They'd already purchased a couple riding horses and met up with the hirelings. The hirelings made it sound like acting as a decoy was a regular part of their job. They had a diverse force of employees for the very purpose. Mia could easily see why they came at Jalett's recommendation.

They made their way back to The Gelland, which was the inn Jalett recommended they use. It was a common waypoint for visiting nobilities who didn't have a local family to stay with. Wearing the hood was much more comfortable than walking openly exposed, though she was curious to see how men would react now that she wore the beautiful dress. Despite the dress's beauty, she didn't like all the extra fabric around her legs. She certainly wouldn't be able to climb well in it.

The Gelland came into view. It was three stories high, but it was quite large. The stone structure was a splendid sight, and it had little ramparts decorated with statues. It bore a large sign on the front of it, the name written in letters so fanciful that Mia could barely read it. The worst part about staying there was that Ven, as a manservant, was required to stay on the bottom floor in a room with all the other servants. The upper floors were only to be accessed by the nobility or specific types of servants. Mia still wasn't sure what all the distinctions were.

Ven heaved the polished doors open and ushered Mia inside. The entry hall had four  decorative stone columns to either side of a red and gold carpet. These led to a table, behind which sat a woman. Two guards stood to either side, their metal breastplates decorated with flower insignias. Mia took her hood off as they approached the table.

"Welcome, Lady Demora," the woman said as she stood. Her dress was slim and elegant. Two additional servants, a man and a woman, entered from open doors on either side of the hall. "How can we be of assistance?"

"I'll be going to my room," Mia said.

"Very well, Lady Demora." The woman nodded to the female servant.

"This way, please, my lady," the servant said with a bright smile and a curtsy.

Ven followed the other servant in the opposite direction. She resisted glancing back at him as they went through separate doors. Would he be safe on his own? At least now he had some form of weapon.

The servant led her up a flight of stairs that opened up into a wide room stuffed with large, soft furniture. Two fireplaces burned with warm light, and there were a few collections of lords and ladies seated together, some of them playing a sort of game at a table. Others sat alone, reading books. Servants passed around food and drink. She caught more than a few looks as she walked through the room.

"Would you like something to eat before you retire, my lady?" the servant asked.

Mia realized she hadn't eaten for several hours, not since the few biscuits at Jalett's. It was hard to remember that sort of thing when she was used to food being a part of a preset schedule run by others. Normal people tended to experience hunger, a pain that her imperviousness had expunged from her. She could at least detect the gurgling motions in her stomach.

"Is it possible to have some food brought to my room?" Mia asked.

The servant nodded back to her. "Certainly, my lady." She handed a key to Mia. "I understand you haven't stayed here before, yes."

"That's true," Mia said.

"Well, my lady, you may come and go from your room as you please and mingle with the other patrons until your stay expires, which is for two nights. Most of the food and drinks are included in your payment, though there are some specialty items which can be ordered upon request." She paused in front of a door. "Any of the servants are happy to help. This is your room." She pointed at the key Mia held.

Mia hadn't used a key before, but she'd seen it used often enough. She inserted the pointed end and twisted it until she heard the click. She opened the door to a room that was more lush than she'd imagined. Velvety drapes hung from the walls and an elaborately carved wooden dresser sat beneath a curtained window. There was also an armoire attached to a small desk with a mirror on top of it. The bed was massive, taking up most of the space.

"I'll bring some roast chicken and steamed vegetables in a moment," the servant said. "Is there anything else I can do for you?"

"That will suffice for now," Mia said, resisting the urge to offer thanks.

The servant curtsied and left, closing the door on her way.

Mia looked back at the bed. She had a feeling she'd sleep very well tonight.

***

"Is this really necessary?" Mia said as a carriage pulled by two horses stopped in front of them.

"It's not expensive," Ven said from beside her, "and it wouldn't make a very good impression if we walked to the castle."

Mia sighed, preferring the freedom of walking outside of the wooden box. Ven opened the door to the carriage and held out a hand to *help her in*. All to keep up appearances. She entered the carriage alone and Ven went to sit beside the driver since it was not customary for servants to ride inside with their masters.

A clattering of hooves echoed as the two horses pulled them along. Mia smelled the distinct stench of the animals. It was one of many wretched smells that existed in this city, but she wasn't altogether annoyed by them. It felt more natural, rather than the sterility of the facility.

They paused outside the massive gates of the castle, much larger and more impressive than those that stood with the city walls. After a brief exchange between Ven and the guards, they passed through. Mia peeked through the window. This gate was made of heavy, iron reinforced wood, and a metal portcullis rose overhead before they were able to enter. Inside, stone walls rose high around an enclosure just large enough for a few carriages to enter and turn around.

The carriage stopped before a flight of steps. A few guards wearing metal breastplates stood to either side of the stairs. They were armed with a variety of weapons, including spears, axes, swords, and maces. They also had matching white shirts that stuck out beneath their breastplates.

The stairs led up to a large set of double doors leading into the castle. Two men, one older, one younger, came out of the doors. They looked much alike, black, cropped hair, fit bodies, and light brown skin. They wore well-fitted red clothing with white tufts sewn in at the shoulders and elbows. Swords dangled at their waists. The younger of the two approached the carriage, accompanied by two guards.

Ven opened the door to the carriage and held a hand out for Mia as she stepped down.

The finely dressed young man's mouth hung open as he looked at her, but he quickly snapped it shut.

Ven bowed to him and introduced Mia. "The Lady Nesua Demora of Lota." It was the one phrase he was allowed to say without first being addressed.

"Lady Nesua," the man said without glancing at Ven. He offered her a small smile. "I am Lord Siwen Huan. It's a pleasure to meet you."

"Thank you for accommodating me on such short notice," Mia said. Everyone in the courtyard stood motionless as they stared at her. She tried not to be nervous at the hyper attention, and she resisted the urge to chew on her lower lip.

"Not a problem," Siwen said. "I'm glad you caught me while we're here. My father and I," he paused and gestured to the older gentlemen in fine clothes who still stood on the stairs, "were about to go to a mountain lodge for a hunting trip this morning."

"Oh," Mia took a step closer. "I'm sorry to have interrupted your plans."

"Again," Siwen said, smile widening to show neat, white teeth, "it's not a problem. Adjusting my plans to accommodate a young lady such as yourself is something I can live with. Come, meet my father, and I'll show you inside. There's more to this castle than dreary stone walls, I assure you."

"Oh good," Mia said. "I was beginning to worry."

Siwen laughed, catching her sarcasm. He led the way and Mia followed. Every time she looked at one of the guards, they'd quickly blink away and stare at the ground. She decided it best not to look at them at all.

Siwen paused one step up the flight of stairs. "Father, please meet Lady Nesua Demora of Lota."

Lord Yubo Huan regarded Mia with narrowed eyes. "Welcome, Lady Nesua. We've not seen many from Endel lately. I hope you find your time here amenable."

Mia nodded her head in a small bow. "Thank you, Lord Huan."

"Come, I'll show you inside," Siwen said, he stuck out his arm for Mia so she held on as he led her up the stairs and through the large double doors. The entry room had a high, arched ceiling. Several tall windows, some stained in crude images, cast brilliant light into the room from the outside. A single, massive rug, intricately detailed with leaves, vines, and geometric patterns covered the floor. There were a few padded benches symmetrically laid out across from each other. Where there weren't windows, large, red drapes hung in ruffles. Two thirds of the way across the room were matching doors to either side, and another directly ahead of them. Two candelabras stood to either side of each door, but with enough light from outside, neither of them were lit.

"This room is clearly meant to impress," Mia said.

Siwen laughed. "Well, are you impressed?"

Mia smiled and gave her answer carefully. "By you? Certainly. By the castle? Yet to be determined." Jalett had instructed her to be flirtatious, but also coy enough to not be throwing herself at him, whatever that meant. She wasn't sure how to measure that scale, but Siwen's smile seemed genuine as he continued to lead her across the room.

Siwen was an attractive man. She liked his hair and strong jaw. She'd be lying if she didn't admit enjoying his gentlemanly mannerisms. Still not as physically attractive as Dami, but the dragonblood was much to blame for that.

They rounded a table in the middle of the room, dodging under the large leaves of a plant that grew from a planter on top of it.

"I bet you'd like to see our gardens," Siwen said.

Mia snapped her jaw shut, realizing she'd been gaping at the beautiful leaves. She *would* like to see their garden, but she needed to focus on getting to their weapons and trophy room.

"Certainly," Mia said. "Perhaps after we explore more inside. You know, I have heard of course, of the famed dragonsbane swords held by your family."

"You have an interest in weapons?" Siwen glanced back at the three of his guards who walked behind, Ven following at their rear.

Had she mentioned the swords too soon? She tried to laugh it off. "I'm the only child of a lesser lord. After my mother died a few years ago, I had no ladies to look after me. My father, an officer in the army, taught me much about combat." She smiled at Siwen and leaned in and lowered her voice like Jalett told her. "You could say I have an interest."

He took the opportunity to eye her up and down again just as they passed through the door on the far side of the room. She felt him measuring her. "You seem the type. Do you have a favored weapon, then?"

Mia nodded. Jalett had told her various conversation points, and this was a topic Mia felt versed enough on. "Sword. About the length of my elbow to my fingertips. It allows for quick maneuvers, and I can double with a small shield or buckler in the other arm." She'd often sparred with both combinations. "I do like longswords as well. They have their own artform, but I don't feel they're as versatile. What about you, Lord Siwen?"

Siwen barked a laugh. "The longsword can be quite heavy. You'll have to show me some forms. I haven't seen much from Endellan combat styles. But as for me," he paused and glanced down at the sword hanging from his hip. "I also favor swords. Longer than your preference." They stopped walking inside a large room, this one lit by several candles. There was a stage built into one side with several musical instruments laid out.

Siwen took a step away from her and drew out his sword. It was curved, and there was a small groove in the middle that extended the whole length.

He gripped it with both hands and went through a couple stances just for show. "I like this weapon because it can be used with both hands or one. It's light and strong enough to do both. A shield isn't necessary when properly trained in some defensive techniques." He held the weapon out to her, hilt first.

"Is this really the place to be swinging weapons around?" Mia said, looking around at the room.

"We're in a castle, Lady Nesua. Everywhere here is the proper place for that."

Mia took hold of the handle, and Siwen gingerly let go of the blade and took a step back. The sword was light. Mia was impressed enough that she found it quite natural to move through a few of her own battle stances. To her, it felt like the same weight as a short sword or even a long knife, but she knew she was much stronger than Siwen.

He gaped at her openly. Even a couple of the guards muttered to each other. She stopped immediately and lowered the weapon.

Siwen held out his hand and she passed the sword back to him. "I'm convinced," he said, sheathing the weapon. "I'm impressed. You moved so fluidly, I may as well have handed you a sheaf of paper. Your father did well to train you. It's always wise for a parent to pass down their knowledge."

"If you're lucky, we could spar someday," Mia said. "Though not today, of course. Not while I'm wearing this."

Siwen nodded. "I would find sparring with a beautiful young lady to be very odd indeed, but I will have to consider."

They continued to walk, passing through other rooms, all decadently decorated. She even forgot for a moment that Ven and the guards were walking with them until they paused in a lush room for drinks and sweet, crunchy treats that Siwen called "cookies." The situation reminded her of the facility. Eating while others watched her.

"And for the moment you've been waiting for," Siwen said, leading her through another set of doors.

The floor was covered by a deep red carpet with no additional embellishments. The walls were clothed in racks and weapons, some concealed in glass containers or bearing plaques with short descriptions. Additionally there were two rows of display glasses that stretched the length of the room and a table where sat an older man who appeared to be cleaning an ancient weapon with some kind of solution.

"Wow," Mia said.

"It's a lot to take in," Siwen said, "but this is what a thousand years of soldiering gets you. Most of these are the weapons and armor of my ancestors, though some were collected as curios. It's a small museum of sorts."

"I'll say," Mia said, tapping a pauldron made with many jagged pieces of metal. Her eyes rested on a section of the wall that looked entirely dedicated to the two dragonsbane swords that hung there horizontally. The plaque beside them was the largest in the room. At least, she assumed that's what they were, given the intricate image of dragons forming the guards and pommels. "Ah, there they are." She took a few steps in their direction. "Did your family kill many dragons?"

Siwen smiled and hurried to walk beside her. "More than any other family as far as I know. We were one of the first to overthrow our dragon overlord, but we knew that to maintain our freedom, we'd need to eliminate the other dragons."

"I haven't heard people talk much about dragons. Were they powerful?" She thought of her own operation using their blood and her resultant imperviousness. Were dragons also adaptive or impervious? Why was that how she'd become?

"Oh, yes. Very powerful." He tapped a depiction of a dragon. It had a monstrous, lizardlike head with several horns. "And they were massive, as big as a cottage, some older ones even bigger."

"I couldn't imagine facing a creature so large," Mia said. Picturing an animal that big didn't seem reasonable. How much of this information was even true?

"It would not have been easy," Siwen said. His voice was light and solemn.

How would Siwen feel if he knew that a dragon still lived somewhere and that people were harvesting its blood? Possibly even here in his own home. "Are there any dragons left?"

"Oh, no." Siwen shook his head and laughed. "They were all killed many years ago. If any were left, trust me, my father and I would be the first to respond."

"How do you explain all the dragonblood research, then?" Mia glanced back at the soldiers in the room. The three guards who'd accompanied them were still standing by the door. Ven stood with them, staring across at her intently.

Siwen's expression turned sour. "It's an abomination. Dark magic or something. Nothing good came from dragons. I'm not sure how things are in Endel, but I'm sure you noticed here in Peskan, dragonblood tech is all but nonexistent. We have a long outstanding law here that bans such technologies. I've personally ousted several of these illegal operations. So yes, we still have windmills, candles, and horse-drawn carriages, but at least the souls of our people are not tainted."

He didn't answer her question, but Mia smiled, playing on his side. "I certainly noticed the difference. It's nice to have a place free of those influences." She could understand why Zein was not in good standing with the rest of the Huan family. He wasn't a soldier, nor did he uphold their same disdain for dragonblood research. And, despite saving her life, he was a monster for many of the things he'd done.

Siwen nodded at her. "I'm glad you see it that way. Many nobility tend not to care and are more concerned about what luxuries life has to offer."

Mia gulped with the memory of the investors Dami had killed. Wealthy individuals. Perhaps they all had the hope that they could obtain what Mia had. Imperviousness. Agelessness. This made her wealthier than them all. If only she had freedom. Instead she had poison in her neck.

"I'm surprised there are only two dragonsbane weapons," Mia said. "Were there not more?"

Siwen sighed. "Yes." He stood close to her, their elbows brushing as he looked back up at the swords. "We once had five such weapons, but two of them are gone. One went missing several years back and another that had nearly rusted away was sold off. Not all of my ancestors were as dedicated to their preservation. Since my great grandfather, we've done a much better job of that." He stepped forward and took down one of the dragonsbane broadswords, taking the handle in one hand and holding the blade in the other. "Feel the edge. We keep the weapons sharp."

Mia hesitated. She remembered what Zein said—that she could not handle the weapon or it would cause her great pain. What would happen to her if she touched it just a little? Her mortality was staring her in the face, but she discovered she *wanted* to test it. Without another thought, she placed a finger against the sharp end of the blade. It *hurt*. The pain was sharp. She whipped her hand back and looked at her finger with wide eyes. She'd only touched it lightly, but the weapon left its mark, leaving a thin cut.

"Oh, my apologies," Siwen said, putting the weapon back. "Maybe it's sharper than I thought."

"Not to worry," Mia said, staring at the small bead of blood slowly growing out. She couldn't remember the last time she'd seen her own blood. And the pain didn't fade. It remained exquisite. Her body's imperviousness didn't even trigger. No tingling sensation from adaptation. Though it didn't heal immediately as she was accustomed to, it was nothing compared to the pain of swallowing a vial of poison.

Siwen held Mia's hand and dabbed at her finger with a white handkerchief, wiping the blood away. His touch was warm.

"Thank you," she said. "I must seem novice to cut myself like that."

He laughed. "It happens."

Mia looked back to the wall of weapons. "I notice you didn't mention the third weapon."

"Ah, yes," he said with a frown. He tapped a spot on the wall where the prongs to hold a smaller weapon were empty. He turned to the old man seated at the table. "Torus, do you know where the dragonsbane dagger is?"

Torus stood from his seat and bowed with a straight back. "My lord, I believe it has been requisitioned for rust treatments."

"When?"

"Three days ago now, lord."

"But it wasn't here a month ago either when I came through," Siwen said. "Does it really need treatments so frequently?"

Torus stroked his chin. "Erm, no my lord. It would not."

Siwen cocked his head. "Who ordered the treatment? Are you not the one in charge of that?"

"Yes, lord." Torus's head bobbed with a nod. "Your father is the one who requested it."

The door behind Ven and the guards banged open and several soldiers entered the room, Lord Yubo Huan among them. "She's an imposter," he announced.

"Father? What do you mean?" Siwen said, stepping toward his father as if to defend Mia.

Yubo folded his arms as soldiers surrounded Mia and Ven, weapons drawn. "I checked the ledgers. We keep record of noble families and births. There is a lord of Lota with a young daughter named Nesua, but she would only be ten years old at present."

"Your ledger must be wrong, sir, clearly," Mia said, heart pounding. They weren't supposed to be discovered.

Yubo regarded her impassively. It was the same look Zein often gave. "We are sent updates directly from the king of Endel's office. I could potentially understand a year of inaccuracy, but not seven. Are you thieves then? Who sent you? Don't tell me Zein is after my swords again."

Mia gulped hard. She wasn't sure how to negotiate her way out of this one. She looked around. There were perhaps twenty guards in the room. She could easily dispatch all of them, so long as nobody got the idea about using the dragonsbane weapons against her, but they didn't have the dagger. Maybe *she* could question *them* after she gained the upper hand. She caught a glimpse of Ven's worried expression as he stared across at her with no regard to the men holding weapons to his side. They might hurt him.

As she clenched her fists and started bending her knees, ready to fight, Ven shook his head and whispered, "Wait," just loud enough for her to hear.

"It was my idea, lord," Ven said, dropping to his knees and bowing his head.

"Explain yourself," Yubo said.

"We are not from here, but I lost my parents to dragonblood research, lord," Ven said. "Since then, I have dedicated myself to eradicating it, mostly undercover. I wanted to find the source. I'd heard of a dagger used to bleed out a dragon. I followed a trail of leads that eventually led me here, to your castle."

"I'll hear no more of that nonsense," Yubo said, raising a hand to silence him. "A rumor spread by Zein, no doubt. As if his existence wasn't enough of a scar across our family. Take them to the dungeon."

The soldiers started dragging them off.

"Then where is the dagger now, Lord Huan," Mia said coolly as a guard unsuccessfully tried to push her shoulder. She allowed them to make her move a couple steps

"Take them away," was all he said in response, not even addressing her.

Ven gasped as a soldier twisted his arm. Mia barely restrained herself from throwing the soldiers across the room to go rescue him as he was dragged away, but she needed to find the dagger first.

"Father," Siwen said, stepping between Yubo and Mia. "Where *is* the dagger?"

Yubo grunted a sigh and reached into his coat. "If you must know, it is right here." He pulled out a dagger covered in an elaborate, emerald-studded sheath, his fingers packed with rings. "I had taken it to my study to write some notes about it. I'm drafting an updated history." He scowled in Mia's direction. "Why is she still here?"

Two soldiers tried to shove Mia through the room with little success. One of them poked her back with a sword. She felt the pressure of the blade against her, but it wasn't sharp. Realistically, a normal person would have relented, but she stood firm.

If anything, now was her chance. She could see the dagger. All she had to do now was take it and run. But she couldn't take it. It would burn her at the very touch. She needed Ven. He'd already been forced out of the room. Her anxiety spiked.

"He's lying," Mia said, looking to Siwen and putting on a sad frown. She originally thought Jalett's idea of them bleeding a dragon somewhere in the castle to be ludicrous, but if she could just get Siwen to bring Ven back into the room, then she could take care of the rest. "He's using the dagger to bleed a dragon, Siwen."

They ignored her. "Whose is that?" Yubo asked softly, pointing at the bloodied handkerchief still in Siwen's hand.

Siwen said nothing, but handed it over to his father.

Mia realized that the blade point being pressed into her back was hard enough that a normal person would be bleeding already. They really wanted her to move. She took a few steps with them toward the door.

Siwen made no further attempt to stop them, but merely frowned at Mia. "Let me know if you see any dragons down there."

Mia ground her teeth. Where was Ven? She let the soldiers lead her to the doorway and out into the hall. *Great.* Ven was out of sight. Maybe she should rush back into the room and subdue the Huans. Could she rip off a curtain and use it to hold the dagger? That way there wouldn't be any direct contact. She also hesitated around the idea of Yubo using the dagger against her. It could kill her. But she was confident in her ability to gain the upper hand. The risk of killing them was real also, but she was doing this to stop Dami. She wouldn't be *like* Dami. She could fight to *save* lives, not to take them. Also, without securing Ven's safety, they could easily use him as a hostage.

She groaned. "Fine, hurry up and take me to these dungeons," she said to the soldiers. As she walked faster, the soldiers holding onto her arms quickened their pace to keep up. They tried slowing her down, but she didn't have the patience for that. Eventually, they nudged her down a side corridor that wasn't decorated as lavishly as the rest of the castle. It ended in a double door bound in iron and guarded by four more soldiers. The door was already open, revealing a flight of stairs that led downward. Torches cast flickering light into the darkness beyond.

The sight made Mia hesitate, but the soldiers urged her forward, and she still hadn't seen Ven yet. Were they taking her to the same place? She worried that perhaps they would be separated.

"Is this where you took my servant?" she asked.

They ignored her question.

A third soldier armed with a torch led the way down the stairs ahead of them, holding the torch high enough for all of them to watch their footing. Each step echoed loudly, muting Mia's ability to listen ahead, but she could hear other sounds further in the distance.

When they reached the bottom, rows of metal bars lined the hall to either side. More bars divided areas into small rooms. To her right, at the very top of the ceiling, a couple of tiny windows blocked with more iron bars provided the only natural light. There was an occupant in both of the two cells beneath the windows. They sat in the corners, sad faces looking up as Mia walked by.

This seemed more like the proper place for her testing to have occurred. Dark, dreary, and painful.

They led her through another door. Even without the firelight, Mia could see fairly well in the dark, though everything tended to take on a darker, colorless hue. In the previous room, she'd been able to see the faces of each person they passed, but here, the rooms were sectioned off by stone walls and wooden doors. The doors had small, open windows with metal grating. She was too far away to see into the rooms, though there were still a couple prisoners with their faces up against the windows, watching. One final door at the very end had no window, and it was studded in metal.

"Ven?" Mia called out, but there was no reply. She let her captors lead her into one of the small rooms near the end of the hall. Flashbacks of the box, the isolation room, hammered at her conscience and gripped her with rising terror. The door was closed behind her. Keys rattled as they locked the door.

She immediately went to the window on her door and looked out, listening. Surely she would have heard Ven by now. Where had they taken him? She wasn't about to stay in this box to find out. Her grip on the iron bars tightened, the metal groaning. Seemed like the only option at this point.

# Chapter 26

## Prison Break

Everything was bright white. Slowly, details came back into focus. Stone floor, stone wall, stone ceiling. White dragonlight shone overhead. The back of his head hurt. Ven couldn't remember how he'd gotten here. He was sprawled on his back. He rolled over with a groan and struggled to his hands and knees. Three men stood around him in the small room, weapons drawn.

"Who told you about a dragon here in the dungeons?" demanded the harsh voice of one of the soldiers. Ven blinked in his direction. He remembered now. They'd dragged him into the dungeons, led him into a cell, and then opened a secret door at the back of the small room that took him inside here. That's when something struck his head.

"What dragon?" Ven said.

Ven gulped. His throat felt so dry. Perhaps he made a mistake in sharing that bit about bleeding a dragon. Would they kill him? All this just to learn about his parents. What had he gotten himself into? He hoped this wouldn't somehow get back to Jalett. That was probably who they were after. He needed to focus. There was always a way forward. His eyes narrowed at the guard. "Hitting people doesn't help them remember things. It actually has quite the opposite effect. Do you lead interrogations often?"

"Maybe we should try the girl. See if a few blows to her head will jog your memory. That way your mind stays sharp."

Ven breathed a laugh. "She would probably end up being the one asking questions while you took a beating."

*Uh oh.* The soldiers looked at each other. Maybe he'd said too much there.

"So she's a warrior, then. An assassin. Was she sent to kill the Huans?"

"No," Ven said. "If she wanted to, they'd already be dead. Trust me."

The other two soldiers laughed, but the interrogator only narrowed his eyes. "That's a bold assertion. So it was just about the dragon, then? Tell me, where did you hear about that?"

Ven shrugged. "It's not an uncommon rumor. I first heard it from a trading caravan while on the road. I was tracking a dragonblood shipment supposedly sourced from around here. People spoke less freely of it the closer I got to the city, which was naturally suspicious." His stomach twisted at the lies, but they were necessary.

"How did you suspect anything about a dragonblood shipment coming from around here?"

"I heard it firsthand at a remote dragonblood research facility," Ven said. He was gaining more confidence in his story as it went along.

"And what dragonblood research facility was that?"

"Doesn't matter now," Ven said. "It's no longer operational."

"Answer the question," interjected a different soldier.

Ven shook his head, stretching the truth to fit his narrative. "It didn't have a name. You know how those places are. I only knew about it because somebody came to me directly and let me know. I helped them bring down the operation." He decided he didn't make a very good spy if he let out information that easily. At least he hadn't said any names.

"Could it be..?" said one soldier.

"Shut up," said the interrogator.

The walls shook as something thudded into the door. Dust loosened from the stones overhead.

"What the..." said the interrogator. The three soldiers turned to face the door, brandishing their weapons.

Ven scooted away from the door. A second later, the door snapped open, breaking free of its hinges and crashing into the interrogator, sending him sprawling back into the wall. Through the dust of splintered wood and stone charged Mia. The soldiers only had time to gasp before she was upon them. She streamed through the air with a high kick that struck one soldier in the head. After landing, she spun on her hands like a windmill and kicked the other soldier square in the jaw with enough force that he tumbled to the floor and didn't move again.

The interrogator rose from the rubble of the shattered door, sword in hand. Mia ran to him, dodged a single swing of the blade, and punched him with an uppercut so hard that his feet lifted off the floor. He fell, dead or unconscious. The first soldier was the only one to remain, and he dragged himself over beside Ven. Blood slowly seeped from a wound in his head. He held a hand over it, eyes blinking up at Mia with horror.

"I told you she's good," Ven said, getting to his feet.

Mia walked to the soldier, kicking his weapon away. She'd torn off the skirt of her dress, revealing the knee-length pants beneath. "Back up against the wall and don't move," she said to the one soldier. He did as she asked without question.

"Did you kill them?" Ven asked.

Mia frowned at him. "I don't know, but they hurt you. I didn't want them to hurt you more."

Ven nodded. "How did you find me?"

"Yours was one of two cells with a guard outside of it," she said, leading the way back outside the cell. "I checked the other room first, then came to this one and heard sounds behind the pretend wall." It was dark outside the interrogation room—apparently the only room in the whole castle that used dragonlights.

As they came out of the cell, Ven had to step over the body of another soldier. "Who was in the other cell?" he asked. He squinted down the hall to the far end where he could vaguely see another soldier crumpled on the ground.

"Not sure, just some woman who was heavily chained."

Ven bent down to pick up the guard's metal mace, hoping he wouldn't have to use it. The weapon fit in the loop of his belt.

"Hurry," Mia said, rushing down the hall.

She moved so silently that Ven had to follow the subtle visage of her silhouette. A few other prisoners banged on their doors and shouted at him as he passed. Yelling ahead signaled that Mia had come across more soldiers. By the time he arrived at the base of the stairs, two soldiers lay slumped on the ground and two more stood above them on the stairs. Mia leapt towards them, dodging jabs from their swords, and grabbed their arms. She flung them down the stairs.

Ven skipped to the side as the soldiers tumbled down beside him. He grabbed a torch off the wall, and together with Mia, he hurried up the stairs, the soldiers groaning behind him. They'd claim she was strong, but Ven was sure they could still get away without people realizing she was superhuman. "Do you know where the dagger is?" Ven asked.

"Yubo has it."

"Then we should make our way back to that weapons room."

"I think I remember the way," Mia said. She led as they jogged up the stairs. Three more guards met them at the top as they came through the door.

One of the guard's spoke before looking at them. "Hey, we're not meant to do a shift change until—" Mia's fist to his throat cut his words short.

Another guard took off running, shouting about the escapees. Mia sprinted after him, slid across the tiled floor, and tripped him with her feet.

Ven tried to pull out his mace, but it got caught on the loop of his belt. The remaining soldier brandished a short ax and took a quick swing at Ven. He screamed and jumped back, tripping over the first guard who still laid on the floor clutching his throat. The soldier raised his ax to swing again, but fell over as a metal helmet struck him in the head, thrown by Mia from down the hall.

"I almost had him," Ven said, getting back to his feet, finally wresting the mace out of the loop. They jogged down the hall.

"I could see that," Mia said, returning his sarcasm, but her eyes were fierce. "Sorry I took away your opportunity." She pointed at the guard who'd tried running away as they passed him. "I figured I'd stop him from raising the alarm first, but your scream might have done the job anyway."

"Right. Sorry. I'll need to work on my battlecry."

"It was very high-pitched. I'm impressed."

"Thanks."

"Hopefully you never need to use it again."

"Agreed."

They turned the corner to a long hallway. Two more soldiers approached from the other end, weapons drawn. Apparently his scream *had* caught some attention. They yelled back down the hall behind them, probably warning others.

"Look," Ven said, placing a hand on Mia's arm. "Try not to be too... obvious."

"What do you mean?"

"Like, don't go running twice the speed of a normal human. That kind of thing."

A crossbow bolt shattered across Mia's chest. She only grunted in response. The soldiers down the hall hurried to wind their crossbows back.

She charged down the hall, definitely fast, but not abnormally so. It took her four seconds.

Ven only covered half the distance by the time Mia took care of them, mainly by disarming them and slapping their fists with a mace she'd stolen. They wouldn't be using their hands anytime soon. Mia threw all the weapons out a window, shattering the glass.

The soldiers cringed away from Mia, and Ven ran by them unabated.

They continued through the hall until they came upon the weapons room, its door guarded by ten soldiers, several of them wielding crossbows. Yubo and Siwen both stood behind the line of soldiers. Ven stopped short, breathing heavily. He wasn't impervious like Mia. Those crossbow bolts would easily kill him.

"Lay down your weapons," Yubo demanded, then noticed Mia carried no weapon at all. Ven kept his mace in hand. "State your true business in coming here."

"That's classified information," Ven said.

"We need the dagger to kill a dragon," Mia interjected.

Ven gave her a sharp look, but Yubo smiled at her.

"The dragons are dead," Yubo said.

"No they aren't," Mia said. "And you know it. We'll only borrow the dagger and return it after we've completed our task."

Yubo's face turned harsh. "It's not for lease. Kill them—"

"Wait," Siwen cut in. "Where is the dragon you speak of?"

"You mean in addition to the woman chained in the dungeon?" Mia said.

"The traitor? She is not a dragon," Yubo said. "These people have no information to offer us."

"She's a dragon in human form," Mia pressed.

Ven groaned inwardly. She was guessing. He could already tell Yubo was determined to kill them. If not for spreading rumors, then for revealing his darkest secret. "We don't care what's in your dungeon," Ven said. "The dragon we're after is loose, but we know where it's headed, so we have a chance to cut it short."

Yubo drew his sword. "A fanciful story. As I said, we're not lending it out. Kill them."

This time, the order went through. Ven flinched as the crossbows triggered with the sound of snapping springs. He moved to hold up his mace, but Mia was faster. She twisted, dodging several bolts and slapping one away that would have otherwise struck Ven square in the chest. She regarded Yubo and his soldiers with an angry growl.

There were a few gasps as soldiers dropped their crossbows and brandished their melee weapons.

Mia leapt unarmed into the fray. She moved quickly, aiming for one soldier at a time. She disarmed one, taking his mace and using it to smash the arms of the others. She struck wrists, elbows, and shoulders, her movements almost completely unhindered as she moved too fast for most to know how to defend themselves.

Yubo stepped back, sheathing his sword and drawing forth the dagger. That's what Ven had been afraid of. Siwen still watched the fight, his own sword in hand, but not engaging himself.

Ven ran to join the fight. He'd never actually used a mace before, but how hard could it be? One soldier noticed Ven approaching, so he turned to engage. Ven raised the mace to take a swing, but the soldier merely kicked Ven in the gut. He stumbled back, unable to breathe for a moment. Yubo closed in on Mia.

Ven swung at the soldier, but the attack was deflected by a wave of his sword. Ven had to jump back just to avoid getting hacked. "Oh, I'm dead," he mumbled to himself.

One soldier managed to stab Mia in the back with his sword, but his weapon glanced away. It left only a small tear in her dress. In response, she kicked him in the face and snapped his arm back at the elbow with a blow from her mace. She shoved his screaming body into another soldier.

Ven stumbled away to avoid another attack. He was too intent on watching Mia that he was going to get himself killed. That's when he had the great idea. "Ah! She's coming!" he screamed, pointing behind the soldier.

A look of horror crossed his face as he turned around. Ven stepped forward and swung the mace, striking the man on the back of the head with a nasty thunk. He could barely believe that ploy had worked.

Yubo took a careful jab at Mia, scoring a glancing blow across her shoulder with the dragonsbane dagger. With a spinning kick, her heel collided with Yubo's elbow, loosing the weapon from his grip. It slid across the floor just beside Ven.

Siwen made eye contact with him but didn't attempt an attack. Ven stepped over and picked up the dagger. Siwen and Yubo retreated into the weapons room while Mia dispatched the final soldier by holding an arm around his throat until he passed out.

"I have the dagger," Ven said. "We should run for it."

"They know," Mia said, frowning at the cut on her shoulder.

"Maybe. Not much we can do about it now. We should hurry before they come back with the dragonsbane swords."

Mia sighed then led the way down their planned route of escape. They met no other resistance blocking them from proceeding, though a few soldiers did start to pursue them. When they burst out onto the balcony, two soldiers jumped with alarm, one of them throwing something over the edge of the wall as though afraid to be caught with it.

After one look at them, their expressions changed and they went to draw their weapons, but Mia leapt forward and shoved them both off the wall.

They landed ungracefully, one of them screaming about his arm. Footsteps clattered down the stairs behind them.

"Ready?" Mia said, looking down the edge of the wall.

Ven came and stood beside her. It was higher than the wall he'd jumped when escaping the research facility, but certainly doable, as long as he avoided landing on his left hand where his fingers were still healing. Hopefully he'd land with better results than the two soldiers still rolling and groaning.

"Let's do it," Ven said.

Mia jumped down without another word, landing easily. Ven came down beside her, landing on his feet, then rolling across his shoulder to ease the impact. His ankle had pinched a little, but it didn't seem too bad. Together, they ran across the small, open field that lay below. Behind them, the guards had reached the balcony. A glance back revealed that a couple of them also jumped down, but most remained on top. Two crossbow bolts whizzed past harmlessly.

At the far end of the field was a short wall. Mia crouched and lowered her hands, lacing the fingers together. "I'll boost you up," she said.

Ven stepped on her hands, and she threw him up. With his own jump, he was well above the edge of the wall. He hoisted himself over with his elbows, but Mia managed to drop down the other side of the wall before him. There were several buildings just behind the wall. One of them would be housing their decoys. Mia led them over to a two-story stone building with a few horses tethered outside. This was a busy part of the city, and several people looked at them as they hurried across the street. The more witnesses, the better. Jalett had planned out the escape well.

When they disappeared inside the front door of the building, their decoys greeted them.

"Ready?" Ven asked.

"Always," replied one of them. Two people stepped forward, one of them dressed like Ven, the other dressed like Mia. Their hair and skin tones were a good fit. The woman's dress wasn't as fancy, but the colors matched well.

"We'll need to remove the skirt," Mia said.

"I see that," said her decoy, already moving to pull the skirt off. She wore similar pants beneath. "You can get changed back there." She pointed at a small room behind her. "We'll go out the front, as planned. You sneak out the back." She pulled a hood over her head and the two decoys exited out the front door. They'd mount the horses and ride out of town for a couple days.

Ven worried they'd get caught, but they said they had good ways of disappearing when they needed to. He let Mia enter the small room first. She'd have a change of clothes ready for her. The building was otherwise empty, save for a few scraps of empty crates pushed up against one of the walls. It smelled of dust, and he sneezed just thinking about it. Mia came out with a dark cloak and hood drawn. Ven took his turn, but all he needed to do was change his shirt and throw on a similar cloak.

When Ven came back out, a member of the decoy company addressed them. "Your decoys have already taken off. Guards took note of them and dispatched soldiers in pursuit, but they have enough of a lead that they should be able to get out of the city without a problem. They will likely check this building very soon since you were seen entering. You should depart with haste." He pointed to a door at the back of the open floor. "I recommend heading due west from here. Pass through a couple streets, then take the road north. That should put you well enough off the trail of pursuit."

"Thank you," Ven said. "Well done."

"There's a reason we can charge top coin," he said with a smile.

Ven shrugged and went out the back door, Mia following behind. They entered a narrow alleyway and had to jump over a wooden fence to reach the next street over. There was decent enough traffic here that Ven already felt that they had good cover, but they followed the instructions carefully, making their way over one more street before heading north. People were already talking about escapees from the castle. Word was spreading faster than he could have imagined.

They finally paused after a few minutes of walking.

They'd escaped.

# Chapter Twenty-Seven

# Chapter 27

## Juns Hall

"It hurts," Mia said, poking gingerly at her shoulder.

Ven gasped, short of breath. Oliver back home wouldn't believe what he'd gotten himself into. "Mia, I'm sorry," he said, his voice quiet. They leaned against a small building. The traffic in this part of town had thinned. "We should have stopped to look at it sooner. I wish I knew more about dragonsbane. I don't understand how it doesn't have any effect on me at all, but it burns you just by touching it. Can I look at it?"

Maybe it worked like an allergy? They rounded the side of the building to get out of sight, then Mia threw her cloak up past her shoulder and stretched her neckline down enough to show the cut.

Ven leaned in to inspect it under the midday sun. Her skin was so smooth when he touched it. He traced the outline of the cut and applied a small amount of pressure, but Mia had no reaction. *She has a high pain tolerance*, he remembered. The cut wasn't very long or deep, and under normal circumstances, he wouldn't have done any stitches, not that he *could* stitch her up. Nonetheless, the skin was quite red.

"Zein said that it would require a stab to the torso, neck, or head in order to kill Dami," Ven said. "I assume the same must be true for you, but there's poison at work. The skin is irritated. Your body is probably mad it can't adapt to this. We'll have to ask Zein if he knows what we're supposed to do to it. We should hurry to Juns Hall."

Mia nodded and adjusted her clothes and they went back out onto the street.

Ven stopped the first person they saw, a tall woman with bright red hair, and asked, "Do you know where I can find Juns Hall?"

The woman grunted and pointed back south. "Other end of the city, near the southern wall. You should head that way for a while and ask again."

"Thank you." Ven shook his head and they turned back south. Of course it was in the opposite direction they'd been going. They walked in silence for some time. Whenever they passed a particularly busy street, Ven couldn't help but pull his hood tighter around his face. He was more acutely aware of soldiers than ever before. There were many of them roaming the streets, but the consensus that Ven overheard was consistent. The two assailants had fled the city on horseback. That put them in the clear.

It almost made Ven want to stop among the shops and look for the tool that could remove the trigger device from Mia's neck. He wanted one, just in case, but still wasn't sure if he'd actually use it. Dayelle's words lingered with him. They wouldn't truly be safe as long as that power was out there. If what Dami said was true, then their imperviousness was also somehow genetic. If Mia ever had children, she'd pass the impervious trait on to them. He'd heard enough stories of children falling away and making enemies of their parents that the prospect was actually frightening.

He'd seen what Mia was capable of. Though she didn't maniacally slaughter like Dami and Ambrose, she glided lithely through the soldiers, breaking bones like they were made of dry spaghetti noodles. He just hoped that all those people who stopped moving were merely unconscious.

They walked for several minutes until they drew close to the other end of the city.

Everyone had probably heard of the incident by now. That only made him more nervous to talk to people. It was the same feeling he got after stealing something back home on Earth. He had to acknowledge how silly the fear was. It wasn't like everyone would somehow recognize him by his voice and turn him in. He decidedly approached a pair of passing strangers. "Excuse me, do you know where I'd find Juns Hall?"

It was a man and a woman, both with swords on hips, but they weren't dressed in uniforms.

"Just two streets that way," the woman said, squinting at him and pointing to her right.

"Thank you," Ven said, letting his head drop from view beneath his hood. He led Mia away, but glanced back a few steps later to see if they were being watched. The pair he'd talked to was no longer in sight. He imagined some bounty on his head and that everyone in the world was after it.

Juns Hall was unmistakable. The building was four stories tall, and mostly made of well-cut stones, but the wood that ringed the fourth floor was painted dark red. A large sign with the building's name dangled above the door.

"Ah, there it is," Mia said with a sigh. She was probably as tense as he was, but the sight of their destination brought mixed feelings for Ven. Some relief, yes, but it was quickly replaced by worry about what now lay before them. They'd face Dami again. This time, Ven would be asked to stab him. How would he, a person with no combat training, manage to stab someone who could move and react twice as fast as him? Even Yubo had struggled to get a small cut on Mia.

Juns Hall was loud. Raucous voices echoed from its doorway, which opened frequently. It was like Ven was quickly plugging and unplugging his ears. People came and went in a constant flow. They looked to be of all classes. As Zein surmised, finding the place had been easy enough.

Ven and Mia followed a vagabond in ragged clothes into the building. A burly guard greeted them just inside the door, and to Ven's surprise, the vagabond was not turned away. In fact, he seemed to know exactly where he was going. Ven on the other hand, was staggered by the sudden chaos. There were several tables inside the main room, and several open doors led to other rooms that looked similarly packed, and people were either eating or playing games of dice, cards, or other assemblages that involved devices Ven was unfamiliar with. It was a casino.

The guard chuckled at them. "First time to Juns Hall?"

A few people shouldered their way by.

"Yes," Ven answered. "We just need a table for now."

The guard nodded. "Head to the back of the room. Miss Kenna at the bench will help you find what you're looking for."

Ven looked to the back of the room and indeed saw a long bench spanning the length of the room. People didn't sit at the bench, but came to it and spoke to the woman who stood behind it, then they veered off elsewhere after conversing, sometimes exchanging something with her before turning away.

From beneath their hoods, Ven and Mia shared a glance, but did as the guard suggested and made their way toward the back of the room. It involved navigating through a maze of tables and patrons, many of whom, Ven realized, also wore discreet clothing with hoods or high collars.

"How are we supposed to find him here?" Mia said to him. They walked close together, and she had to speak louder to be heard over the noise.

Ven shrugged. "I don't know, but I can see why he picked this place."

More than once, Ven was jostled by others as he steered through the crowd. He kept a tight hand held over the small fortune that still remained in his coin pouch. This seemed like the perfect place to get robbed.

One man in particular walked straight into Ven.

"Humblest apologies, sir," the man said. He was short, and was able to look straight up Ven's hood and into his eyes. The man had a crooked nose and a stark pink scar just across his right eyebrow.

Ven pushed the man away and continued without a word, but now Mia led the way, easily slicing a path between the other patrons. Ven squeezed at his money pouch again. If only they used credit cards. Everyone here would try and rob him if they could.

Before they reached the back of the room however, the same man stood in their way, standing directly in front of Mia.

"Don't make any trouble," Ven told the man harshly as he stopped shoulder to shoulder with Mia.

"I don't bring trouble," he said, "but we've been watching for you. I can take you to the man you seek."

"And just who is that?" Mia said.

The man leaned in. "A certain doctor who wishes to remain discreet. Follow me." He waved for them to follow and began weaving through the crowd and tables.

Ven shrugged at Mia and followed. The man could have been leading them to a trap, but how many people would have known they'd be coming here? They eventually ended up in a room with considerably fewer people, and the tables were more sparse. Conversations were quieter, and any gaming at the tables was engaged in with less enthusiasm. The excellent smell of food made Ven's stomach rumble. He hadn't eaten anything besides meager stew and a lump of bread from the morning.

The scarred man led them to the back of the room behind a divider. A single man was seated at a small table there. He wore a hood, but it was loose enough that Ven could tell it was Zein Huan.

Zein stood immediately and gestured to the two empty chairs at the table. He nodded to the scarred man, who returned the way he'd come. Zein waited a moment before speaking. "I heard news from the castle. I assume you've secured the item."

"We have," Ven said. He patted the dagger where it hid in an inner pocket but didn't pull it out. He realized that if he'd been worried about getting robbed this whole time, the dagger held greater value than all the coins in his pouch.

Zein heaved a sigh of relief and sat back down. "Very good. I take it you weren't as discreet as we'd hoped, correct?"

"Jalett did provide a good method of infiltration," Ven said, "but our ruse was uncovered by Yubo. We found the item in time however, which enabled us to acquire it even after it got... violent."

"Speaking of which." Mia pulled down the collar of her dress to reveal the cut on her shoulder. "Any advice?"

Zein rose and approached Mia. It was the fastest he'd ever seen Zein move. He inspected and dabbed at the cut with squinted eyes. After a moment, his features softened. "I'm glad it's not any deeper and only seems to have penetrated skin. In reality, there's nothing we can do. It will heal in time. It will be difficult for your body to redistribute and excrete the toxins. Otherwise, I don't believe it will cause further harm."

He went back to his seat and Mia covered her shoulder again. "It is at least reassuring to see that this will remain a reliable method of achieving victory."

"Is he here, then? Dami?" Ven asked, voice soft. His heartbeat quickened at the thought.

"If he is, we will find out very shortly," Zein said, then raised an eyebrow at Ven. "Do you need something to drink? You look like you've tanned recently, but even still, you're quite pale."

"Actually, that would be great," Ven said. "I haven't eaten for a while either."

"I did feel a little bad eating in front of you while we were in the castle," Mia said.

Ven laughed. "I was wondering how out of place it would be for me to ask you to share."

Zein waved down a servant to bring food over and a short time later, a roasted duck, seasoned rice, and a plate of fruits was set at their table, enough food for all three of them.

Ven threw back his hood and dug in quickly, knowing Mia could sometimes have an insatiable appetite. Her body was highly efficient at maximizing energy usage, but she always had an apparent need of more food. The flavor of the duck was so rich that he suspected they'd somehow injected it with seasoned juices. He was so engrossed in enjoying the food that he jumped when he realized the man with the crooked nose and pink scar was at their table again.

"He's attacking," was all the man said.

"Lead them there," Zein said, rising from his chair slowly and dabbing at the corners of his mouth with a napkin. "Go now. Waste no time," he said to Ven and Mia.

Ven and Mia snapped to their feet, and the scarred man led them away. Ven's body felt electrifyingly charged. This was it. At least he wouldn't die hungry.

# Chapter Twenty-Eight

# Chapter 28

## Chase

Mia and Ven ran side-by-side, sprinting down streets as they followed the scarred man. The pace was crawling, and it was all Mia could do to keep from bursting ahead of them. She ignored the looks people gave them as they ran. Ven breathed heavily beside her after only two blocks. Her own heart pumped rapidly, not from exertion, but anxiety.

She wanted to get this over with. No more chasing anyone, just freedom. They had the dagger now. Mia wasn't alone. She could do this.

"There," said the scarred man, pointing at smoke trailing into the sky, black tendrils scarring the cloudless blue.

Mia jolted ahead of them. It felt good to run at full speed. It brought a thrill, like every heartbeat was pushing her to move even faster. The soft boots she wore impeded her ability to reach full speed. Dami probably ran barefoot.

How much had Dami's body developed since their last encounter? While she'd been riding in carriages, he'd been sprinting cross-country at full speed. He'd no doubt strengthened his adaptations, testing his limits in ways that were actually useful.

The smoke came from a large mansion. One side of it had caught flame, but the fire seemed minor in comparison to the rubble that remained of its gate and front door. How Dami was able to obliterate buildings so quickly was beyond Mia's comprehension.

Mia stopped just in front of the crumpled iron gate. The metal was bent and torn apart as if it were made of cheap wood. A giant, gaping hole two stories high was all that remained of the front entrance to the building. From the entrance stumbled a woman, tripping over the rubble. One of her arms was missing. She passed out and didn't rise. A man came crawling out behind her, his legs twisted at odd angles.

Mia's lips curled back in disgust. Dami wasn't just killing people. What he was doing was even worse. *I have to help them.* She dashed across the yard to the crippled man. After picking him up and carrying him across the rubble, she asked, "Where is he? Where's the man who did this?"

The man sobbed back at Mia and shook his head. Mia sighed and went to the woman who was missing an arm. She was dead. Mia growled in frustration.

A distant thundering sounded from the southern walls, and a cloud of dust billowed up. There were enough handholds that Mia easily climbed to the third floor of the building from the outside. This gave her enough of a vantage to see that a portion of the city wall near the top had collapsed.

"Dami!" Mia shouted, her voice echoing off the stone buildings. Was he afraid to confront her again? *He should be.* She clenched her fists and kicked a potted plant that went soaring into the neighbor's yard.

Ven and the scarred man came sprinting to the front of the building.

Ven stepped gingerly around the metal shards of the gate and spotted Mia on the building. "Is he gone, then?" He hollered up to her through his panting.

"Yes," Mia said. "We should have been here the whole time." She threw up her hands and bit back a scream. She jumped down to a patio on the second floor, then jumped down beside the rubble that remained of the front door.

"Agreed," Ven said, wincing as he beheld the scene. He bent down to inspect the man with the crippled legs who was now lying still on the ground with eyes closed. Ven felt at the man's neck, then stood. "We should get medical help," he said to the scarred man. "Dami is no longer here. This man has fainted. It looks like both his legs are broken."

"Other help will come," the man said with a scowl. "I'll report back to Zein." He took off running the way he'd come.

Curious citizens gathered in the streets to observe the destruction. Mia and Ven pulled their hoods back on.

"We should go," Mia said, putting a hand on Ven's elbow and tugging him away. He resisted only slightly with a final glance at the injured man, then hurried away with Mia.

"You're right, Mia," he said. "We need to get to the next place ahead of him. I wonder if he's worried now knowing that there's something out there that can kill him."

A group of soldiers came pushing their way through the gathering crowd. Mia and Ven quickly melded into the throng and made their way towards Juns Hall. They'd only made it halfway down the next street when the scarred man stopped them, this time accompanied by Zein.

"We need to get ahead of him," Mia said sharply.

"I was a fool," Zein said. "I should have sent you straight to Tromar's home as soon as I confirmed you had the dagger."

"It's my fault," Ven said. "I was hungry."

"Nonsense, I could have sent you along with food just as easily." Zein laced his fingers in front of him.

Mia folded her arms. Zein's decisions would always be full of mistakes. "How do we get ahead of him? Where do we go?"

Zein sighed. "Inevitably, he will end up at—"

Ven rose his hand sharply and grabbed Zein's arm. "Wait. Don't say anything."

"What is this about?" Zein said.

"We should go somewhere private to talk," Ven said. "I'll explain there, but we shouldn't discuss anything more out here."

Zein sighed again. "Very well. Come with me." He led them further down the street until they were nearly at the wall, then paused in front of a small, quaint home and removed his hood. The building looked empty, but a squat woman appeared beside the tiny gate and opened it for them.

"My family owns many of the buildings in this part of the city," Zein explained as he led the way up two stairs then opened the front door. He took them to a small sitting room.

Ven removed his hood and held a finger to his mouth. He motioned with his hands as if he were trying to write something.

Zein nodded slowly and left them in the room. He came back a moment later with paper and a stick of graphite.

Ven wrote on the paper and held it back up for them to see.

*"You're still wearing your vest,"* was all it said.

Zein frowned at first, then said, "I see. Wait a moment." He left the room once again.

"What's this about, Ven?" Mia asked.

Ven shook his head. "I've been wondering how Dami is always a step ahead of us. There are dragonblood tech devices that allow people to listen in. What if his undercoat is somehow rigged with one?"

Mia put a hand over her mouth. "Dami would know everything."

"Practically, yes."

Zein returned a moment later wearing completely different clothing. Wordlessly, he started a fire in the small hearth then held up a device in his fingers that was roughly the size of a few coins, then placed it in the fire. He led them to a different room.

"That was a very wise assumption, Ven," Zein said. "I would not have guessed that they'd somehow gotten one of those into my vest. It would certainly explain how Dami seemed aware of our plans. Whoever is assisting or directing him has good resources. They must also be using a similar device that allows for communication across distances. Both of which are very rare and expensive dragonblood technology. They are well-funded."

"They know everything, then?" Mia said.

"No, I don't believe so," Zein said. "I have three vests which I wear on rotation. Though I don't know which information they *do* have, I know they don't have all of it."

"What about the dagger?" Ven said.

"It's unclear what they know," Zein said. "I intentionally avoided using specific words while we were at Juns Hall, but I don't recall which vest I wore when we originally discussed the plan to come here to Peskan. I mentioned Peskan on other occasions since that meeting, so it's possible he learned of our coming here on other days."

Ven rubbed his forehead with a knuckle. "My advantage with the dagger was supposed to be a surprise."

"It might still work, even without the surprise," Mia said. "We just need to be in the right place. You were about to recommend something before Ven stopped you." She looked to Zein.

"Yes," Zein said. "You should go to the compound of Sitena Rosars. She was the primary investor in our research. She will know about the attacks on the other investors and will have retreated to her fort, Castia Mont. I believe she has a swordsman in her employ there who also possesses a dragonsbane weapon, but I don't know if she is aware of its effectiveness against subjects. I tried to keep such information as secret as possible."

"Will we get there before Dami this time?" Ven asked.

"Now that he doesn't know where we're going? We stand a good chance," Zein said. "It's also possible that they've been tracking the movement of my carriage. It has been equipped with various devices over the years in my enthusiasm. You must use another means of transportation."

"That's easy enough for me," Mia said. "How will Ven get around?"

"Horse."

"Alright," Mia said, leaning against a wall and folding her arms. "We'll go hole up with this Sitena. Let me reaffirm something. What happens to me when this is all done?"

Zein held up his hands. "As I stated before, I will hold you to no further obligation. You will be free to go, but the toxin in your neck will remain as a failsafe. You will live a very long life, Mia. Who you are now as a young woman is a commendable character, but at any risk of you taking a turn for the worst, it will be absolutely necessary."

Mia reactively traced the device on the back of her neck with a frown. Could she pinch it hard enough and pull it out? Was there a way she could remove it herself without causing the poison to spill out and kill her? Her one hope was Ven.

After a moment of silence, letting the message sink in, Zein spoke again. "You must depart now. We traveled off the path to reach Peskan, and Sitena's fort will be a three day's ride from here. Dami could likely run there in half that time, if it's his next objective. I'm not sure how many investors remain, but he tends to kill the others nearby wherever he goes, so I assume he's busy for now taking care of two others around here. He would finish with those by this evening however, and we are far too late to reach those ones first. Of our 36 investors, I estimate that he's slain about 25 of them. Those remaining will be difficult for him to root out, but Sitena is not one to go into hiding. She will make an easy target."

Zein turned to Ven directly. "Ven, there is a stable here that usually has a couple Zebadons for sale. They are ancient horses of great strength and stamina. Acquiring one of those may be sufficient enough for you to reach Castia Mont in time. There is a gate to the east of the city that leads across the river. You will exit there and follow the main road until it veers south at the base of the mountain. Eventually, a path will open up that cuts between two mountain ridges. Take that route through the other side and continue southeast from there. You should pass a small village there where people can further direct you to Castia Mont. It would be about a day's journey from the village."

"Great," Mia said. "Anything else we should know? Sitena won't try and kill me when I show up, will she?"

Zein stroked his chin. "She will recognize you. She may be alarmed at your appearance, so it may be prudent to have Ven first reveal your intentions there before you unveil yourself. It would also be wise to refer to her as Lady Rosars. She is indisputably the number one financier and distributor for dragonblood technology. She is wealthier and more powerful than the king and queen."

A frown darkened Ven's face. "Alright, then. I guess we'll be off."

"There is... one more thing you should be aware of." Zein waited a moment before speaking again. "I cannot confirm anything of course, but there is the chance that Lady Rosars is the very person responsible for directing Dami."

"What?" Mia hissed.

Ven rubbed at his forehead. "I also considered the possibility that one of the investors could be attempting to monopolize the research. If she's really the top investor, why wouldn't Dami have killed her first?"

"There are many possible explanations," Zein said. "I would prefer Lady Rosars not be a suspect in the matter. She has been known to be aggressive in her business dealings, but never violent."

"Yes, maybe because she never had access to the best assassin in the world," Mia said.

Zein shrugged. "As I said, there are reasons to be suspicious, but I believe her to be intelligent enough to know that Dami cannot be controlled.

All I'm saying is that you should be cautious. Stay close together, and be prepared to flee if you must."

"Excellent," Ven said. "Any other advice on how not to die this week?"

Zein gave him a flat stare. "You seem tenacious enough to pull through on your own from here." He then gave directions to the stable and handed Ven a few extra coins just in case he didn't have enough.

Ven and Mia moved to leave.

"I will be a day's journey behind you," Zein said as they left. "Ride hard, Ven."

Mia pulled her hood up and stepped out the door. The street outside was empty. Smoke no longer curled up from the mansion, so the fire must have gone out.

"What do you think would be faster?" Ven asked from behind her. "You could sling me over your shoulders or I could ride a horse. Do you think they make backpacks for holding people?"

Mia gave a fake laugh. "Let's stick with the horse."

"Alright. I know how much you hated the last stable. Why don't you go on ahead to the gate, and I'll meet you there with this horse," Ven said. "We might be less suspicious walking around individually anyway."

Mia looked back at Ven but his face was covered by the hood. Ditching her was suspicious. It didn't sit well, but she tried to justify his decision anyway. He wasn't avoiding her, he was trying to be nice because she didn't like the smell of horses.

"If you say so," was all Mia said, but she knew it came out snarkier than she intended.

Ven stopped walking.

"I'll see you soon," he said, and hurried off in a different direction.

Mia grunted and slowly meandered in the direction of the eastern gate. She stuffed her hands in the pockets of her cloak, wishing she had something to punch or throw across the city. This would have been a great time to spar with another subject, but only Dami remained. Their sparring would come soon enough. She clenched her fist, pressing her nails against her palms. *If only I'd killed him right after Ambrose.*

The memory returned of Ambrose suddenly crumpling lifeless beneath her after the poison had been injected. That had been her friend. They'd been like sisters. Sure, they didn't see eye-to-eye on everything, but the other subjects were the only family Mia had ever known. It was an ultimate act of betrayal. She tried forcing away her emotions as the thoughts happened, but this time she struggled to hide them. Her lower lip trembled and tears blurred her vision.

*I made my choice*, she reminded herself. Dami was out of control. He was basically responsible for all the other subjects' deaths. She had to remind herself that she was the only person who could stop him. Defenseless people would continue to die.

Zein's methods in saving her life and developing her imperviousness had been cruel and tortuous, but his motive was to save other lives. This was the reason she existed. But in this way, she was free to save lives how *she* chose.

Mia wandered through a part of the city that was nearly empty. Her heightened sense of hearing didn't fail to notice quiet shuffling behind her. She adjusted her hood to increase sight range. The shuffling stopped, then began again. It was like swift footsteps that continued to pause and then continue.

She picked up her pace, dodging through a narrow alley. At the end of the alley, she heaved herself over a fence as tall as her head then sprinted to the next street and slowed to a walk. She fell in behind a small group of people who also turned right to head down the main road to the eastern gate. Anybody following her would have struggled to take the same route at her pace. Hopefully she'd lost them.

The eastern gate was ahead, equally as tall and formidable as the western gate through which she'd originally entered, but the doors were smaller.

This passage had significantly fewer people coming and going, but at least a dozen soldiers guarded its perimeter.

She knew she should hunker down and wait for Ven to arrive, but the possibility that she was being followed left her feeling uncertain. Ven would know what to do. She'd wait inside the city limits until Ven arrived. Pausing at an intersection, she looked behind her. A shadow of a person came out of the same street she'd entered the thoroughfare from, movements lithe. The personage vanished behind a hand-pulled cart.

Mia bit her tongue hard. She'd never been followed before. Was that really what was happening, or was she just nervous? She crossed the intersection and found a quiet spot to wait against a stone wall and an empty crate.

When the cart passed her she saw nothing suspicious. Whoever had followed her was good at what they were doing.

# Chapter 29

## The Road

Ven rode at a slow pace through the streets of Peskan from atop the Zebadon. He'd never heard of this kind of horse, but he could see why Zein recommended it. The beast was massive, and its body was a bulk of rippling muscles. Its dark brown coat shimmered with an almost metallic glow. If this kind of horse had existed on Earth, it would have been the medieval equivalent of a tank. The reins hung limply in one of Ven's hands. It required no additional guidance other than an occasional nudge with his knee to know which direction to go.

He wanted to name the beast, but couldn't think of anything very good. So far, all his brain could muster was Big Brown and Horsey. Both options made him feel like an idiot, so he chose not to call it anything. Maybe Mia would have a better idea.

The saddlebags were stocked with some food from the market. Ven also made extra effort to look through medical supplies, hoping to locate the tool that would extract the poison from Mia's neck. He found no luck there, but after showing the drawing of the device, he'd been directed to a group of artisans and craftsmen who did metalworking and construction.

They'd had two of the tools and were hesitant to part with one until Ven flashed a hefty sum of money.

In hindsight, it probably would have been wise to find out what store they got theirs from, but for all he knew, maybe it was custom made, and he certainly didn't have time for that. He wasn't sure if he should tell Mia that he'd acquired the device. Once the poison was out, he wondered if she would take off and start her own life of freedom. *Shouldn't that be her choice to make?* He wondered how he'd feel if a gun were held to the back of his head at all times. Why did he get the tool in the first place if he didn't intend to use it? It made him question his own sanity.

She hadn't turned on him so far, so he wanted to trust that it would remain the same whether she had the poison or not.

The gate was ahead. He scanned the road for signs of a Mia, worried about the prospect of approaching the guards without her. The idea made him realize how heavily he'd come to rely on her.

Two soldiers near the gate eyed him. If they caught sight of him, he worried they'd recognize his face. He knew the idea was ludicrous. They'd have to be one of the soldiers who'd seen him in the castle, and most of those were probably getting treated for broken bones.

Relief came as Mia walked out of the last street before the gate and followed behind him.

The soldiers weren't stopping anybody as they strolled out of the city, but when Ven got close, an officer pointed at him and two soldiers moved to block the way. They pointedly observed his horse.

"Sir, please uncover your face," said the officer. "In light of recent activity we have orders to check everyone's faces before they leave."

Ven set his jaw. A description like his was probably commonplace enough that it would be fine, but he worried more for Mia. She'd be identified the moment her face was revealed. They'd be able to make a run for it. None of the soldiers were mounted, and once on the road they could easily get away.

He was just about to heel his horse into a gallop when another figure stepped in front of them.

"I'll handle this," the man said, turning to face them. It was Siwen Huan.

The soldiers saluted him and stepped aside.

"Only for formalities," Siwen said. "Let me see your face."

Ven didn't respond, but instead urged his horse on. It responded by charging forward into a quick gallop. Siwen dove out of the way, and Ven zoomed out under the gate. He spared a glance back. Mia followed, running at a fast pace, but nothing abnormal. A few soldiers ran to catch up, but Siwen stood and stared after them.

The road diverged ahead. One route led north and east, into the mountains, another route led south. A small thicket obscured the south road. Ven steered his horse there and waited for Mia to catch up.

"Looks like you lost some of your speed there, Mia," he said as she entered the brief cover.

She rolled her eyes at him but wasn't winded. "Had to play the part."

"We should keep moving. I wouldn't be surprised if they pursued on horseback. I noticed a stable near the gatehouse."

"Then we should run. I'll keep myself angled behind your horse so they can't tell I'm running so fast."

Ven looked between her and the horse. "Half of your body will be visible beneath it."

She shrugged. "At least they won't see my head."

"Better than nothing." He heeled the horse forward and Mia easily kept pace as Ven pushed to a full gallop. The walls of the city passed in and out of view between the trees which grew thicker as they progressed along the road. The Zebadon ran faster than any horse Ven had ever ridden. It moved faster than the dragonblood powered carriage. He whooped at the exhilaration

Mia laughed beside him. "I could go faster, but I'm impressed by its speed." He believed her. She spoke without trouble but had to shout loud enough to be heard over the horse's tromping and the rushing wind. No wonder Dami got everywhere ahead of them.

The road remained empty for a long distance, but Mia pointed ahead and slowed down when somebody came into view. Ven reduced to a trot, and despite its great stamina, the horse whinnied and slowed eagerly. It had been a long sprint. They would have a good lead on any pursuers.

"I'll slip into the trees and follow out of sight," Mia said. "I'll converge again after we pass them."

"Good idea."

Mia disappeared into the trees to their left. The sun was getting low off to the right. They could probably ride for another hour before they'd need to find a good place to set up camp. He wished he knew more about finding a good campsite.

The approaching person turned out to be five people, one walking behind the other in a straight line, hauling bags on their backs. Ven waved at them as they passed. His hood had fallen back during the gallop, and he hadn't bothered putting it back on. It was unlikely that he would be recognized, and their decoys had gone out the western gate, so all their pursuers were probably off in that direction. Excepting Siwen.

Once they passed, Ven slowed to a walk. He didn't catch sight of Mia until several minutes later. She sprinted up the road, and then walked beside him. "You had me worried for a while there," he said.

"I ran up the mountain a little ways. I wanted to see if I could spot our pursuers."

"Any luck?"

"Not really. We must have outpaced them by quite a bit. Zein was right about that horse."

"Speaking of which, I was hoping you'd help me name it." Ven patted the horse's shoulder.

"People give names to horses?"

Ven shrugged. "It's a thing."

"You're not really asking an expert here, Ven."

"You can't possibly think of worse names than I did."

"How about Horsey?" Mia suggested.

Ven slapped his forehead. "We're doomed."

"That's a bad name?"

"Yeah, it's horrible. That was one of the two names I thought of. That's what a child might call a horse."

"What was the other name you thought of?"

"Don't ask. Maybe we should name it after something fast or strong."

"We're not naming the horse after me," Mia said with a smirk.

"Oh, that's a great idea actually. Maybe we could name him 'Subject.'"

"Please don't."

"Well, unless you come up with something better, I'm just calling him Subject from now on."

"Hold off on that idea for a while. How about we sleep on it, and I'll give you a new idea in the morning." She looked west to the setting sun. It was low enough now that it hid mostly behind the trees lining the road. "How's he doing though? Do you think we could put in another sprint before dusk?"

"He probably could," Ven said. "Keep your eyes out for some water, and we'll try to camp nearby. I noticed a couple streams that went under the road."

"Sounds good. I can scout ahead for that." Mia stretched her arms. "It feels great to run at full speed. I can feel my body stretching to adapt. I'm not sure I can run much faster or if speed reaches a peak eventually. I'm sure our bodies must be able to reach a maximum. If so, I wouldn't be surprised if Dami has already reached it. I'd like to catch up as much as I can."

"That's reasonable," Ven said hesitantly. He glanced at the road behind them. He didn't feel inclined to admit that he was feeling somewhat afraid of riding a strange road alone.

Mia paused to reach down and remove her shoes and socks. "I don't technically need them," she explained as Ven stared, "and they get in the way." She found an empty bag on the horse's saddle and stuffed them inside.

"See you soon," she said, and took off at a full sprint, running faster than he'd ever seen.

Ven led the Zebadon back to a gallop, but Mia disappeared ahead of him as the road curved slightly. He frequently looked behind himself. With no experience as a fugitive, he wasn't sure how he was supposed to behave. Would it be wise for them to set up camp beside the road? He'd watched a few movies. No fires. Cover their trail somehow. Keep watch to make sure nobody snuck up on them while they were sleeping. That's how it always happened. They'd wake up surrounded by a gang.

The sun dipped below the horizon before he met up with Mia again.

She had a smile on her face and panted a couple of times before her breathing became normal. She even stroked a bit of sweat from her forehead.

"You look like you had fun," Ven said.

Mia shrugged, and her smile remained. "I found water. Sorry, I couldn't find any for a while. We're actually fairly close. I let you get close while I looked around the area, and I found a good spot to stay under the cover of some thick bushes."

"Wow. I bet you had time to take a nap and snack on fresh berries that you scrounged out of the woods too."

"It was only a short nap," she teased.

Ven followed her to a small stream where the Zebadon drank greedily. Once the horse had his fill, they went a little ways into the woods to a good, flat surface relatively clear of twigs. Thick grasses grew nearby and provided excellent food for the horse.

"Not bad," Ven said, tying up the Zebadon.

"It's perfect," Mia said. "I did a great job."

Ven smiled. It was good to see Mia in such a happy mood, even in the face of their current task. His body ached. He hadn't ridden that much in a long time. They decided against lighting a fire as the temperature seemed relatively warm enough, and they had enough fresh food that they didn't require any cooking. Ven rolled out a couple mats for both of them and he fell asleep quickly after laying down.

# Chapter 30

## Not Alone

**M**ia woke abruptly. She sat up and looked around the trees. It was still relatively dark, but the sky overhead was turning a beautiful shade of purple, and stars were vanishing from sight. *Did I hear something?* It had been something like a twig snapping or a leaf crunching. She rose to a crouch and scanned the woods around them. The horse stirred a little. It could have been the horse, but she didn't want to discount the possibility of something else out there.

The nearby stream made small noises as well. It might have been a bad idea to sleep near the stream. It *did* impede her ability to hear other sounds. She hadn't thought of that. Ven slept soundly. She didn't want to wake him unless there was an actual issue. He needed a lot more sleep than she did.

Rising from the crouch, she decided to investigate. She tiptoed through their camp and inched towards the road. If someone was sneaking up on them, it seemed like the most likely direction to be coming from. Stealth was a skill, not an adaptive trait. She grit her teeth at every noisy step she took, but at least Ven didn't seem to mind.

Eventually, she made it around their bushy hideout and started slinking toward the road. The sky continued to brighten, stars winking out. Her advantage with advanced night vision wouldn't last much longer, but the road ahead appeared empty. She sighed and straightened, dropping her stealthy approach. After a few more steps however, she froze. Further down the road, visible between the trunks of trees, a few people moved quietly.

"Shh."

The sound came from behind her. She spun. There, crouching in the tall grass, was Siwen Huan, a single finger held over his mouth. How had she missed him? And what was he doing here?

She took a step towards him, ready to hurl him across the stream. When she opened her mouth to speak, he repeated the gesture. He was clearly more concerned about silence than he was about her attacking him.

He made another gesture, urging her to follow him back towards the camp. A bow remained slung over one shoulder, a sword strapped over the other, and a quiver and dagger hooked to his belt. No weapons were drawn.

Mia frowned but followed, reminding herself that she could reach him before he'd be able to draw any of those weapons as long as she kept a close eye on him.

"Rouse your companion," Siwen whispered. "You must flee immediately. Over sixty soldiers follow your trail."

"So you are helping us?" Mia said, her voice louder than it should have been. She could defeat sixty soldiers. She could defeat hundreds.

"I am," Siwen said, voice still lowered, a frown creasing his brow. "Do not be so bold as to assume you can face them." Ven started to stir at their conversation. "I understand you are a capable warrior. I witnessed that firsthand, but I doubt you'd be able to prevent your friend from coming to harm."

"What?" Ven said, bouncing to his feet. He stumbled away from Siwen.

Mia shushed him. "We've been discovered. Soldiers are coming. We need to leave." She could defeat sixty soldiers easily, but Siwen was right. She wouldn't be able to keep all of them off of Ven.

"How did you find us?" Ven asked, rolling up his mat.

"Easily," Siwen said. "And they have trackers who are better than me. We can talk more later. I know a way to lose their trail."

Mia stayed close to Siwen while Ven continued to pack. He made no complaint about her not helping, but he got everything back onto the horse in about a minute.

"This way," Siwen said, heading towards the stream.

"Do we trust him?" Ven asked in a voice quiet enough that only Mia would hear. He mounted the Zebadon and waited for Mia's answer.

"No, but I'll play along at least until we have full daylight," Mia said. She took a couple steps after Siwen. She knew she should be more circumspect, but if Siwen wanted to kill Ven, wasn't it possible that he could have already done so? There was also the likelihood that he'd want to use Ven's life against her.

"He could be leading us to a trap. Is that a dragonsbane sword on his back?" Ven asked. They'd just stepped down into the water as Siwen quickened the pace and led them further upstream. With no trees overhead and the sky getting lighter every second, it was much easier to see him. The sword on his back seemed the right size, and the etchings on the pommel bore the likeness of serpentine dragons.

That detail was all the information Mia felt she needed. With two leaping steps, she sprang onto Siwen's back and ripped the weapon free, holding it only by the scabbard. Even through the scabbard, there was a dull pain emanating from it. The pain was bearable, like holding her hand a little too close to a fire. She tossed the weapon up to Ven who caught it.

Siwen struggled beneath her, his face underwater.

Mia pulled his head out of the water. "I think you need to explain what's happening here."

Siwen tried to stifle a cough. "I will explain everything, I swear it. We just need more distance from those soldiers. My horse is a little further upstream, and then we can ride hard, parallel to the road. Stony ground by the mountain will mask the trail of the horses' hooves. It will buy us more time."

"If you intend to trick us, you will die," Mia said.

"I believe you, and I have no intention of dying."

Mia dragged Siwen back up to his feet, lifting him by his collar. He stifled another cough and continued forward without looking back.

Ven shrugged at Mia, but they resumed following him. "We run at the first sign of trouble," he whispered. She barely caught the words over the sound of the water.

Mia's bare feet slapped through the cold river water. The ground beneath her feet was often hard clay or smooth rocks. Her body tingled with adaptation. The facility hadn't done much experimentation using cold, only heat.

After another couple minutes of walking up the stream, they saw Siwen's horse. It wasn't tethered, but stood watching them as they approached. It was large like Ven's. Probably another Zebadon.

True to his word, the stream poured down from an outcropping of stone. Mia couldn't imagine people being able to track them fast enough by following the horse's footprints, but if Siwen had been able to find them, then there must have been some truth to his words.

Siwen went to mount his horse. "Following your trajectory, I assume you were going to be continuing south, correct?" He kept his voice low. Were the other soldiers really still in pursuit? She left the water and climbed up the nearest boulder, looking downstream. She could see nothing.

"For a while," Ven said.

"We can ride along here for a couple miles, then slow to talk for a while," Siwen said. "I'll be willing to answer your questions then, but we should go now. We need some speed, but we can't run at a full gallop across the stony ground. We need to allow the horses room to be more careful in their steps."

Ven chewed his lip and held a hand out to Mia.

When she raised an eyebrow at him, he cast a careful glance at Siwen before whispering, "You'll need to ride with me. Best if he knows as little as possible. You can sit directly behind me and hold on. The Zebadon rides smoothly."

Siwen led his horse a few steps ahead of them so his back was turned. Mia had never ridden a horse. Hopefully it wouldn't be too obvious, but if Ven could do it, it shouldn't be too difficult.

"Step there to heave yourself up." Ven pointed at a stirrup.

Mia sighed, grabbed Ven's hand, and stepped up using the stirrup. She swung a leg over the horse. The seat sloped behind her, pressing her against Ven's back. The saddle was rather large, and could have fit a much bigger person, but both she and Ven were built smaller.

"Hold onto my waist," he said, easing the horse into a slow walk at first.

"Hurry," Siwen called from ahead of them. "We need distance or the sound of the horses' hooves will give us away." His own horse began trotting.

They picked up the pace. At first, it felt awkward, bouncing with the horse's steps, but she quickly got accustomed to the rhythm. The most awkward part was how close she was to Ven. Something about the situation brought warmth to her cheeks, and she was grateful he couldn't see her face. She kept her hands firmly in place, faintly aware of her pinky fingers pressing against the bone of his hip.

Their speed increased and decreased at varying intervals. None of them spoke for over an hour. The sun cast its light into the plains below and slowly grew towards them. Eventually they came upon a small pond, and Siwen slowed to a walk ahead of them.

"Now should be a good enough time as any," Siwen said. "What questions do you have?"

"How did you find us?" Mia asked. It felt odd to talk to him while sitting behind Ven.

"I, like everyone else, suspected you'd fled the city on horseback," Siwen said. "That's what the witnesses attested to. A force of about one-hundred soldiers were dispatched in pursuit. I did not attend with them. To me, it was clear that you had not entered the castle with the intention of killing anyone. Your companion—no offense, sir—is obviously not a trained soldier. And, while you had many opportunities to do so, I noticed you made particular effort not to kill my soldiers. I had to believe that your primary interest truly was in obtaining the dragonsbane dagger."

"We didn't lie to you about that," Ven said.

Siwen nodded. "Furthermore, I found your points interesting when you questioned my father about the dagger and a possible dragon in the dungeons."

"Did you look into it?" Mia asked.

"I did." Siwen's expression grew dark. "I had soldiers and servants helping clear up the dungeons after the mess you left behind. My father was distracted by the pursuit, so I took the opportunity to slip into the other cell that you'd broken into where there is a woman in heavy chains. I've heard only that she is a dangerous traitor, imprisoned there for life since before I could remember. I found it odd that she was so heavily chained, and her cell included chairs, a table, and much more lighting than others, including a small dragonlight candelabra. We often destroy such devices when they are confiscated, but I do know that dragonlights are often preserved. Even my father can't deny the convenience.

"That aside, the woman has several scars across her arms, which was the only exposed skin aside from her face. A few of the cuts on her arms looked fresh. When I spoke to her, she would not respond. If there was ever the chance that what you said about us keeping a dragon in the dungeon in human form, preserving its life to drain its blood, then you certainly have a suspicious enough case to potentially prove the point. It still seems wild to me, but I can't deny what I saw there."

"You didn't free her?" Mia said.

"By stars, no," Siwen said. "If she truly is a dragon, she needs to be slain, if anything. Releasing her is the last thing I'd do."

Ven grunted. "You didn't answer how you found us though."

"That was the easy part," Siwen said. "Do you want the short answer, or the long one?"

"You seem like the type who likes giving long answers," Mia said.

"I'm a warrior and a politician," Siwen said, flashing Mia a smile. "Once word reached me regarding the attack on the Taladia residence, I rode over. Witnesses saw a man moving with incredible speed who demolished the gate and door. Evidence on site was also consistent. A couple people mentioned seeing a woman jumping down from the building. I assumed it was you.

"Nobody knew where you'd gone, but you were close to a lot of property owned by my father's cousin, Zein Huan. The Taladia's were also suspected of being involved in dragonblood research somehow, but we could never prove anything. The fact that he'd been ripped apart in his own home just before you two had visited didn't seem like a coincidence." Siwen shrugged. "I checked nearby, heading towards one of Zein's known hideouts when I saw both of you emerge from a building. Even with hoods on, I assumed it was you. From there, I followed Lady Nesua to the gate and had a servant prepare my Zebadon in case she made a run for it."

"If you had identified us at the gates, why didn't you order us to be detained?" Ven asked.

Siwen laughed. "I have genuine interest in whatever you're doing. And clearly, my father is hiding something."

"If that's truly a dragon in the dungeon, wouldn't it have been there for generations?" Mia asked.

Siwen's smile disappeared as he gazed down at the trees stretched out below them. "Many generations, yes. It must explain my family's extensive wealth. It makes me ponder the schism between Zein and my father."

"What do you know of Zein?" Mia said.

Siwen grunted. "I'd ask you the same thing. I only saw him one time when I was a young boy. From what I've heard though, he was always different from the rest of us. Huans have always been raised as warriors, but he instead studied health and medicine, stating that saving a life is more important than taking one. It was really quite tragic then when his wife and daughter were killed by some kind of disease. When he publicly opposed the ban on dragonblood research, my grandfather was forced to ostracize him and he was banished from the city. Oddly enough, he still maintains quite a large estate and operates a few businesses within the city even though he's not allowed to visit. What about you two? Do you work for him?"

Ven looked back at Mia. "Not exactly," he said. "As I said in the castle, I was hired to destroy dragonblood research. I'm determined to stop it, however I can. It was Zein's research facility that I helped to take down. Mia was... assisting me."

"Mia," Siwen said. "Nice to know your real name." He placed a hand to his chest and offered her a small bow of the head.

Mia almost rolled her eyes at him before she realized he was being sincere.

"So what of your current quest?" Siwen said. "Why did you need the dagger?"

"The less you know, the better," Mia said, narrowing her eyes at him. "And thank you for helping us evade the soldiers, but I think you should return to Peskan now."

"I see," Siwen said, looking forward. "You know, if there is someone you're after, I can aid you. I don't claim to be as talented as Mia, but I'm quite skilled with a broadsword. Is it the man who attacked that home yesterday?"

Ven sighed and looked back at Mia.

She ground her teeth. *The last thing I need is another person waving around a deathstick.* Would it increase their chances for success? Probably.

"Our mission requires utmost discretion," Ven said. "I'm not sure our organization would approve."

"I understand," Siwen said. "But know that I am a man of the law. From what I can gather, you are seeking to enforce the laws our kingdom has had well established for many years. I would swear secrecy if it meant bringing a murderer to justice."

Mia rubbed her forehead. "We would need to discuss. Ride on to the edge of the trees there."

Siwen obliged and rode off to the edge of the trees while Ven brought his horse to a halt. Mia leaned back in the saddle.

"What do you think?" Mia said in a whisper. "Can we trust him?"

"Of course not. As soon as you and Dami start fighting, he'd see that the two of you have the same abilities. What would keep him from trying to kill you as well?"

"He said it would be in pursuit of justice. Dami has been killing people unlawfully. Am I not guilty of the same thing?" She remembered the two men she'd killed during their first assignment. That was the first time she'd ever attacked a normal human, ignorant of how easily that would kill them.

She winced at the memory. There was also the possibility that she'd killed one of the men back at the castle when she kicked the door in.

"That's a harsh comparison," Ven said. "You haven't acted maliciously."

"Does the intent matter when it comes to enforcing the law?"

"It does where I come from, but I don't know about this country."

"What would keep him from turning on us?"

Ven sighed in thought. "I guess I don't know. I mean, it would be convenient to have an actual soldier armed with a dragonsbane weapon, but it might be too risky."

"We could always ask him about it now. Have him swear to secrecy on anything that might be revealing about myself."

"I'm surprised you'd be willing to risk it," Ven said. He placed a hand on her knee as he looked back at her. "I won't mention any details. That should come from you."

Mia nodded and yelled over to Siwen. "We have questions for you."

Siwen rode back toward them as Ven's horse took a few steps forward. "What would you ask of me?" Siwen said.

"First, we need you to swear to secrecy," Mia said. "This doesn't mean we're accepting your offer to join us, but our questions can also be revealing."

Siwen nodded. "Understood. Normally, I'd be hesitant to accept, but under the circumstances, I swear to secrecy."

"Would you hold me to justice for impersonating a lady, escaping the prison, and harming some of the soldiers?"

Siwen let out a breath and stroked his lower lip. "That's definitely a hard question. As it stands, I'm not sure I can justify everything you've done. I understand you may be in a pinch for time, and so an escape there was necessary on a moral standpoint. I probably would need to know more to offer a straight answer."

"We need to catch the man who attacked that house," Mia said. "He's responsible for murdering over a hundred people by now. It will only get worse once his primary targets are dead. He has shared with us plans to dominate the human race essentially."

Siwen raised his eyebrows, eyes wide. "Are you saying this man is a dragon? That's why you need the dragonsbane weapons?"

"Not exactly," Mia said. "Zein ran... experiments on him. He can only be killed by few other means. Though he isn't a dragon, dragonsbane poison would be the easiest solution. We know that eventually he'll go to the place we're currently traveling. We hope to head him off there and prevent the next murders by stopping him."

"So Zein created a monster... how ironic," Siwen mused with a sad frown.

"Zein didn't create the monster," Ven said. "He merely ran his experiment on a person who chose a monstrous path. Zein's goal was still to save lives, but the consequences were pretty bad. He knew the risk as well. It's part of why I was brought in to bring down his facility, but I'm also partially to blame for this man's escape. We need to stop him before he kills others."

"I see," Siwen said. "I understand why you'd want to keep this all a secret. This information is frightening to say the least. I would be honored to help you bring this man down, but I must ask that at the conclusion of this task you return the dragonsbane weapons to me."

"We only intended to borrow the dagger," Mia said. "Once he's taken care of, we won't need them anymore. You should know, however, that this task will not be easy. These experiments have made this man extremely strong and fast. He almost killed me the last time I faced him."

"Stronger and faster than you?"

Mia blinked. This was where she worried about saying too much. "Likely, yes."

"I can tell you're both resisting sharing some more information with me," Siwen said. "You should know that I already understand that this man and Mia probably share these qualities. I have witnessed many soldiers fight, but never have I seen someone move with such speed and strength as Mia."

Mia ground her teeth. "I'm not a monster."

"Of course you aren't," Siwen said. "A monster doesn't make conscious effort to spare those who attack her as you have. I was not tactful in how I used that word earlier. Your actions have spoken differently than his."

"That's probably about all we have to share, then," Ven said. "So what's your response?"

"If your goal is to bring this man down, I will aid you. I wish things had happened differently at the castle. I likely couldn't absolve all that you've done, but I personally will not hold you to justice there. Some of those soldiers will never return to fighting condition. But, consider it a fair trade if you return the weapons to me when we're done."

"You won't try to arrest or kill me?" Mia said, seeking assurance.

"I will not," Siwen said. "At least not based on your current list of activities."

Ven shrugged and looked back at Mia.

"Very well," Mia said. "We've wasted enough time." She hopped down from her seat behind Ven. "Try to keep up." She took off at a sprint.

# Chapter 31

## Castia Mont

Ven cast a sideways glance at Siwen as they sat around eating a hasty meal of dried meat and bread the next morning. It had been difficult for him to sleep last night. He had to remind himself that if Siwen wanted him dead, he would have already killed him. But that didn't mean the same thing for Mia.

Siwen often stared at her when she or Ven weren't watching, but Ven caught him doing it. He wanted to call him out, but couldn't muster the courage.

Ven went and sat beside a tiny stream near their camp.

Mia tucked her rolled mat back into a saddlebag, retrieved an apple from a bag, and sat beside Ven. "Why the brooding face?" she whispered so that only he could hear. Her bare feet were quite filthy. They'd run across a bit of muddy ground yesterday, and she hadn't bothered to wash them. She mentioned enjoying the feeling of the mud drying on her skin and cracking off. It was heartwarming to see her free to enjoy simple things in life that Ven might have otherwise taken for granted.

Siwen turned away from them.

"I don't like how he stares at you," Ven said honestly.

Mia smiled. "I didn't think you were the jealous type."

Ven's mouth hung open, a bit of apple remaining unchewed as he tried to figure out how to respond.

"I'm only teasing," Mia said, bumping him softly with her elbow. "I know you only have the most professional opinion of me."

That was it. He knew he could seize this moment to clarify everything, but what would he even say? He wasn't sure what his feelings really were. Sure, he was a boy, and she was a girl. An absolutely gorgeous, determined, empathetic, strong, compassionate girl who actually seemed to care about him. *Stars, maybe I* do *like her*. His mind spun with what to say but all he could sputter was, "You aren't my patient, Mia. Professionalism doesn't have anything to do with it at this point."

Mia nodded at him, eyes calculating as they stared deep into his. "That's because you're not a doctor."

He smiled as she scooted forward and lowered her feet into the water, rubbing the mud off her feet.

Ven took off his cloak. It was like wearing a blanket, but he'd put it on to ward off the morning chill. He tossed it to the ground behind him and pushed back his sleeves as he kneeled beside the water, upstream from Mia. He bent and splashed water on his face.

When he lifted his head back up, Mia was standing beside the horse, digging through the saddlebags for more food.

"Not that one," Ven said as Mia opened a flap, his heart lurching. He bounced over to her as she reached in and pulled out the trigger device.

Her eyes widened with horror as though she'd been stung, and she dropped it back in immediately. A low hiss escaped her lips, and she threw him a scowl.

"Someone gave it to me, Mia," Ven said, but she already turned away from him.

"Let's go," Mia shouted and took off at a jog.

Oblivious to what had just happened, Siwen narrowed his eyes at Ven, then sprang onto his horse.

Ven threw his apple core at the stream, snatched up his cloak, then mounted as well. The Zebadon responded quickly, heaving into motion as it took off at a sprint. He growled at himself for leaving the device in a bag by itself. He should have at least put something else on top of it. Why did he still have it anyway? He should have destroyed it as soon as Dayelle gave it to him. Her idea to kill Mia was insane. There was no way he'd be able to do it anyway, but now he'd probably just lost all her trust in him.

He wanted to scream, but even though Mia was several paces ahead of them, he worried she'd hear. Instead, he clenched his fists on the reins and stared ahead, branches whipping by.

They traveled through the mountain pass all morning without pause, Mia keeping her distance ahead of them. If only she'd stop so he could explain.

The mountain itself was not very large, at least not compared to the Rocky Mountains. By late afternoon, they were already through to the other side.

"There should be a village up ahead," Siwen said. "I recommend we go around it. The less eyes on us, the better. There will also be a few more people on the road."

"Not a bad idea," Ven said. They had to shout at each other to be heard over the thundering hooves and rushing wind. Ven was sure that Mia, running just a few steps ahead of them, had heard without issue.

They stopped after coming up behind a pair of men heading back to the village. The Zebadons devoured any bit of greenery they could find as soon as their riders were down.

Mia kept her distance and only allowed Siwen to toss her a block of cheese.

"Are you alright?" Siwen asked.

"Fine," Mia said, stepping off into the trees.

When he glanced at Ven with a questioning look, Ven merely shrugged. He wasn't about to explain that he could kill Mia with the click of a button.

Siwen climbed onto the branch of a tree and looked out to the east. "I have a good idea for the route. We'll want to go around the north end. There's less tree coverage, but at least we won't have to cross the river. I've only been near Castia Mont once, but I know the road that leads there."

"Is it hidden?" Ven asked.

"Not necessarily," Siwen said. "It's a very large plain from here. The trees thin out more the further east we go, which means we'll also have greater visibility. The fort sits atop a plateau. I remember seeing it from the road. It will be difficult to miss if we stick to the path."

"Sounds like a plan," Ven said.

"Very well," Siwen said. "I'll lead the way."

Mia returned from the trees and finished off her cheese.

They mounted back up and Siwen led them at a brisk gallop. They crossed the road to the north side and rode hard, passing between the trees which grew up in clusters.

They changed directions after riding northeast for a while, and instead steered hard east. The trees grew more sparse, but Ven still never caught sight of the village or any people.

"We should be on the other side of the village now," Siwen said as he slowed to a trot. "I'll lead us back towards the road."

"Castia Mont is only a day's journey from here, right?" Mia asked.

"Hopefully less than that," Siwen said.

"Mia, I—" Ven started in a low voice.

"I'm sure you have your reasons," Mia said, cutting him off with a plastered smile that flickered away.

***

The next morning, they reached the road.

"You could ride behind Ven again," Siwen suggested to Mia, "to keep up appearances."

"I'd rather jog if that's not too much of a tell," Mia said.

"I suppose that would be fine," Siwen said, glancing at Ven.

Ven avoided eye contact, setting his jaw and staring at the road ahead.

They kept a steady pace for a few hours. Many more people frequented the roads here. Siwen said that a few cities connected along this route. Nobody paid them any special attention unless they caught sight of Mia.

Ven spent most of his energy trying to figure out how to explain things to Mia. He also had to think of what he'd do when they faced Dami. Dami likely knew he had the dagger. The image of Dami ripping off Ven's arms was more frequent than he liked. His broken fingers were still weeks away from full recovery.

Trees were much more sparse, despite there being a small lake that they passed to the south of the road. The sky overhead was a clear blue. Dark clouds over the mountains behind them hinted at rain that they managed to dodge. The road curved towards the south, and gray, slab rockfaces were visible to their left, sometimes protruding like giant monoliths.

"We're getting close," Siwen said. "You don't mind if I have my sword back, do you?"

"He's not leading us to a trap is he?" Ven whispered to Mia.

Mia glanced over her shoulder at him and shrugged.

"We can return it to you once we arrive," Ven said.

Siwen only nodded in response.

Their view to the left opened up with no trees blocking their sight. A large, walled castle rested atop a cliff of bare rocks. From a distance, the structure looked impressively large. Certainly the type of thing that would be owned by the wealthiest woman in the nation. Its walls appeared built from the same stone that surrounded it, though it was a little lighter in hue. A flag hung limply. A few towers rose independent of the castle itself.

Stretching between them and the castle was an expanse of two or three large farms, one field empty, another ready to harvest, growing what Ven assumed was some kind of root or vegetable.

They proceeded down the path for a few more minutes before a split-off led left to the castle. The road was a deep, blackish color, littered with stones and gravel that made it look as though it were once paved. The ground was quite level until they got closer to the walls, then it wound to the left and had two switchbacks as they ascended the hill. An iron portcullis remained closed as they reached the walls. A few soldiers watched them from behind the iron bars, and a few others looked down at them from the walls, all heavily armored with weapons drawn.

"State your business," called a harsh voice from above.

Ven pulled his horse up beside Siwen.

"I could announce myself as a visiting lord," Siwen said to Ven, "but I'm not sure she cares about us. Do you have a better introduction?"

Ven shrugged but called up, "My name is Ven Yashke. My companions are Lord Siwen Huan of Peskan, and Mia. Doctor Huan sent us here."

"Wait here," the voice called down again.

They ended up waiting several minutes, long enough that the horses started stamping with impatience.

Finally, the portcullis began to rise. Ten mounted riders came out to surround them. Ven worried at first that they were going to attack.

One of the riders spoke. "Come with us. We'll lead you inside."

"Is there a problem?" Siwen asked.

"Her ladyship wishes to exercise certain precautions," answered the rider at the front.

The road went up at a mild incline. The fort was more spacious than Ven originally thought. It included two additional tiers with their own walls. The first level contained several buildings, some of them bunkered down against the walls. Fires burned and many soldiers crowded the area. On the second level, the buildings were taller, and several people bustled around, hauling water, carrying laundry, and so on. The final tier was where the castle rested, nestled back against the cliffs. Ven wondered how people ever managed to build walls right up against cliffs without the use of cranes.

Two tall, narrow towers rose at either end of the large courtyard. Only a stable and another large building shared the space with the castle, which of itself rose five stories high. The courtyard was not what Ven expected to see. There was hardly any adornment, save for two statues and a few manicured bushes at their bases. The rest of the space was empty.

"Dismount here," the soldiers ordered them as they stopped in front of the stable. A few stablehands emerged from the building, ready to help. An open, double door on the stable revealed a couple carriages.

Ven, Siwen, and all the soldiers dismounted as stablehands led the mounts off.

"Follow us inside," the leader said, keeping a hand lightly gripped over the pommel of his sword. Five soldiers marched in front of and behind them as they were led across the courtyard and through the massive doors of the castle. Sun-colored dragonblood lights glowed from golden chandeliers that hung from the tall ceiling. They were taken through a door that stood immediately to the left of the room. This took them to a windowless room of bare stone. More soldiers peered in at them through crevices in the walls.

The door closed behind them, and a metal portcullis dropped into place. The only other feature in the cramped room was another opening on the far end, closed off by two additional portcullises. All ten soldiers had accompanied them into the room, though nine of them hung back by the entrance. The lead soldier walked to the two portcullises at the far end and announced, "I have brought Mia, Ven, and Lord Siwen Huan."

"Bring them forward, I will speak with them." The womanly voice came from beyond the opening, but she was not visible.

The soldier gestured for them to step forward. Once they stopped before the first portcullis, a woman stepped into view, wearing an elegant blue dress. She was mature and striking, her brown hair tied up and decorated with a silver chain that hung across her forehead.

"I'm Lady Sitena Rosars," she announced, her voice rich and lilting. Her eyes shifted to Ven. "Doctor Yashke, I read good reports of your work with Mia. I'm glad you could both make it here. I've heard word of what's been happening, so I hope you don't mind the precautions I've made. Lord Huan, did Doctor Huan drag you into this as well?"

"No, milady," Siwen said, bowing his head before speaking. "I chose to come with them. It sounded as though there was a threat against which I could be of assistance."

"Your words may prove true," Sitena said. She shifted her steady gaze to Mia. "Mia, I am aware of your weakness." She held up a triggering device like those from the facility. One click from it and Mia would die. Ven's heart sank, and his cheeks burned with shame for also possessing one. Sitena continued. "I hope never to use it. I also have two very capable soldiers here in my employ armed with dragonsbane weapons, likewise capable of delivering mortal damage. If you've come with ill intent, you will not succeed."

Mia took a step toward the gate until her face was almost touching the metal portcullis. Ven put out a hand and held her arm with a light touch. She pulled her arm out of Ven's grip, but took a step back.

"We've come intending to help you," Ven said. "Dami is likely to come here soon. Possibly within a day. He's usually one step ahead of us, so we're glad he hasn't come already."

"I am prepared to meet him," Sitena said. "He has been wise to avoid this place."

Ven shook his head. "I don't doubt the ability of your soldiers, but I doubt anybody besides Mia would be able to stop him. I'm sure he could kill everybody here and depart unscathed. He's faster and stronger than you could imagine."

"You assume much for one so young," Sitena said.

"He does not speak lightly, milady," Siwen said. "If this man fights anything like Mia, he's the equal of an army."

"I see," Sitena said with a blink. "I am glad to have Mia here. I worried that all the other subjects died attempting to escape. I would like to speak with you another time without a doctor looking over your shoulder."

*She'd use Mia,* Ven thought. Just like Dami was somehow being manipulated by somebody else.

"Lord Huan, I assume you are trained in the use of a dragonsbane sword as your fathers before you," Sitena said.

"I am, milady."

"And my soldiers reported seeing a dragonsbane sword in your party's possession when you arrived," Sitena said. "I assume that weapon is still with your horses. I will have it retrieved for you. You are welcome to be armed with it while you remain here. I've had detailed reports from other attacks. Armor would not help very much in favor of mobility. Your current attire is suitable."

"I would be glad to assist you, Lady Rosars," Siwen said with a slight dip of his head.

"We stand a greater chance of success if we have your participation, Mia." Sitena raised her eyebrows and stepped back from the portcullis. "I would like to speak with you more." Both the portcullises in front of them rose slowly with the sound of grinding metal. Sitena held the trigger in her hand as she beckoned Mia forward. "Your companions here look haggard with travel. They will be taken to the dining hall to relax for a moment while you and I chat."

Mia looked over at Ven, her eyes hard. "Alright then," she said to Sitena.

Ven shook his head at Mia. He thought to object, but she turned her head away from him.

"We will rejoin your companions shortly," Sitena said, leading Mia off down a separate hallway.

"I'm surprised you'd let her out of your sight," Siwen said to Ven through the side of his mouth.

"Yeah," Ven said as a sinking feeling dropped into his stomach.

"Follow me," a soldier said, interrupting them. He beckoned them under the two raised portcullises. They proceeded down the hall in the opposite direction Mia had gone. To Ven's surprise, the hallways were relatively unadorned. He expected somebody as wealthy as Sitena to have every surface decorated, but he'd gone on assuming that wealthy people were all the same, and he knew a lot of wealthy people. He had to remember that they were free to be conservative in some ways and ostentatious in others.

They entered the dining hall through a large door. The room and tables were much too large to seat only the two of them, but they were led to two seats at the end of a long, wooden table, a white cloth draped across its surface. Five soldiers accompanied them to the room. Ven hated how exposed and helpless he felt without Mia beside him. He wished he'd taken the opportunity to learn some fighting techniques from her if only to boost his self-confidence. But he was a stranger here in a strange world.

A servant wearing a white and black suit scuttled into the room, holding her hands so stiffly to her sides unnaturally. She paused beside them and offered a bow. "We will have food brought to you shortly." She gestured toward another servant who approached with a silver jug and two glasses.

He poured magenta liquid into the glasses and placed them before Siwen and Ven.

The two servants scurried back through the door they'd entered.

"Not even my servants move like that," Siwen muttered.

"I only have one servant back home," Ven said, remembering Oliver with great fondness, and it felt weird to call him a servant rather than an employee. "And he was about as improper as servants get. I'd often come home to him playing one game or another."

"Surely not," Siwen said with a snicker.

"He did," Ven said. "He still kept the place clean and prepared food and everything, but he always found time to play. We often played together in fact. He was one of my few friends growing up."

Siwen grunted and nodded. "I can respect that." He glanced at the soldiers standing near the doors. "I can't say I'm fond of her ladyship. I don't like that she separated Mia from us. I'm surprised you aren't more distressed by it."

Ven pursed his lips. The sinking feeling in his stomach had not dissipated, and only seemed to expand with each passing second. "I know when to hide my own fears." It was practically a requirement of treating the sick and dying.

Siwen nodded knowingly. "What was that device she threatened Mia with?" He took a sip of the drink.

"Another detail that it might be better you don't know," Ven said.

"Surely you can trust me by now."

"You might be a little too blunt."

A door opened, and a soldier came in holding Siwen's dragonsbane sword in front of him with both hands, mouth parted in awed reverence.

"Ah." Siwen stood and accepted his weapon with a relieved sigh. The soldier bowed and left.

The dragonsbane dagger was still tucked in the front of Ven's pants, hidden beneath his shirt. The hidden weapon.

"You know she has a fondness for you, right?" Siwen said as he sat back down.

"We've saved each other's lives. I suppose it's natural."

Siwen leaned forward. "No, more than that. I'd say she was attracted to you."

"Nonsense," Ven said, shaking his head and barely holding back a snort. He took a sip of the drink and found it very sweet, but it somehow left a burning sensation on his throat. Was this wine or port or something? He'd never had alcohol before. He put it back down.

"I do act more coy than I truly am," Siwen said, "and I know I would envy the attention of a woman like her. She sneaks glances at you when you aren't looking. She leans in when you speak. These are subtle signs, but they speak verses. She is stronger and more beautiful than any woman I've ever met. Intelligent too. And free. A rare combination."

Despite the unsavory sensation, Ven was tempted to take another sip, so he pushed the drink further away. The thought of Mia finding him attractive was exciting, but maybe she didn't feel that way anymore. Maybe she hated him. He just hoped that Sitena wasn't somehow corrupting her.

# Chapter 32

## Crumble

M ia eyed the back of Sitena's head as they walked down the hall. No soldiers accompanied them. Sitena was supposed to be smart, but a smart woman didn't walk down a hall with her back unguarded like this. Perhaps there was some other ploy at work.

She wasn't without defenses though. The trigger in Sitena's hand was instant death for Mia, and Mia wasn't exactly sure how it worked. Did she only need to push a button, or did she need to aim it at her?

Ven had one too. She wanted to scream at him. She would have if Siwen wasn't around. She'd *trusted* Ven. A feeling that apparently hadn't been mutual.

Sitena opened a door and led the way inside. A single room of Jalett's modest home was easily more lavish than Sitena's entire fort. There was nothing in the room except a dragonblood light overhead and four un-adorned chairs. Mia sat in the one furthest from Sitena. *At least they're comfortable.*

"You must find it odd that I want to speak with you," Sitena said, "but I worry about your future. With the facility in ruins and Doctor Huan's research ended, I don't believe he had much of a plan for what to do from here. I would hate for you to lose your way. I can only imagine how confined you've felt all your life, and I sympathize for the circumstances you've lived in for so long. Once Dami is subdued, what do you plan to do?"

Mia eyed the older woman. Her brow was slightly furrowed, and a faint hint of wrinkles showed at the edges of her eyes. It was the most emotion she'd seen from her. Her hands remained folded on her lap, lightly settled over the trigger device.

"What do you want?" Mia asked, ignoring Sitena's question.

Sitena nodded—a slight movement of her chin. "Your caution is justified. Look, I've accomplished much in my life, but I have no husband or children. What's my legacy, then?"

Sitena straightened in her seat before continuing. "I spend much of my fortune investing in technological advances not simply for the profit, but to aid the rest of the human population. I fund the establishment and maintenance of orphanages, schools, and hospitals." She paused and raised an eyebrow at Mia. "You, Mia, have no family. Those you may have considered your family have all died. Tragically. You spent your whole life being tortured. I can only imagine the horrors you've been through. Even still, you have a good heart. I believe you want to make an honest living for yourself and be free of the worry that someone will abuse you. I'd want to help you in any way. That is why I wanted to speak with you."

Mia picked at her fingernail. Sitena was good. She seemed genuine. If not for the fact that she was basically holding a sword to her throat, Mia might even believe her. "Would you remove the poison from my neck?" Mia asked.

"I believe its necessity has been explained to you."

Mia nodded. How was Sitena aware of her conversations with Zein? Her chest tightened. "What are you proposing?"

"Just an opportunity to restart," Sitena said. "I could provide you with an honest living." Her eyes narrowed just slightly. "This will be necessary if you hope to have a real life. You should be aware that information regarding what you are has leaked. It is already beyond my ability to control. As long as you live, people will be looking for you. Hunting after you. You will never be able to rest."

Mia set her jaw. She couldn't tell if Sitena was proposing a warning or a threat. Perhaps it was both. Perhaps *Sitena* would be the one hunting for Mia if she ever got away.

Sitena gestured at the castle. "But I could offer you safety."

Another prison. More experiments. Passed from one facility to another. "Safety," Mia scoffed. "I'm not sure I could ever be safe around one of those." She pointed her chin at the trigger device.

"Yes." Sitena's expression returned to that of emotionless glass. "Again, a necessity. I would hate to deprive you of the one thing maintaining your humanity."

Mia grit her teeth. Poison in her neck was all that made her human, was it? The tightness in her chest boiled into rage.

Her face must have shown it because Sitena frowned at her and said, "I can assure you that I have no ill will toward you, Mia. That's why we are having this conversation. There are others who would sooner see you dead. They would not have hesitated to pull the trigger on this device, but as of yet, the connection between you and these devices is knowledge limited only to a select few. Those hunting you would be unlikely to know of this. Here in the castle, I could keep you safe from them. Nobody gets through the gates of the keep without my explicit permission."

"A prisoner," Mia said with surprisingly more calm than she would have expected, though years of being a subject had taught her to suppress much of her emotion.

"Hardly. You would enjoy significantly better accommodation than any prisoner. You would have a job here among my staff. Perhaps as the arborist." She raised an eyebrow. "I'm sure you noted the lack of decadence here at the castle. A bit of fresh life could make this feel more like home."

Mia had no desire in being Sitena's arborist. The fact that she was trying to appeal to Mia's interests only made her more cautious. She'd play it safe. "Then I'll be able to leave if I want."

Sitena's answer didn't come immediately. She tapped the weapon in her lap. "No. We all know how dangerous you can be. It wouldn't be right of me to let a force like that run wild. That was an error on Doctor Huan's part. I asked you to stay here to be polite. You would not like the alternative."

Mia suppressed her growl. "And what if I didn't have the dragonsbane in my neck any more? What would you do then?" She rose slowly to her feet. She was bluffing, of course, but she had to know if Sitena's threats were founded.

Sitena's grip settled over the trigger. "I have other means in place. Soldiers armed with dragonsbane blades, yes, but as the dragon slayers of old, I have many troops armed with dragonsbane crossbows that are equally effective." She tilted her head at Mia's growing sneer. "I want you here as my guest, Mia, when all of this mess is resolved in Dami."

"Prisoner."

"Call it what you will, but perhaps things will change eventually. Time will tell."

"I see," Mia said, holding back the tears that threatened to swell in her eyes. "May I rejoin my companions, then?"

"If you wish," Sitena said, rising to her feet. "But consider your options, Mia. There aren't many to choose from."

***

An hour later, Mia stood on the balcony adjacent to her room, looking out across the courtyard below.

Footsteps bustled outside her door every few minutes, but when somebody stopped in front of her door, she turned to look. Silence stretched for a full minute before there was a knock.

"It's me," Ven said, voice haltering.

A breath escaped through Mia's teeth. She chewed her cheek then strode to the door and swung it open.

Ven took one look at her face, then redirected his eyes to the floor and walked into the room after closing the door behind himself. He immediately took the trigger device from a pocket, but Mia punched his wrist in a quick motion, sending the device across the room to land on a couch.

Ven gasped in pain.

"Is this what you came here for? To kill me?"

Ven blinked rapidly, as if holding back tears. "What? No, I disassembled it. I was going to show you how I took it apart so it can't work." He looked down at his wrist then slowly managed to hide his grimace. "That was the frame you just knocked out of my hand." He awkwardly used his other hand to pull out a few more pieces from his pocket and set them down on a small round table. "Here are the other parts. I wanted you to break them with me."

"Oh," Mia said. Her gut twisted with guilt for punching his wrist. "Did I break your wrist?" She asked, putting a hand over her mouth as she looked at his wrist.

"No," Ven said, feeling at it with his other hand, "but the bruises will be awesome."

"Where did you even get the trigger from?"

Ven sighed and sat on a chair opposite the couch. As far as furnishing went, Mia's room had more than any other room she'd seen in the castle. "There's something you should know."

"What is it?" Mia said, narrowing her eyes. She went and stood in front of Ven.

"That secret employer of mine? They found me right when we arrived in Peskan and gave me the trigger. I was asked to kill you. They want you dead once we take care of Dami. They say your power shouldn't exist."

Mia blinked. Her legs went weak, and she dropped to the couch behind her. Those words struck a chord. It seemed to be a common sentiment. "Maybe they're right. And they're not the only ones who think so."

"No," Ven leaned forward in his seat, eyes pleading. "They couldn't be more wrong. Your life is worth saving. There's no way I'd kill you, and there's no way I'm letting anyone try."

"Like you'd be able to stop anyone if you wanted," Mia said, striding back to the balcony.

Ven charged after her. "That wouldn't stop me from trying." He grabbed the railing as they looked out over the balcony at the courtyard below. In his hand, he held up a different tool. "I can remove it."

Mia let out a shuddering breath, heart pounding. She clenched then unclenched her fists, all remnants of her anger at Ven dissipating. She remembered what he'd said to her the night before Dami broke out. He told her to try some affirmations. She'd memorized the words. Even started to believe them. *You are important. You are beautiful. You are good, and smart, and caring. You have value. You have the ability to do great things.*

She wasn't a monster. But she wasn't completely human either. She'd never be free of it. Sitena was right. She'd be hunted all her life. Even if the poison was removed.

Then a question occurred to her and she looked up at Ven, biting her lip. "Do you," she whispered, "love me?"

Ven stared at her unblinkingly, his blue eyes glowing in the fading sunlight. Goosebumps ran across her arms and back. "Yeah," he sighed. "I do."

She swallowed against the blossoming warmth in her chest before grabbing the tool from his hand and flinging it back into the room.

He blinked back at her in confusion.

She gestured down to the castle courtyard below. "This is where I'll die."

He shook his head. "Impossible. I won't let it happen. Besides, you're practically immortal."

"We both know how this has to end." Her eyes watered despite the resolution that settled in her shoulders. "I have to die. And you'll be the one to kill me."

"Mia, no." He gripped her shoulder, eyes searching hers frantically.

"I will never be free, Ven," Mia said. "Once we stop Dami, Sitena won't let me go. If I try to run, she will kill me, and if I stay, she will make me her prisoner, no doubt succumbing to a resumption of experiments. I won't live a life like that."

Ven shook his head slowly, his Adam's apple bobbing. "I won't."

"You must, Ven. I will not subject myself to being a prisoner again. I've already thought this through. Once Dami is taken care of, you need to be the one that kills me. This will earn you their trust. Then you must take my body away so they cannot keep it."

As Ven shook his head again, Mia growled and strode back into the room, grabbing the device. She slapped it back into Ven's hands. "If you love me as you say you do, then you must do this for me. Please."

This time, Ven bit his lip, eyebrows furrowed. "I will do what must be done," he said, voice barely more than a whisper. The sadness in his eyes broke Mia. She turned away, unable to bear it.

This was the only way it could be done.

***

Mia breathed in the crisp morning air as the sun slowly crept up. Clouds covered most of the sky, and there was a smell that she'd come to recognize that hinted of a coming storm.

Behind her, Ven slept soundly on one of the couches. He'd tried arguing with her more last night, but she would hear none of it. This was her life. She would choose how to live it, regardless of how much it pained him.

Perhaps he was right. Maybe she *should* run. Maybe she *should* stay to at least see what kind of life Sitena really offered here at the castle. But she also knew that living in captivity wasn't truly living. The pain of being stuck would never leave her. What she yearned for was freedom, and her plan was the one true way to achieve it.

She only hoped Ven would understand in time.

Ven stirred on the couch. His feet shuffled as he came up behind her. "Did you sleep?" he asked.

"A little," Mia said, feeling bad for lying to him. She was trying to protect him to minimize the damage of what might happen in the next couple days. In truth, she hadn't slept at all.

There were some things Ven was better off not knowing.

Ven touched her elbow, and when she turned to look at him, his blue eyes were deep and penetrating. "I want you to be free, Mia. To run among the mountains and see the wildflowers. There's a town in the mountains I used to visit called Mavenda. I only wish you could see it in the summer."

"Yeah, I guess that would be nice," Mia said with a smile.

"What's wrong?" Ven asked, though he probably knew.

"I'm afraid."

"I know." He squeezed her hand. "I'm so sorry. I'm a little scared too." He said nothing for several minutes, and her fear started to diminish.

"I can beat Dami, Ven."

"I know you can."

"I just... don't want him dead."

Ven let out a long sigh. "I know. I wish there was another way."

Mia took a deep breath and looked into Ven's blue eyes. "I'll do it. I'll end him."

"You'd better, otherwise, I'll die."

"We should probably avoid you dying."

"I'd have to agree," Ven said.

She felt a pang of guilt for the pain she would cause him, but as he still held her hand, something giddy wiggled in her stomach. He admitted to loving her last night. Did she love him? Could that explain the fluttering feeling and the waves of warm emotion that flowed across her body, ebbing from where their skin touched?

Was that what love felt like? She looked back up into his eyes.

He shuffled one step closer to her, leaning forward. He glanced down at her lips, and for a moment, she expected him to give her a kiss. Her heart pounded as she tilted her head up in anticipation, looking at his lips, slightly parted, warm breath blowing softly down her face.

He leaned down and closed his eyes. Her heart pounded, and she threw a hand around his neck, rising up on her toes to meet him. A loud knock rebounded on the door.

Ven shot back a step, and they both looked across the room. The door opened and three soldiers stepped in. A bell rang from another tower.

Brown eyes wide, nostrils flared, the soldier stated, "He's coming."

# Chapter Thirty-Three

---

# Chapter 33

## Defenses

The thundering in Ven's chest shifted to a different beat. He patted his pockets, finding the dragonsbane dagger still sheathed to his belt. Hopefully he wouldn't need to use it.

His cheeks burned as he looked over at Mia. They'd been so close to kissing. The anticipation of it left his skin tingling. Admitting that he loved Mia felt bittersweet. It seemed like a silly thing to say. What was love anyway? And his frustration still simmered beneath the surface. How dare she ask him to kill her?

The reassembled trigger was tucked in a large pocket of his tunic. Another weapon he didn't plan on using.

"What do you mean he's coming?" Mia snapped.

The soldier shrugged. "I don't make assumptions. I follow orders. My orders right now are to escort you to Lady Rosars." He stood aside, holding the door open.

Ven took the liberty of taking the first step away from the balcony. They followed the soldiers at a brisk pace up a flight of stairs. They were in the main castle tower. Sitena had given them rooms in which to rest just below her own quarters. She made it no secret that she wanted Mia to remain close.

Despite the rugs that covered the stone floor, their footsteps echoed loudly.

"I understand your question," Ven said to Mia. "How do we know he's coming? Usually there's no notice."

"Exactly," she said with a sideways glance at him.

A group of twenty soldiers stood at the top of the stairs outside the entry room to Sitena's bedchamber. Ven caught sight of one of them tucking a glass vial into his cloak right as they entered the room. The soldiers stopped shuffling around and stood at attention as Ven and Mia crossed the threshold, all eyes on them.

Siwen stood near Sitena's door, his large dragonsbane sword sheathed on his back. He gave them a nod. Two other soldiers stood beside him with similar weapons sheathed at their waists.

A guard opened the door and led Ven and Mia inside, as well as Siwen and the other two dragonsbane sword wielders.

Sitena stood inside beside a wooden writing desk, and she regarded them with her expressionless face. She wasn't wearing her usual dress, but instead wore a plain off-white shirt, pants with little adornment, and small riding boots.

"If his attack here is similar to other reports, he'll come straight to me," Sitena said. "I want you all to be ready for him. It must be a concerted effort. No matter how fast or resilient, he can't dodge all attacks at once."

"How do we know he's coming?" Mia asked, repeating her question from earlier.

Sitena gave Mia a hard look. "He deliberately destroyed one of my outposts about eight miles from here, but not before they sent off a message using a device I have that allows for immediate communication."

Ven frowned. That was certainly a different approach than what Dami had done before. "Lady Rosars, that does seem odd to me. Previously, he would only show up at the last moment, complete the job, and then flee. Destroying the outpost almost seems ostentatious."

"He wants us to know he's coming," Mia said quietly.

"I thought the same thing," Ven said.

"Overconfidence," Siwen said. "We can use that to our advantage."

Sitena held up a hand. "We'll want to seize whatever advantage we can get. If he's being bolder, would he come straight through the gates? Is it possible that he could take another approach?"

"If it were me, I'd scale the cliffs," Mia said. "I could probably climb all the way up here to your room and come through that window." She pointed at a large window on the other end of the room.

Sitena raised an eyebrow. The expression was subtle, but Ven could detect the doubt it signified. If Ven hadn't seen Mia's incredible ability to climb, he'd probably disbelieve the possibility as well.

"He could climb the cliffs?" Sitena asked.

"Easily." Mia shrugged. "He could probably attack from any angle he wanted."

"You seem confident," Sitena said. "We'll maintain wall patrols in all areas to notify us of his approach."

"Milady, he'll also likely kill or maim anybody that crosses his path," Ven said, still feeling a sense of awkwardness when talking to nobility in such a way. "I would recommend that most people get tucked out of the way so that casualties can be minimized."

"Also wise council," Sitena said. She pointed at an officer. "Have nonessentials retreat to the eastern outpost immediately." The officer dashed out of the room. "Mia should be the first to engage him. From what I understand of dragonsbane weapons, you may not be able to wield them, Mia, is that correct?"

Mia regarded the dragonsbane weapons in the room. "Not for very long. A second or two at most. The feeling reminds me of grabbing a hot coal for the first time."

Sitena blinked in acknowledgement. "Then your objective is to lead him to those who wield the dragonsbane weapons. Their objective is clear." She looked at each of the three men with their dragonsbane swords.

What objective? To kill both Dami *and* Mia? He clenched his jaw tight.

"Where will you position yourself, Lady Rosars?" Siwen asked.

"I will hurry out to the balustrade above the front door of the keep where I should pose maximum visibility," Sitena said. "I will keep Lend at my side in case Dami finds another way around," she pointed at one of the soldiers beside Siwen. "But hopefully he crosses through the yard which is where I'd hope Mia can confront him."

"Where should the rest of us be?" Ven asked.

Sitena offered a subtle smile. "You should seek hiding, Doctor Yashke. I don't imagine Dami is fond of you. If I represent Dami's ultimate target, then Mia should remain near me until she can confront him. I will have Teamon concealed in the yard." She nodded at the other soldier armed with a dragonsbane sword. "Siwen will be posted halfway between me and Teamon at a balcony that's already rigged so he can drop down to the yard or climb up to reach me depending on where Dami and Mia fight."

Mia and Ven looked at each other. She gave him the slightest shake of her head. There was something about this plan that she didn't agree with, but didn't get the chance to ask as an attendant came bursting into the room.

The soldiers instinctively drew their weapons, but the attendant quickly dropped to her knees in a low bow. "My lady," she said, "the Dayawen outpost has been destroyed. Message just arrived."

Sitena gasped. "Leave the room," she ordered the attendant. The woman left as quickly as she'd come. Sitena's eyes were wide. "I did not fathom how quickly Dami can move. The two outposts he attacked are four miles apart, and he destroyed both of them in a few minutes." She pointed to an officer who stood by the door. "Issue the orders. Maximum wall patrols. Everyone else will be ushered outside the walls and flee to the east camp. Go!"

The officer saluted and dashed out the door.

"The rest of you, assume positions," Sitena said. "We have less than fifteen minutes."

Ven exhaled, heart pounding, a shiver running down his arms, thoughts returning to his parents. He was here for them. Not for Dami, not for Dayelle, not for Sitena. Not even for Mia. He was here for justice. For truth.

He would do what was necessary.

# Chapter 34

## Dami

There was a flurry of activity as Mia stepped into the hall. The combined panic of so many people made the very air feel claustrophobic and smothering. She kept her eyes focused on Lady Sitena Rosars and her soldier, Lend, as they led the way. Everyone dodged aside as they recognized their lady.

They made it down two flights of stairs before Mia looked back. She blanched, realizing Ven wasn't behind her. Anxiety rippled through her chest. "Where is Ven?" she called ahead to Sitena.

"He'll have gone somewhere safe," Sitena said as they strode through a door that led outside. The afternoon sun shined down into their eyes.

"I need him here," Mia protested, clenching her fists. "He wasn't supposed to be separated from me."

"Mia." Sitena turned and regarded her with a frown. "I have read your entire file. With or without Doctor Yashke, you are more than capable enough to deal with Dami. And believe me, he will be much safer away from the confrontation."

"He made preparations to assist me," Mia said. She clenched her fists. She had to trust that Ven would find his way to the courtyard.

Sitena continued walking to the edge of the balcony. "I have full confidence in our plan, Mia. I wouldn't be exposing myself in such a way otherwise. Ven is perfectly capable of making his own decisions. Right now, it looks like he's hiding."

Mia grunted and walked to the balcony. Ven wasn't hiding. He wouldn't abandon her. She resisted the urge to touch the back of her neck.

The balcony offered a good view of the whole fort and the surrounding area, except for behind them where the view was blocked by the higher levels of the keep. She was barefoot, and the stones felt smooth. Dark dark clouds rolled toward them from the east.

Down below, people scrambled. She doubted there was enough time for people to leave the gates. By the time word got around that they needed to flee, it would be too late for most of them. She only hoped Ven was somewhere nearby.

There was a distant flash of lightning from the east, followed a few seconds later by thunder. The clouds were getting closer. Another rumble echoed through the air, this one much closer. A tower on the lower wall started to crumble.

Sitena cursed silently. "So much for climbing the cliffs."

Bells rang out a moment later, signaling the assault and joining in with a cacophony of voices that shouted, echoing up from below.

Lend drew his dragonsbane sword. Mia could practically smell its metallic surface singeing her nostrils. She scanned ahead. The ground level of the first tier was hidden behind walls and buildings. A man screamed as his body flew through the air and fell back out of sight.

"He's slaughtering them," Sitena hissed, lips curling in anger. The cries of death rose even louder than the bells, shouts, and distant thunder. The older woman slapped the parapet before her.

Mia clenched the stone, leaning forward. She wanted to dive down and confront Dami immediately. "I have to stop him," she snarled.

"Wait," Sitena said, giving her a sharp look. "He must come here where we are most prepared to receive him. Remember, those are *my* people he's killing. I feel the loss of their lives, but we must hold to the plan. If we don't stop him here, then the whole world will know how dangerous he is."

Mia swallowed the words bitterly. She hated the truth behind them, but she stared ahead. The screams. She shook her head. They were too reminiscent of their first job when they'd stolen the crate of dragonsbane poison.

The dark clouds passed overhead when another building collapsed and Sitena cursed again. The chorus of screams was too much. Mia squirmed.

A figure emerged from the last gate. Her eyesight was sharp, but Mia hardly recognized the man. He was clothed in dark leather and wore metal gauntlets on his hands. He looked like a monster, his body spattered in red blood. As expected, he was barefoot.

He stared back up at her, eyes as black as she remembered.

Dami.

Energy surged through Mia's veins. She clenched her jaw and sprang from the balcony.

# Chapter 35

## Freedom

Ven coughed through the dust that billowed around him after the building's collapse. Two of Sitena's soldiers had forced him to evacuate the castle, but they'd only made it to the second tier before Dami arrived. Once they saw Dami, the soldiers shoved Ven into the nearest building and tried to hide with him.

To no avail.

Dami smashed through half the wall. It appeared his intent was just to create havoc before approaching the keep itself.

The building was missing half a wall, and rubble had poured down, crushing many people within. Ven was one of the lucky ones who was virtually unharmed. The two soldiers who'd *escorted* him were less fortunate.

One of the soldiers cried out, his arm hanging slack as he sat up against the ruined wall. Dislocated. Ven gripped the soldier's elbow and the back of the shoulder, then gave it a gradual rotation upward while applying slight pressure. The man screamed, but the shoulder returned to its proper position.

It was the best he could do for now. Ven climbed over the rubble, scanning the streets. For all he knew, Mia and Dami were already locked in combat.

No soldiers bothered to stop Ven now that Dami had arrived. Most people hid, but some ran for the gates. A woman lay sprawled in front of him with a broken leg, her toddler screaming for her to get up. They hadn't been able to flee in time. Dami was too fast. Cries shook Ven to the core. They rattled in his brain, almost making him dizzy. *I can't help them all. Mia is my priority right now.*

Thunder rumbled around him just as Ven felt the first drop of rain patter against his forehead. He could taste moisture in the air. His legs pounded up the street. The final gate to the top tier of the fort was open without a single soldier manning it. Two other people passed him heading the opposite direction, but nobody else went up.

Dead and injured littered the road. Ven frowned in anger and disgust, the fiery emotions boiling his insides. Dayelle was right. This kind of power had such cruel potential.

Ven passed under the gate and went up the slight incline, the keep rising ahead of him. He arrived in time to see Dami throw Mia across the courtyard.

Mia twisted in the air and came down on her feet. She looked at Ven, her expression strained.

"I was wondering where you were, Doctor Yashke," Dami said. His voice had deepend since they'd last spoken, though it had only been a few days. Perhaps he was *trying* to make his voice deeper.

Ven looked around. Sitena was still at her spot atop the keep. Lend hadn't moved from her side. Teamon stood just a couple steps away from the keep, dragonsbane sword held before him in both hands.

"Someone's playing you, Dami," Ven shouted. The rain picked up, dotting the cobblestones of the courtyard. "Someone's using you as their assassin. One of the investors is trying to control you."

"I pull the strings, little doctor," Dami said. He pointed at himself with a blood spattered gauntlet. "My informant knows to serve me well, otherwise he's next on the list. I'm nobody's puppet. Not anymore. Unlike Mia." He jerked his chin in Mia's direction. She made no response, but crouched where she'd landed. He could tell she was prepared to charge at Dami at a moment's notice.

"You're the one who ruined her, you know that?" Dami continued. "Before you came, she was mine. We were going to rule everything together."

Teamon inched closer.

"She had a heart long before I arrived, Dami," Ven said. "She never would have become a monster like you."

Dami sneered. Lightning flashed, and he came sprinting at Ven.

Ven's guts lurched, and he took a step back, reaching to draw the dagger.

Mia intercepted just before Dami got to him. She dove into Dami, snatching at him like a lion. Together they rolled across the pavement. Dami rose to his feet, holding one of Mia's legs. He went to throw her, but she grabbed his arm and twisted around, kicking him in the face with her other leg.

An involuntary whoop of exhilaration escaped Ven's lips. He freed the dagger from its sheath and approached them at a careful walk.

Teamon also approached from the other side, though he moved in faster with the courage of a soldier.

Dami and Mia spun and tumbled, wrestling in constant motion so that each action blurred. It was like watching a superhero movie, but there were no pauses in the fight. Mia never let go of Dami. Ven knew he'd die as soon as the man was free to move. His life was literally in Mia's hands.

Dami pinned Mia on her back against the ground.

Teamon took that moment to jab at Dami.

"Just what I needed," Dami said, glancing up at Teamon. Dami grabbed the blade with his gauntleted hand and pulled it. Teamon kept his grip and came tumbling towards Dami, who promptly kicked him in the chest. The soldier soared across the courtyard.

Dami kept Mia pinned as he flipped the weapon around and held its handle. "You know the funny thing about these gauntlets is that I don't have to touch the poison laced into the sword. It only burns a little. I bet nobody told you how easy the solution was, did they?"

Ven's jaw dropped in horror. He sprinted toward them as Dami placed the sword against Mia's neck. She gasped in pain as the metal burned her flesh. Ven withdrew his last vial from his pocket and hurled it at Dami.

Dami didn't even react. The vial burst open as it hit a metal clip on Dami's shoulder.

Some of the poisonous liquid spattered Dami on his neck and the back of his head. He roared and sprang back.

Mia kicked Dami away and rose to her feet, a dark red sore flaring on her neck.

A shout came from the keep as Siwen ran towards them. Two other soldiers, armed with crossbows, emerged behind him. *What good are those two?*

Dami jumped towards Ven, soaring over Mia's head. His blade passed inches in front of Ven's nose as Mia grabbed Dami from the air. He fell to his back and whipped the sword at Mia. She dodged away and stood between Dami and Ven.

"Mia. You need to let me kill him. I will free you," Dami growled, rising to his feet.

"I will destroy you before I let you touch him," she snarled back.

Siwen took a quick jab at Dami, but the subject deflected the blow easily. Siwen kept at it, but even for a master swordsman, he was no match for Dami. Dami caught every feint and stroke, then battered back at Siwen, swings so powerful that Siwen was nearly disarmed each time he blocked. Dami kicked Siwen in the hip, sending the soldier clattering across the stones.

Ven stepped around Mia sneaking toward Dami from behind, the dagger held out. He lashed at Dami's arm, leaving a small cut near his elbow. Dami whipped around. He punched Ven's hand, crunching the fingerbones, the same ones that had already been broken merely a week ago, and the dagger sailed out his grip. The next thing he knew, something sliced one of his thighs and then Dami was holding him by the throat, lifting his whole body off the ground with one arm.

Stars exploded across Ven's vision. He blinked through the rain down at Dami. The subject's lips were curled back in a sneer. Mia stood a few steps away, eyes wide in horror. She was too afraid. Ven tried to say her name, but only a strangled gurgle emerged. *You can do this, Mia.* He willed the thoughts to her as his vision began to fade.

"You're almost free, Mia," Dami said. "Once he's dead, nothing will hold you back." The voice seemed distant or muted.

"You won't hurt him," was all Mia said before she charged Dami. Her movements were a blur as she stepped forward, ducked under a swing from Dami, and snapped her hands up to snatch his arm as it arced above her.

Ven dropped to the ground, gasping.

Dami swung through the air as Mia spun him around. She sprang onto Dami's back while he was still in the air. Her legs wrapped around his from behind, preventing him from catching himself. She held his sword arm behind him, the dragonsbane weapon digging into Dami's side as they crashed to the ground with a meaty thunk.

Now. The moment was now.

Ven's breath was ragged as he rose to his feet, scooping the dragonsbane dagger off the ground, limping on his bad leg. Dami tried to loose himself using his one free hand, but Mia latched onto it with her own free hand and forced it behind him. The dragonsbane sword was still pressing against both their sides. Dami and Mia screamed as the poisoned metal burned at their skin.

Dami shouted and managed to jerk them to their side.

"Now!" Sitena's voice screamed across the courtyard.

Bolts whistled through the air. Ven glanced up. Several crossbowmen had entered the courtyard. The bolts crashed against Dami's body, glass shattering as poison vials exploded. Mia screamed and rolled away.

Dami tried to rise, but fell to his back. Steam rose from his face and neck where the poison burned his flesh. His screams were that of pure agony.

Mia groaned and shook her arms where some of her skin sizzled. Just her arms. Not fatal. Ven's body trembled at what needed to happen next.

The soldiers moved in, reloading their crossbows.

No time to think.

Dami's screams burned the air as he writhed on the ground. Ven dropped to his knees beside Dami, gripping the dagger in his good hand. He had to prove himself to Dayelle. He would finish the job. He'd learn the truth about his parents.

He plunged the dagger with a powerful thrust, piercing straight to Dami's heart with a fleshy thunk and a sickening spurt of blood. Ven's nostrils flared, lips curling in disgust as he panted. Dami's screaming stopped immediately.

The soldiers continued to close in, still reloading their crossbows, though many of them had now turned their eyes to Mia. Even Lend was coming around Mia's back, dragonsbane sword raised to the ready.

"Wait!" Ven shouted.

"We have our orders," muttered one of the soldiers, raising his bow to point it at Mia.

They would kill her. Mia was right. Sitena had no intention to let Mia go. It was all a trap.

He locked eyes with Mia, tears welling in his eyes. Her own eyes were already wet with tears, and her lips trembled, but she gave him a nod.

Ven shivered, anger burning in his chest. He wanted to roar. He'd never felt a stronger urge to fight than he did at that time. As futile as it would be, he'd fight all of them.

But reason took hold.

Mia's plan was the only possible outcome.

He withdrew the trigger from his pocket, aiming it at Mia.

"Let me do it," he said, voice more a growl than anything. He locked eyes with Mia, both of them crying as the rain poured harder. He was out of time.

He pulled the trigger.

Mia collapsed.

A flash of lightning streaked directly overhead, and thunder rumbled across the courtyard.

The soldiers lowered their crossbows.

Sitena pulled the wet hair back from her face and smiled. "Doctor Yashke, you killed both of them. I underestimated you."

Ven stood, dropping the trigger and leaving the dagger in Dami's chest. His hand throbbed. His thigh stung. His heart ached. "I did my job," he said, voice monotone as he tried to steel himself from the pain that wracked his brain.

"It's done then." Sitena waved a hand. "Let's get things cleaned up."

Ven stumbled down beside Mia. Her body was soaked. She looked so peaceful he could almost believe she was merely sleeping.

This was what he'd been hired for all along. He succeeded. But why did it feel like such a failure?

He held back the pain as he leveraged his injured hand under her legs and put his other arm under her shoulder.

"We'll handle that, Doctor Yashke," Sitena said.

Ven grunted as he heaved Mia up into his arms. He faced Sitena. "No. I will take her body where she wanted it to go." He didn't pause for an answer, but turned and limped his way toward the stables. He wouldn't let them have her body.

Sitena's soldiers moved to stop him.

"Let him go," Siwen said, retrieving his dragonsbane dagger from Dami's chest.

Ven sighed in relief to have someone else's support.

"Lady Rosars," Siwen said as her men remained blocking Ven's path. "You have Dami's body. Let that be enough. Let him take her. He is the only person who truly cared for her. She deserves that respect for what she has done."

"He killed her," Sitena said.

"He did what was necessary," Siwen said. He nodded to Ven.

Ven continued to walk and Sitena made no further argument, but her eyes flicked to Lend before she turned back toward the castle.

Ven's heart pounded. It was all he could do to keep from falling to his knees.

Siwen ran up ahead of him and began saddling Ven's Zebadon for him. "You showed a warrior's courage today," Siwen said, tightening the final strap.

"I'm not sure that's a compliment," Ven said. The sickening feeling of piercing Dami's flesh and the light leaving Mia's eyes was still too fresh.

He jerked away when Siwen offered to help place Mia's body on the horse. "I will do it." he said. It was extremely difficult, but Ven managed to heave her body up over the front of the saddle so that she was lying on her stomach. Then he mounted up on the saddle behind her.

"Thanks for your help, Siwen."

"You're welcome," Siwen said, his eyes sad. "I wish I could convince Sitena to relinquish Dami's body as well. I don't trust her." He let out a sigh. "I am sorry for your loss."

Ven gulped past the pain in his throat. He gave Siwen a final nod, then steered out of the stable, riding at a half gallop into the rain.

# Chapter 36

## Home

I t took Ven two days to find a suitable place to leave Mia's body, nearly getting lost in the process. It was in a forest at the base of a mountain, hoping nobody would find her. He dug a hole in the soft soil with his bare hands and dragged her inside, fighting back tears the whole time. He wished there'd been another way. Some path that didn't involve her dying. If Sitena's soldiers hadn't been there, he would have never done it. But at least now he could get his answers. As long as he could find Dayelle.

Though in truth, he suspected she would be the one to find him.

Six days was all it took for him to relocate the spot where Dayelle had brought him into Orund. He wasn't sure if it would take him back to Florida or if he'd land in some other place completely. Were there other worlds? What if he accidentally went to a whole different planet?

He looked around the dusty landscape, unable to believe that this whole thing had lasted no more than two months. It felt like two years. Hopefully time passed the same on Earth as it did here.

Sorrow welled up in his chest. He failed Mia. He still hadn't learned what he came here for. Why were his parents dead? He forced the emotions away, ignoring his mother's voice in his head that urged him to be emotionally self-reliant. It wasn't plausible right now.

Hooves approached from behind him.

Ven whipped around, prepared to mount back up on his Zebadon if he needed to flee, but the person who rode to meet him was familiar.

Dayelle.

Ven released his breath and folded his arms as Dayelle brought her horse to a stop in front of him. The animal wouldn't settle though, even as Dayelle patted its neck. He had the feeling she didn't ride very often. When she dismounted, the beast tramped off to hide behind the nearest scraggly tree.

"Ven," Dayelle said with a smile. "Well done. I knew you were the right man for the job."

"So you didn't forget our arrangement," Ven said, still wary of the woman.

"Of course not," she said, head shaking. "But look, before we get to all the business, I'm sorry about Mia. I know you cared for her, but necessary measures had to be taken."

"I did as you asked," Ven said, masking his tone.

"You did. You've helped save an entire planet. I only wish you hadn't had to work with Sitena Rosars." Dayelle's eyes narrowed with a dark look. "She's next on my list." Her smile returned in a flash. "Not that you need to worry about that. Let's focus on your payment, eh?"

Ven nodded, only too eager to finally learn the truth.

"Your parents were, in fact, murdered, though I will offer you some context so that you might understand how events came about. Your parents were involved in dragonblood research. My agents had been watching them for years. They wanted to find ways that dragonblood could be used to treat physical or mental pain and maladies, so they often portaled to Orund for their own studies."

"How did they ever find out how to get to Orund?"

Dayelle shrugged. "That, I do not know. I only became aware of them after they'd seemingly been using the portals for some time. At some point in their travels and studies however, they met Doctor Huan and consulted him before he established his study involving Mia, Dami, and the others. Once you were born, they backed out for several years, but Doctor Huan and other researchers would occasionally write to them. Your parents never wrote back. Until just over a year ago."

Dayelle withdrew a letter from her pocket and handed it to Ven. "The letter was the first time Doctor Huan explicitly stated that their research had been successful and the operations had cured various maladies. That seemed to pique your parents' interest."

"Why do you know what all the letters said?" Ven said, eyes narrowing as he studied her face.

Dayelle smirked. "My organization has a good hand in the delivery service."

Ven read the letter, recognizing Zein's familiar scribble, stating exactly as Dayelle had said.

"We can assume he wanted your parents' help to try and make the dragonblood transfusions into a more selective treatment rather than a collective imperviousness, as that remained his focus. After your parents met with him, we intercepted a letter only a week later that was delivered to an organization well known for assassinations. Your parents were dead a week later."

Ven shook his head. "Zein killed my parents?" He'd spoken with the man. Sat with him. Worked with him.

"All evidence would suggest so."

"And you had me work with him?" Ven's voice took on a fiery tone.

Dayelle's smile turned sinister. "Indeed. Ironic, isn't it? But I couldn't very well give you that detail or you may have jeopardized the mission."

Ven huffed, balling his hands into fists, prepared to ride through all of Orund to hunt Zein back down. "He needs to be brought to justice." His voice was low, dark. He'd killed before, despite how much it pained him to do so, but Zein's life was one he wouldn't regret taking.

"Calm yourself, Ven. We've taken care of Zein as well. We intercepted him as he was on his way to Castia Mont. We only had to wait for the right moment."

Ven shook his head, placing a fist over his lips. "This whole time. Did he know who I was?"

"I suspect he did," Dayelle said. "It's actually why I kept your name the same. I believe it's what got you your placement on the team."

"I don't understand. Why would he do that?"

"Zein was a smart man. He would have wanted to keep a close eye on you. He knew your parents were skilled doctors and would have been intrigued by what you'd have to offer. I knew he wouldn't be able to refuse."

Ven seethed, pacing around his Zebadon as he shook his head more. "How did you catch him?"

"We were following him closely all along," Dayelle said. "I don't believe he was aware of our organization until the moment we came upon him."

Something stirred in Ven's gut. "He's still alive then?"

"Not for long," Dayelle said, "but you needn't concern yourself with that."

But he was concerned. He wanted to see the life escape Zein's eyes. He recognized the thought as something dark, but that didn't prevent him from savoring the idea. He focused his eyes on Dayelle. Something about her organization confused him. What was their aim? Eliminate drag-onblood usage? And then another thought occurred to him.

"Is Siwen one of your agents?"

"Very astute," Dayelle said. "He is being treated for his injury, by the way. He wasn't too happy to discover what his father was up to. The person in their dungeon was in fact a dragon. Yours and Mia's escape from their castle left Yubo Huan unprepared. Let's just say that dragon issue of theirs has also been resolved. A very fortunate side-effect of your endeavors."

Ven cared little for the dragon issues. His mind still reeled at the revelation regarding his parents and Zein. He took a sharp breath. "Why did my parents stop working with Zein? All those years ago."

Dayelle tapped her chin. "You were born. Priorities shifted. They must have wanted you to have a normal life."

Ven huffed. His life had been anything but normal.

But it was done.

He knew the truth.

And justice would be serviced.

All that remained was to return home and attend Harvard. He'd finish his schooling and do as his parents had wanted him to. To heal people. To help them. He withdrew the marble from his pocket and nodded to Dayelle. "Thank you."

"Indeed." Dayelle took a step backward, glancing at the marble in Ven's hand. "Be careful with that. If you intend to return to Florida, you need to focus on that bayou with intensity, otherwise you'll cross into New Mexico."

Ven gave a curt nod. "Thanks for the tip." He patted his horse. "Can you take care of him?"

"I'll see to it." Dayelle said nothing else as she took his Zebadon's reins and started leading it toward her own horse.

Ven turned, facing the invisible threshold that would take him back to earth, only too pleased to leave Orund. This place had killed his parents. It had only brought him pain. With every blink, a flash of Mia's face flicked across his vision, eyes closed. Lifeless.

A deep breath filled his lungs before he swallowed back the pain.

He put the marble in his mouth, envisioning the bayou back in Florida, and stepped forward, the world twisting around him. He could hear the croaking and buzzing of life and smell the sulfuric stench of ancient mud even before the flickering sunlight barely breaking through the cypress trees came into view.

He dropped as soon as he got through, knees smushing into the soft earth.

Home.

Alone and broken.

He'd wished the truth would bring him peace, but instead it flushed him with sorrow and anger. Tears fell from his cheeks. Why couldn't his parents have just left it all behind?

*The peace will come*, he told himself, taking deep breaths. *The peace will come.*

# Chapter Thirty-Seven

# Chapter 37

## Grave

"I swear it was here!" Trefal said as he hurled another scoop of dirt to the side before tossing his shovel to the ground in frustration.

Four other Drekis stood around the site, arms folded. The late day sun dipped beneath the treeline, casting the setting into shadow. A stretch of wildflowers decorated the mountainside anywhere the trees weren't too thick, the scent of sweet pollen heavy in the air as insects buzzed about.

"Are you sure this is the right place?" Malar asked in her condescending tone as the others muttered.

"Positive! I followed him here," Trefal said. "I watched as he dug the hole and buried her, then marked it with the flags so we'd be able to return." It was true. He'd followed closely behind Ven, easily tracking the untrained boy's path as he'd carried Mia's body into the forest.

"It's the right place," Dayelle said, emerging from the trees.

Trefal jumped back in surprise, tripping over his discarded shovel.

The others fell into silence, watching as their leader knelt in the soil beside the upturned gravesite.

Only Malar was bold enough to speak. "Perhaps somebody else got to her first. Maybe Sintena had followers as well."

Dayelle ignored Malar. She took a deep breath, her nostrils flaring, eyelids fluttering shut. Her fingers laced across the freshly turned soil. "The scent of her is all over."

Her eyes snapped open, and she regarded Trefal, the color of her eyes having faded to a misty white before returning to the normal brown.

Dayelle pursed her lips, but nobody else dared speak. "This *was* where Mia was buried, but I detect no other interference."

"Then who took her?" Malar asked.

"Nobody," Dayelle said. "She got up and walked away." She rose to her feet, tongue clicking as she shook her head. "Malar, inform the other Drekis. We've a hunt ahead of us."

# Epilogue

## Breathe

Mia let her hood fall back from her head as she turned her face toward the wind. More dirt fell from her clothes, whisked away in the breeze. From atop the mountain, a large forest stretched out to one side, and varied farmland littered the other.

She'd gotten away. Everyone thought she was dead, including Ven. She ran her finger over the metal hole in the back of her neck where she'd removed the poison. Once Ven had fallen asleep at Castia Mont, Mia used the tool herself to extract it. Once removed, she'd hurled it out the window, far out past the castle walls and into the forest beyond.

She felt bad for lying to Ven, but it was necessary. Everyone else needed to buy it when he used the trigger, and she needed to cut him off for good. Not that she didn't care for him—truly she did—but she needed to be on her own. Despite the sadness or the loneliness that would accompany her. She wanted to experience life on her own for once. Perhaps her path would lead her back to Ven someday.

But for now... She took a deep breath. She was free.

# Acknowledgements

Massive shoutout to my beta team who even made the book possible: Sarah, Grace, Penny, Rebecca, Matthew, and Melody. I probably would have thrown it out if not for them. They deserve an award for slogging through that initial mess and for putting up with my constant messages whenever I get random ideas.

I absolutely cannot go without acknowledging my wife, Julia, with all of her patience and support for my authoring ventures. I am so fortunate to have her in my life.

# Also by

Be sure to check out Hunsaker's debut series, The Ringdweller Series. It's very big on fantasy worldbuilding and mindblowing twists.

# About the author

Brady was born in a stronghold at the base of the Rocky Mountains. He currently resides there with his wife, their three daughters, and a few domesticated house lions of a rare breed. He set out with the goal to write fantasy that anybody could read with characters who face real life struggles. Everyone deserves to feel like there is hope.